D1180055

DAWN OF THE JAGUAR

A SHADOW BRUJA NOVEL

BOOK 2

Also by J. C. Cervantes

The Storm Runner Trilogy

The Storm Runner
The Fire Keeper
The Shadow Crosser

Shadow Bruja Novels

The Lords of Night

DAWN OF THE JAGUAR

A SHADOW BRUJA NOVEL

WITHDRAWN BOOK 2

J. C. CERVANTES

RICK RIORDAN PRESENTS

Disney • HYPERION   LOS ANGELES   NEW YORK

First Edition, October 2023
1 3 5 7 9 10 8 6 4 2
FAC-004510-23229
Printed in the United States of America

This book is set in Aldus Nova Pro/Linotype
Designed by Phil Buchanan

Library of Congress Control Number: 2022055038
ISBN 978-1-368-06702-7

Reinforced binding
Follow @ReadRiordan
Visit www.DisneyBooks.com

SUSTAINABLE FORESTRY INITIATIVE

Certified Sourcing

www.forests.org
SFI-01681

Logo Applies to Text Stock Only

For the Seekers. You know who you are.

The End and the Beginning

The god of death kept his promise to Ren.

He wouldn't let the godborn become the Night Lords' queen. At least not for very long.

But more than anything, he wouldn't let her die alone. And so, Ah-Puch stood hidden in the trees near the lake's edge, a god in teen form who could do nothing to save the only being he had ever...loved.

He could only watch in horror as the Aztec hunter Monty let her magical arrow fly at his command. It whizzed through the air—a streak of blue light the Lords of Night didn't see coming until it was too late.

Until it had pierced Renata Santiago's heart.

In that single horrific moment, Ah-Puch held Ren's last gaze. He wished...oh, how he wished he had the power save her. The god's eyes burned with tears for the first time in his existence. But he wouldn't look away from Ren's death.

He watched as the shadow bruja blinked, her black eyes changing back to blue as she experienced an awareness that shattered his heart. He watched as her face contorted in pain, as her hand reached for the magical arrow, as the blood flowed in rivulets down her silver dress.

And he felt her pain, the agony of her death, the grief of an unlived life.

As Ren collapsed into a heap of nothingness, her shadows

rose from her limp form, screaming and writhing with the fury of ancient demons.

A terrible sound filled the forest just then. The last beat of her heart.

The god of death had lived an eternity watching humans take their final breath, seeing the light go out of their eyes. But he had never known true death and darkness and destruction until now.

The world erupted into a storm of chaos.

Great flashes of light filled the night sky. Mighty winds exploded, shaking the trees violently. The Lords of Night raged. As Ren's lifeless body evaporated, the lords grabbed for the crown of jade and shadow they had just placed on her head. But it was too late.

The crown rose into the air, spinning like a cyclone, and then broke like a twig being snapped in two.

The hunter, Monty, inhaled sharply, then leaped down from her perch. "What th-th-the . . . ?" she sputtered. "Ah-Puch . . . the crown . . . Did you see . . . ?"

Yes, he had seen. And the same confusion washed over the god. Why would the crown break? But he didn't have time to think about that. He still had one more card to play, a part of his plan he had shared with no one. He would make himself known. He would let the Lords of Night destroy him; they would explode his powerless teen form with the force of a dying star. And he would welcome it.

Just as he made ready to step out of the forest's shadows, he was gripped by an agonizing heat spreading between his shoulder blades. He felt fire and ice coursing through his veins. He sensed a darkness rising at magnificent speeds that ripped the breath from his lungs. Then, as turmoil continued to explode all around him, silence settled over his heart.

A trail of glimmering mist swirled around his thin frame, a vortex of unimaginable magic that was quickly reduced to a single golden thread, its tail lashing wildly across the dark. In a blink, the thread coiled around the god's feet like a snake, forcing him to his knees. He gasped, struggling to free himself as the thread burned brighter and brighter, hotter and hotter.

On the edge of his consciousness, the god heard Monty calling to him, felt her reaching for him . . . but it was the strange whispers that had his attention: *Do you see?*

Ah-Puch cast his gaze to the white flames igniting from his palms, searing not only his skin, but his blood and bones and very soul.

So, this is how I end, he thought grimly.

But he didn't burn. He didn't turn to ash. His wish for death would have to wait because the flame vanished, and in its place something else materialized. It was so impossible he didn't . . . *couldn't* believe it.

Ren's time rope.

Split into two now, one length tied to each of the god's wrists.

And the twin ropes glowed with the power and rage of a thousand suns.

1

Ren had been to the underworld before, but never as a dead person.

And even though she was trapped in a blacker-than-black darkness, she guessed that's where she had landed. First because that's where the dearly departed go, and second because of the wretched smell—mold and vomit and rot all blended in a concoction of GROSS.

Ren felt like she'd just been put through a wood chipper, twice. But she wasn't worried about the pain—she was fixated on the fact that she had just been stabbed with an arrow and was . . . dead.

As in adios, life.

No. She would *never* accept it. She was the queen of the Night Lords, a powerful shadow bruja. That had to mean something.

A small voice within her whispered, *And what else?*

Ren blinked into the darkness. The air was thick, hot, and near suffocating as she reached back to the moments before she keeled over. But there was nothing. Only fuzzy outlines of people, places, things. And her name: Renata Santiago.

She strained her memory hard—so hard she thought she might pop a blood vessel (if she still had any). A red light flared to life, and then it began to flash once, twice, three times, like a strobe. Ren's eyes scanned the space that was no bigger than a small bedroom.

Whispers floated around her, a symphony of indecipherable voices. And then she saw shapes, shadows climbing the pitted walls.

She inched closer.

Webs. The walls were covered in them, thick and twisted, pulsating even though there wasn't a single breeze in the little space.

Ren stepped back into the center of the room, wondering, hoping, praying that whatever giant spider had spun these webs was long gone.

Her worry was forgotten when broken images began to flicker across the web-covered walls, each flash a different memory filling her mind and heart. Voices, faces, fear, and denial—she saw and heard and felt it all as if she were experiencing each moment all over again.

She was a shadow bruja whose magic was descended from the Aztec Lords of Night. She was also a Maya godborn, the daughter of Pacific, the goddess of time. Ren's heart twisted when she remembered Serena and the other four godborn teens who had plotted to overthrow the Maya gods, and the quest she had taken with her friend Marco to find and stop them. She saw how the journey had led them to her trusted amigo Ah-Puch, the Maya god of death. He had helped by introducing her to new allies like Montero, the Aztec hunter, and Edison, the demon boy who had been raised in the underworld. Together, they had discovered that the rogue godborns (aka the cinco) intended to wake the Aztec Lords of Night, all because Serena had believed she was prophesied to be queen.

Ren felt a dark stab in her chest.

I am the queen.

The cobwebs shuddered. New images played, and Ren saw herself as she was before. Before she knew the truth about the origins of her shadow magic, before she was crowned queen. She didn't like that previous version of herself, the weak, pathetic version with an open and ready heart that had worn a giant sign saying SUCKER.

But then the lords chose Ren. She was consumed by their darkness; it had strengthened her and made her whole. Ren clenched her teeth. *Even as powerful as I was, did it really matter? In the end, I was still struck down.*

The red lights continued to flash as Ren searched for a way out, a way back to the lords.

Somewhere between her thoughts of power and death, she heard the hissing.

She wasn't alone in here.

In the split second it took her to realize this dismal fact, a burning pain slashed across her forearm. And then another.

Ren cried out and reached for her shadows. They gathered, writhed, and churned all around her, but they felt cold and distant—outside of herself for the first time. She willed them to take the shape of a giant scorpion, a dragon, a sharp blade, but they didn't respond.

Seething, she remembered that all this was the god of death's fault. He was the one who'd given the command to release the arrow with enough magic to kill the most power-ful godborn and shadow bruja on the planet. But why would someone who had been her friend want to kill her? That part was still fuzzy.

Ren cursed herself for not seeing Ah-Puch's impending betrayal. But no matter. She would break free of whatever hell-scape she was currently in and get her revenge on the god. And oh, how he would suffer.

Click, click, click.

Ren felt another painful slash, this time across her cheek, but whatever was ripping open her skin was too fast to see. Then, just as she threw up her hands in a protective stance, she remembered her time rope. It could destroy any monster in the universe! Ren grasped at her throat, where she wore the magic item as a necklace....

But it was gone!

She reached for it again and again, refusing to believe it wasn't there.

"No!" she cried.

The rope had been a gift from Pacific; it could never be sto-len, only given freely. And Ren would never ever give it away.

The razor-sharp cuts kept coming, from the left and right, from above and below. The red strobe kept pulsing, the webs kept vibrating. Ren ducked, bobbed, and weaved with tremen-dous agility, but that wasn't enough to prevent her tormentor from slicing her arms, hands, and neck. And though she didn't bleed, she still felt the agonizing pain of each laceration.

I officially hate being dead.

"Let me see you!" Ren shouted. It was a desperate plea, she

realized, but if she was going to be torn to shreds, she at least wanted to look into the wicked eyes of her perpetrator.

"Coward!" she screamed as the darkness inside her exploded.

"A spider caught in her own web," a woman's voice cooed.

Ren gasped. She knew that voice, but from where? "Who are you?" she asked with a growl.

"How do you like the web, little spider?" The woman laughed lightly.

"It's officially the worst welcome to deathdom"—was that even a word?—"in the history of deaths." Ren squinted. "And can you turn off that strobe light?" It was giving her a massive headache.

Instantly, Ren was plunged into darkness.

"I meant the flashing part!" she said.

"You make a lot of demands for a dead girl."

Ren swallowed. "Am I seriously dead?"

"Yes."

"As in forever?"

"Death is final," the woman said. "Conclusive, definitive, and absolute. And we have a strict no-return policy here. So, please, no pleading or whining. And for the love of demons, no more preposterous questions."

Ren swallowed her frustration. She wasn't afraid; she wasn't the anxious bruja she had once been, the one who had always wanted to console or help or save others. The one who had been bullied by strangers and abandoned by friends. She had tasted the darkness, and she liked its power.

Another hiss sounded from her right.

"How about you call off your monster?" Ren suggested.

"Spiders," the woman corrected. "And you are in their house uninvited, I might add. Which means you don't make the rules."

Suddenly, Ren remembered the many houses of trial in the Maya underworld, places of torment like Rattle House, filled with bone-chilling hail, and Bat House, with bloodthirsty creatures shredding visitors with their teeth and claws.

"Yeah, well, I didn't want to come here, either."

"And yet here you are."

The cobwebs vibrated again, and in an instant, half a dozen hairy black spiders as big as cats began to climb across the gossamer strings. Ren began to tremble as their mouths opened and closed, exposing the tiny fangs that made that terrible clicking sound.

Ren's eyes traveled the length of their horrible plump bodies, stopping at the razor-like claws on the ends of their legs. Wait . . . Their legs were made of metal.

"Mechanical?" she whispered.

"See?" the woman said, sounding amused. "You are much more intelligent than you look."

"Can I get out of here now?"

"It's a sad truth," the woman went on, as if Ren hadn't said a word. "But one has to keep up with technology, and this new house of trials does just that. You should see what these beauties can do! Such agony and torment. Each razor cut carries a trace of poison."

"Poison?" Ren's voice was a small, quiet thing.

"Do you feel it?" the woman said. "It should have spread to your heart by now, consumed it with a terrible burning sensation."

Ren clutched her chest, panting like she'd just run ten miles uphill. "You can't kill a dead person," she ground out.

The woman laughed. "Ah, how little you know of my realm."

The floor split open, and Ren plummeted. When she landed, she was on all fours in a stark white room with an onyx floor that had been polished to a mirror shine. The only light came from the open ceiling Ren had fallen through. She looked up to see a marbled gray sky and, suspended from what looked like a rope made of glittering stars, a small golden cage the size of a fish bowl.

"Hello, Renata."

Standing before her was Ixtab, Maya goddess of the under-world.

2

Ren rolled onto her side, writhing and twisting, struggling against the poison that now seemed to live inside of her.

"This will be over much faster if you stop fighting," Ixtab said in an annoying singsong voice. The goddess wore a long, fitted dress made of dark feathers. Her once-golden hair was now raven black and pulled into a tight bun, accentuating her elegant features.

Tears fell as Ren gripped her stomach and curled into a ball. She could feel the poison spreading, its heat multiplying, like her blood was on fire.

At the height of her panic, she thought about her abuelo—his soft brown eyes, the deep lines of his face, the warmth of his hands. And then, sure as breath, the pain vanished.

Slowly, Ren rolled over, and as she did, she saw her hands. The veins under her skin had grown thick and black. With a gasp, she jumped to her feet and pushed up her sleeves to find that the darkness was spreading up her arms as well.

"What did you do?" she shouted at the goddess.

"I put some controls on the evil living inside of you."

Ren knew Ixtab was talking about the darkness that had recently seized her heart. Anger rose in her, igniting the pain again. She inhaled sharply, then exhaled slowly until the pain subsided. "Why am I in . . . Xib'alb'a?" she spat.

Ixtab flashed a sinister smile. "You are a godborn, daughter of time. Or have you forgotten?"

"I am queen of the Aztec Lords of Night," Ren insisted. "A shadow bruja!"

"Would you rather be in their wretched underworld, Mictlan?"

"I'd rather be *alive.*"

"Well, that is a problem, isn't it?" Ixtab came closer. Her eyes flashed yellow, then a silvery lavender. A sudden heat erupted in the empty room as she calmly stated, "There is only room for one queen."

Ren lifted her chin. "Jealous?"

"Always."

That admission surprised Ren, but she wouldn't let it show. She gathered the shadow magic still pulsing in her blood. It was so different from the darkness spreading through her. The shadows were inherited and could be shaped into anything she desired. The darkness was new and all-consuming. She let the magic rise to the surface, and as she did, she noticed only bits of sombra slipping from her wounds, rising into the air like useless specks of ash.

"What did you do to my shadows?" she cried.

"Death has such strange effects on magic, doesn't it?" Ixtab said with feigned curiosity.

Instantly, Ren's wounds began to close, as if making the goddess's point.

Even if Ren's shadows had been in working order, she knew

there was no way she could go up against the goddess of the underworld on her own turf, a goddess who could be friend or foe depending on the circumstances and what was in it for her.

History had taught Ren this simple fact.

Which was so unlike the Lords of Night, who had kept every promise to Ren. They'd made her their queen and were the source of her greatest power: shadow magic. No matter what, she would find a way back to them. She would marry the Prince Lord as promised, and then she would carve out Ah-Puch's heart for his betrayal.

"Thinking dark thoughts?" Ixtab asked, but it came out more like a purr.

"Always," Ren echoed.

"And I was so hoping the poison would be enough."

The goddess's eyes flicked to the top of Ren's head, and the godborn had another flash of memory. Ren's hands flew up to the jade crown she was wearing... but they came up with nothing—only a shadow that vanished into a trail of smoke the moment she reached for it.

"Tsk, tsk... Such a shame." Ixtab sighed, toying with the black diamond bracelet shimmering on her delicate wrist. "Oh well, I didn't expect this to be easy."

Ren glared at the goddess.

"You forget who you are," Ixtab growled, now circling her like a cat on the prowl. "You believe the shadows are your greatest source of power, but they—"

"Are everything!" Ren remembered that much. Her godborn power rested solely in the time rope, an object. But her sombras—those were in her Mexica blood.

"Ah, if that were true, you wouldn't have landed in my realm. You see," the goddess went on, stopping in her tracks to face Ren, "a soul of magic will always be guided to its source of greatest strength."

Lies. All of it, Ren thought, disgusted by the fact that she had ever aided the goddess or any Maya being. She hated them. All of them!

The poison in her veins reignited. Ren clenched her fists at her side. "What do you want from me?" She knew the great goddess wouldn't bother to show up for some nobody's welcome party, which meant that Ixtab had an agenda. And if that were true, maybe they could strike a deal. After all, Ixtab couldn't stand Ah-Puch, either. Once she heard that Ren wanted to destroy him, she might offer Ren a one-way ticket out of the underworld's gates.

Ixtab drew closer, eyes narrowed. She steepled her refined hands, tapping her red nails together. "Why must I always get the dirty work?"

Then, in one swift movement, she thrust her hand into Ren's chest and grabbed hold of her heart. Agony racked the godborn, scorched her from the inside out. Screams echoed from somewhere in the distance, but all Ren could do was stand frozen, staring into the eyes of the queen of the underworld.

Ixtab did not pull out the heart. Instead, she held Ren's gaze as she said, "NEVER forget who you are."

More memories flooded Ren's brain.

She remembered her last moments on the lakeshore with Marco. How the world had contracted, how the forest had closed in. A sensation had spread through Ren like warm water, coursing through every inch of her until all she could feel was the power of her ancient magic from what others called the dead gods. Also known as the Lords of Night, who weren't dead at all. They'd just been asleep for more than a century.

She remembered Marco on his knees, telling her to fight the darkness. Marco thrashing beneath her magic before she stepped into the lake, before a vibrating sensation wrapped around her throat—a spark of light, of something she couldn't name.

Ah-Puch's whisper. *Not like this.*

Ren gasped as Ixtab withdrew her hand, leaving the godborn's chest intact.

Instantly, Ren's knees buckled. She collapsed to the floor and stared up at the ball of pulsing shadow in Ixtab's grasp. It was so small, so weak looking. That couldn't be the extent of Ren's bruja magic, could it?

With a smirk, Ixtab tossed the ball into the tiny gilded cage hanging from the sky. "Now, doesn't that feel better, godborn? No more darkness vying for your attention."

Ren dropped her gaze to her reflection in the onyx floor. Hollow eyes, stringy hair, pointed jaw. A shell of herself.

Terrified and shocked, she stood up on wobbly legs. "I . . . I tried to resist the Lords of Night," she said by way of excuse. It was more for her own soul than for Ixtab. "But their pull was so strong."

"That is often the way of darkness."

Ren felt exhausted, and so weightless that she could float away. Glancing down at her hands, she saw that her veins were back to normal. "It was terrible," she said. "I . . . I thought horrible things and hurt people I love and . . ." Tears streamed down her face.

Ixtab grimaced, looking away with disgust. "For the love of demons, do not dare cry in my presence. It is not only a waste but also quite messy."

"Do you . . . have any tissues?" Ren blubbered, sniffling.

"Does this look like a convenience store?!"

Bleary-eyed, Ren looked up at the imprisoned shadow that was shrinking into a corner. It was an odd feeling to miss something so dangerous, so poisonous, a magic that had mutated into a dark thing that had transformed Ren into something she swore she'd never be: evil.

"Why did you put my magic in a cage?" Ren's voice was a mere whisper.

"I thought perhaps the poison would be enough to keep it in check, but the little beast is quite spirited, so I'm afraid it must stay locked away."

Ren wasn't sure who she was without her shadow magic, without the time rope.

"And now," Ixtab said gleefully, "you and I have some business of a most wicked nature."

3

A few minutes ago, when Ren was still gripped by dark forces, *wicked* would have sounded utterly delightful. Now it just sounded empty and sad, and it reminded Ren of how much she was hurting.

Not just because she was dead, but because she had left her friends under the worst circumstances. They were now likely being held captive by the Lords of Night. Were they okay? Alive?

With a burning twist of nausea, she remembered what the lord named the Smoking Mirror had told her in the last moments of her life when she'd asked about her friends. *They are alive and well. All but one, that is. He was a real fighter.*

Who was *he*? Marco? Edison?

Ren's heart squeezed. *This is my fault. All of it.*

Ixtab waved a hand. At once, glass doors appeared to Ren's right, framing a view of the most majestic garden Ren had ever seen. Each star-like bloom was bursting with color: peach, pink, red, blue, and purple. The flowers climbed up and up and up, as if trying to reach the sky.

"Dahlias," Ixtab said, as if Ren had asked a question.

Maybe Ren had and didn't remember because she was suddenly so exhausted. Every limb felt like it was made of stone.

But Ren refused to close her eyes or get distracted by all this false beauty when her shadow magic was sitting in a golden cage right above her head, her friends were in danger, and she was a ghost.

And what had happened to the rogue godborns who had awakened the ancient Aztec lords in the first place? And Zyanya, the magical bird with the power to put the lords back into their slumber . . . Had she been captured, too?

"What is this place?" Ren asked.

Ixtab swept her gaze across the colorful landscape. "Wretched in so many ways, wouldn't you agree?"

Wretched? Were they looking at the same thing? "You don't like flowers?"

"They are weak, delicate creatures," Ixtab said bitterly. "They die far too easily. And require far too much care."

"Then why do you have the garden?"

Ixtab sneered. "A sacrifice, I know, but it's for your little brain."

Ren wasn't following, and Ixtab must have noticed because she released a melodramatic sigh. "It is a memory garden, you foolish child!"

Ren, suddenly chilled, wrapped her arms around herself. "But my memory is fine."

"You just died—that can be arduous," Ixtab said flatly. "And I've removed a portion of your magic. Quite a shock to the system. For this to work, I need your memory to be sharper than it's ever been before. So go take a whiff of any dahlia and let's get on with this, shall we?"

Ren hesitated. "What do you mean *for this to work*? I really think I should know what I'm agreeing to," she said, collecting her nerve. "How do I know this isn't some trick?"

Scowling, the goddess said, "I've forgotten how impertinent you are."

There was a part of Ren that would rather not know all the nitty-gritty of her story. Maybe certain memories were better locked away. "I mean, if I tell you whatever it is you want to know," she said, "I need something in return."

"I do not negotiate."

"Tell me if my friends are okay." Ren clung to the hope that the Smoking Mirror had lied and none of her friends were dead. They couldn't be.

An expression of pure wrath crossed Ixtab's face, and Ren wondered if she had asked too much. But how could she go on not knowing which of her friends hadn't made it?

"If they were dead, wouldn't they be here in Xib'alb'a?" Ren asked.

"We get thousands of intakes a day!" Ixtab spoke into her bracelet, in a muttering whisper Ren couldn't quite make out. But she was sure Ixtab was calling on a demon snoop to check things out. With a huff, the goddess turned her gaze to Ren. "My soldiers are on it. Now... it's your turn."

Ren wanted to know how long it would take to get the intel, but she shelved the question, knowing she could only push the goddess so far.

The godborn made her way across the threshold and out into the fragrant garden. The sky was a black canvas streaked with silver.

"How about moving with a bit more urgency?" Ixtab said,

following her closely. "And do not touch the flowers—merely select one to smell."

"That's all it takes?"

Ixtab glowered.

Ren took that as a yes. She bent her face to a purple dahlia and inhaled. It was a strange sensation—like dipping her body into warm wax one inch at a time, beginning with her toes. At once she was no longer tired but invigorated. The regret and sorrow she had felt now vanished, replaced with determination and strength.

Then, in a single blink, everything around her came to life in blazing Technicolor, as if her eyes hadn't been working to their full capacity before now. And her mind? Sharp, bright—ready.

When Ren turned back to Ixtab, the goddess was sitting at a long table that hadn't been there a moment ago. It was loaded with pastries, chocolates, truffles, tiny cakes, bowls of berries, and a tower of colorful macarons.

"Did you do all this for me?" Ren asked, suddenly famished.

Ixtab shook her head. "For some reason unbeknownst to me, the dead are fueled by sugar, so, in essence, I did this for me."

"The dead eat?" Ren sat at the table across from the goddess, plucked a perfectly formed chocolate shell from its plate, and popped it into her mouth. The buttery sweetness burst across her tongue. "Delish!"

Ixtab sat back, folded her lithe arms across her chest, and glared at Ren. "My patience is waning. Now, tell me everything you know about these lords."

After swallowing a macaron, Ren said, "Sure, but, uh...
have you heard about my friends yet?" Ren really didn't want
to give away the whole kitchen sink. She needed to reserve a
few key points for negotiation purposes if she was ever going
to get the information she needed.

"You have no choice but to tell me what I seek, godborn. If
you try to hold anything back, it will only make you vomit, and
I would rather not see such a putrid sight."

Ren realized—too late—that the feast before her was
magicked, and she had been the dupe to inhale it. "You used a
truth serum on me?"

"Did you really think I would trust you to give me all the
details otherwise?"

Ren clenched her jaw and held her tongue. Her nostrils
flared. No way. She wasn't going to give up all her knowledge
without a solid trade.

Ixtab laughed lightly. "It is going to come up one way or
another."

Ren could feel the chocolate and macaron churning like a
maelstrom of acid in her gut and then rising in her esophagus.
A vicious heat clawed up her throat, spread across her tongue.
And when she could no longer hold in the truth, she opened her
mouth and released all the details, down to their finest points.

She told Ixtab about each Lord of Night whom she had met.
There was Centeotl, the maize god; Jade Is Her Skirt, god-
dess of water; Piltzintecuhtli, the Prince Lord; the Smoking
Mirror, god of the night sky; and Xiuhtecuhtli, the Fire Lord.
She even told her about Seven Death, the retired Maya demon

who had once worked undercover for Ah-Puch. With each word she spoke, Ren cringed. She cursed herself for falling into the goddess's trap.

Ixtab nodded, waving her hand impatiently. "Yes, we know all this. You think I don't have spies, too?"

"Then why are you asking me?"

"I didn't become queen of the underworld by relying on only one source of information."

"Well, did you know that the Lords of Night hid their magic in a few humans?" Ren spat. She clapped her palm over her traitorous mouth. Her entire body buzzed with frustration. But the more she tried to withhold additional facts, the faster the words flew from her mouth. "A magic that never sleeps? Shadow magic?"

Ixtab shifted. And in that moment, Ren realized she had surprised the goddess, a rare feat. Something about it made Ren feel prideful, powerful, maybe even gleeful.

Ixtab stood, making a sound between a growl and a sigh, and as she rose, the feathers of her dress shifted back and forth like wings preparing to take flight. With a snap of her finger, the cage that held Ren's magic appeared on the center of the table. Ixtab studied it, frowning and pursing her lips. And Ren knew why. The goddess was angry that the lords had been clever, hiding their magic in humans like that. But Ixtab was even angrier that she didn't know about it and Ah-Puch did.

Ixtab said, "Your magic comes directly from those... those...?"

"Technically, from Jade Is Her Skirt."

"That changes things."

"Changes as in I'm not going to stay dead?"

Never taking her now blazing eyes off the ball of shadows, Ixtab traced her fingers along the cage. It rose into the air, spinning on the rope of stars. "It's not possible," she said with a contorted smile, "to separate your shadow magic from the lords' darkness now."

Ren went cold. "How...? Are you saying...?"

Ixtab turned to her. "Let me spell it out for you. There is no way you can possess the shadow magic without also possessing the lords' darkness."

Ren had relinquished herself to the dark before her death. She had let it swallow her whole. There was no way she would ever do that again, even if it meant not having any magic.

And then the memory dawned with such clarity Ren felt ill. She had made Ah-Puch promise to end her life rather than let her live as an evil queen.

She had willed the time rope to him so the lords would never get their hands on it and be able control time.

But had it worked? Did the god of death possess the rope now?

Ren pushed back from the table and stood. "I need to get back to the real world, to save my friends and..." She felt a terrible pressure in her chest, like the weight of the world had settled there. "What if I could put the lords back into their slumber? Would my shadow magic be free of the darkness then?"

"And just how do you propose to do that?"

Okay, so Ren hadn't thought that part through. Not wanting to look entirely unprepared, she went with her first thought. "With your help. Because you're queen of the underworld."

Bah. That had come out all wrong.

A wicked leer fanned out across Ixtab's face. "When will you realize that I sacrificed everything to become queen? Winning my power was one thing, but keeping it? More difficult than your little brain could fathom, so no, Renata, I will not help you. . . . Unless it serves my best interests."

"But it does! You don't want to deal with those nasty lords, do you?"

Ixtab plucked a feather from her gown and twirled it between her fingers. Then, with a sigh, she said, "If you only knew the number of enemies I have to deal with at any given time. One more or less does not tip the scales."

Surely there was something the goddess wanted. But before Ren could figure that out, Ixtab said, "But if I *did* choose to bargain with you . . ." Her voice trailed off as she narrowed her eyes.

Bingo! So Ixtab *did* want something, and whatever it was, Ren would deliver—she'd pay any price. "All you have to do is give me my life back," she blurted. It was the best solution to get her everything she desired: a chance to save her friends and put those lousy lords back to sleep, to fix everything she had somehow broken.

Ixtab paced, her footsteps as silent as the night. "I am in the business of death, not life."

"It's all on the same spectrum . . ." Ren offered, challenging the goddess's ego.

Ixtab stared up at the night sky, clearly dragging out her response. Then the goddess turned to her and said, "The crown of jade and shadow. Bring it to me and I will give you back your life."

Why would Ixtab want the crown the lords had made me wear? Ren wondered, but she was too ecstatic to delve into it. She thrust her hand forward and nearly shouted, *Deal!*

"Do not agree so quickly when you don't know the terms," Ixtab warned. "You will have seven days. And if you do not come to me in that time *with* the crown, then I will release your shadow magic and you will return to this dark world for eternity, dead as dead, locked away here in the bowels of the underworld."

Oh. Perfect. Dead and miserable.

Not exactly what Ren was expecting, but what choice did she have? "Er...I'm not going back to my world as a ghost, though, right? I mean, I'll be alive and stuff?"

Ixtab exhaled. "I suppose you will be at a better advantage as a living being. The dead are far too unpredictable."

Ren had never felt so relieved. She needed to make things right, no matter the cost. And while being alive was a good start, she also needed some power. That part was definitely trickier. "So, I don't have my shadow magic and..." She cleared her throat. "I, uh...don't exactly have the time rope, either."

"Must you always tell me the obvious?"

"You knew?"

"It is no longer around your neck, so yes, I deduced, and it didn't take me long to realize to whom you gave it."

"I gave it away to save it from falling into the lords' hands."

"How very selfless of you." The goddess's voice dripped with sarcasm.

Ren wasn't sure why, but Ixtab's calm unsettled her. She had expected the goddess to blow a gasket, and yet here she was, taking it all in stride like they were talking about a piece of floss and not the most powerful time magic in the universe.

"So you know I gave it to Ah-Puch."

"Mm-hmm ... Let me know how that works out for you now that ..."

"Now that what?"

"You'll find out soon enough," Ixtab said, and then added, "You will need to change out of that revolting dress."

Ren looked down at the silver gown that had been made for her coronation. She hated to admit it, but it was beautiful. Regardless, it wasn't hers and never would be. The tips of her red cowboy boots poked out from the gown's hem, and she smiled, reassured that even when she had been lost to the dark, a flicker inside her knew who she really was.

The goddess looked Ren up and down, and just as she was about to snap her fingers, Ren said, "Wait! If you're going to put me into something else, it needs to be comfortable. Like, I need to be able to run and jump and—"

"So, hideous stretchy pants."

"Stretchy, yes, but hideous, not so much. And don't touch the boots!"

With a sigh, the goddess snapped her fingers, and the next thing Ren knew, she was wearing black yoga pants and a matching sweatshirt. She looked like a cowboy ninja, and ... she absolutely loved it.

Feeling more like herself, Ren walked over to Ixtab, trying to keep her gaze from darting to the caged ball of shadow magic. With each step she was reminded of something Ixtab had said that she couldn't quite shake: *A soul of magic will always be guided to its source of greatest strength.*

The moment the words floated across Ren's mind, the cage swayed, and the ball of darkness trembled and extended toward the bars as if it had read her mind.

Ixtab, taking notice, scowled. When Ren asked her what she had meant, the goddess said, "Have you never wondered about your godborn powers?"

Ren blinked. "I... I controlled the time rope and..." She reached back to all the moments she had inadvertently interrupted time—a minute here or there, but nothing of consequence.

Ixtab steepled her fingers, tapping her nails together again. "You never asked because you had the shadow magic and the time rope, enough magic to make you quite powerful and fearsome," she said. "But your shadow magic masked your godborn powers—and inhibited them. And now... *that* is no longer in the way."

Ren went still, feeling the icy truth spread across her scalp and down her spine. "Then what *is* my godborn power?" she asked, suddenly terrified that whatever it was, it wouldn't be enough.

Ixtab pressed her red lips into an ominous smile. "When you face death a second time, you will realize your full supernatural potential. But by then it will likely be too late."

4

Going from dead to alive wasn't what Ren had expected.

She had thought the goddess would snap her fingers and, presto, Ren would wake up under some shady tree in the world of the living.

Yeah, well, that's what Ren got for thinking.

Instead, Ren ended up in a narrow underground cavern, crossing a dark river in a canoe. Her bony tour guide looked like a hologram—there but not quite there.

"I am Captain Z," the guide said, rowing the boat steadily. His joints creaked and groaned with each paddle of the oar. If he turned to the right, he was a young guy, but when he tilted his face to the left, all Ren saw was a skeleton in a bad wig. His dazzling blue sequined jacket twinkled as they passed the wall torches.

"I'm Ren."

The flickering firelight glinted off the dark waters, which happened to be overflowing with shiny black scorpions as big as rats, all crawling over one another.

Their hissing echoed across the chamber, and Ren shuddered, wishing her guide would hustle his bones.

"Uh . . . are those things going to come inside the boat?" Ren didn't want to sound like a chicken, but without her powers inside her, there was more room for her fear to grow.

"Probably," Captain Z said. "They smell fright, so you should definitely remain calm, centered . . . Zen-like."

Right. Best way to get someone to lose their Zen is to tell them not to lose their Zen. Ren twisted her fingers and tried to do one of her meditative calming techniques, but her nerves were all jumbled.

Captain Z said, "I've never taken someone upriver before. Death is usually a one-way ticket, you know."

Usually?

"Right, but I, uh . . . have some things left to do." People to save, lords to knock out.

A scorpion with plump legs click-clicked across the gunwale. Its arched tail had a vicious red stinger on the end, and its claws were enormous. But the creepiest part of all was its face—human-ish, except for the slimy mouth filled with fangs. Ren stifled a scream and then, with the toe of her cowboy boot, gave the thing a swift kick, sending it over the side.

Captain Z snorted. "Not exactly Zen, but okay." He glanced down at her red boots. "Nice kickers, by the way."

"Good bug squashers, too."

With an approving nod, he circled back to his point. "You've got unfinished business, eh? All the dead say that. But that doesn't get them a ticket back to the land of the living. You must be special. Either that orrr . . . you have only been given a rare leave of absence. In which case, you'll be back."

Sitting up straighter, Ren said, "Leave of absence? What does that mean?"

"It means that if a dead person has been on excellent

behavior, has done their underworld job with absolute perfection, and promises not to haunt, bite, terrorize, or otherwise interfere with human existence, then they might, and I repeat *might*, get a temporary leave."

Ren hated the sounds that came from the oar slicing through the scorpion-infested water. Every once in a while, there would be a *crunch* and then an ear-piercing hiss that chilled her to her bones.

"How long have you been here?" Ren asked, thinking that conversation would mask her fear, and maybe, if she was lucky, make the trip go faster.

Captain Z swept a tangled strand of his wig back over his shoulder. "Eons."

"So you've probably seen lots of wild stuff."

"Indeed."

Ren shifted her weight on the seat cushion. "Like what?"

Captain Z rowed the boat slowly, like he had nowhere else to be. "I am not at liberty to discuss that," he said. "We sign a nondisclosure agreement when we arrive. The secrets of the underworld are vast and . . ." He cleared his throat. "They are not to be revealed, ever."

A stab of disappointment pierced Ren's dead heart. She was a sucker for secrets, especially the delicious kind found in places like Xib'alb'a.

"I won't tell," she said, pretending to zip her mouth closed. "Ask anyone who knows me, and they'll tell you I am seriously the most amazing secret keeper."

A few scorpions slinked up an oar. Captain Z sighed, then

opened his mouth, and the sound that came out shattered Ren's illusion of Zen. It was a screech so loud, she had to cover her ears. Apparently, the nasty little monsters didn't like it, either, because they leaped off the boat like it was sinking.

"Sorry 'bout that," said Captain Z. "Now, where were we? Oh, right! Secrets. Yeah, well, I can't tell you any, but"—he leaned forward and whispered—"I know who you are."

Ren froze, unsure of what to say. But she didn't want to show her surprise or sudden edginess because, after all, she was in the underworld with a dead guy rowing her across a river of monsters that wanted to eat her for dinner.

"You're the powerful bruja," he went on. "A godborn, too."

I'm not so powerful, Ren wanted to say, but strength was the only currency that seemed to matter down here, so she went with "How did you know?"

"Let's just say that there is a potent and vast whisper network in the underworld. And you've been watched."

"Watched?"

"You have mighty fine friends."

Ren was about to ask more when the little boat bumped up against a dock that had appeared out of nowhere.

"And we have arrived," Captain Z announced, as if he were talking to an entire cruise ship of passengers instead of a single lonely soul trying to get out of hell. "Take the path straight up," he said as he stood to leave. "You'll land where your heart most desires to be."

Ren wondered where that was. Would she end up back home in Texas with her abuelo? Or maybe she'd wake up in

SHIHOM, the Shaman Institute of Higher-Order Magic, where she had spent the summer training with her friends and fellow godborns.

Her insides buzzed with anticipation. "Thanks, Captain Z."

He turned his face to the right, and there, in the glow of the torches, he looked entirely human. Ren wanted to ask how he ended up here, who he'd been before, but she figured that was too personal. And besides, maybe he didn't want to remember.

"I hope I don't see you again," Ren said, and immediately realized that had come out all wrong. "I mean..."

Captain Z laughed. "I know what you meant. But everyone will meet me again...eventually."

Ren gave his bony hand a high five as she walked past him to step onto the dock. "Then how about not anytime soon?"

"Oh, speaking of timing, we try to get it just right on the rare occasions when we send souls back, but sometimes we can be off by a moment or two. Or even a decade. So, you know... just go with the flow and all that."

Ren's mouth fell open. A decade?!

It had never occurred to her to ask how much time had passed since she'd died. And she knew the Maya realm well enough to understand that time passed differently in the magical spheres. A few minutes here could've been a week or more in the real world.

"I bet you got it just right," Ren said, because even after everything, her spirit was still optimistic.

"Good luck, and say hi to Ah-Puch for me."

"You know Ah-Puch?"

Captain Z laughed and pushed the boat away from the dock. "We all know the former king."

"Because he used to run things down here?" Ren guessed. He had, until Ixtab overthrew all the underlords and took over the place.

"Just be careful."

Ren wanted to laugh. A.P. was her best friend and greatest protector. Okay, so maybe he hated the world and everyone in it, but she knew she had a place in his dark heart. "I'll be fine."

Captain Z clucked his tongue. "Well, rumor has it that . . ."

"That what?"

Captain Z chortled as he rowed into the darkness. His voice echoed across the rock walls when he said, "Our former king is out for blood."

Out for blood? The scrawny teen who'd lost all of his godly powers? *Captain Z has it all wrong,* Ren thought as she stood there all alone on the slippery dock. She wished she had even an ounce of magic, a speck of power. Something to help her with what was probably the biggest quest of her life.

When you face death a second time, you will realize your full supernatural potential.

"Lot of good it'll do me, then," Ren said under her breath as she started walking up the dirt path. Her shadow loomed across the torchlit walls, looking larger and more menacing than she actually was. It made her miss her sombras, but she couldn't think about what she didn't have. She couldn't long for the magic that was locked in a cage, especially not when it was a part of the darkness that had consumed her before.

Ren took a few more steps. A cool draft wafted from up ahead.

This for sure does not feel like my heart's desire.

And she wondered where exactly the skeleton had left her.

5

Ren put one foot in front of the other, slowly at first, and then fast. Too fast, because in the next moment she walked into—and bounced off—an invisible surface that felt rubbery, like a giant balloon. She was thrust backward and landed on her bottom with a painful thud.

She widened her eyes, trying to make out the nature of the obstacle. Why couldn't Ixtab have just set her on some sandy shore and called it a day?

And why was she still in the underworld?

Ren got to her feet and took a few tentative steps forward. The barrier now began to glow a faint blue. She pressed her hands against the slimy membrane and was just about to poke her hand through when she saw a dim light flicker awake on the other side. The wall became transparent enough for her to see a room there.

It was a familiar place back in the above world, a place she'd been in only a few weeks ago—Ah-Puch's safe house, the one tucked away in a thick forest that was protected by mountain spirits. She recognized the large stone fireplace, the elegant furniture, the massive window that overlooked the trees. But the living room was darker than before, as if it had been swallowed by gloom and shadow. *Why would Ixtab drop me here?*

she wondered. And then Ren remembered what Captain Z had said: *You'll land where your heart most desires to be.*

In the next blink, a crowd materialized like mist. Ren peered closer. The guests seemed to know each other as they mingled with drinks in their hands. Their necks, faces, and arms were painted with eye-catching tattoos: huge red birds, green-and-gold snakes, blue-and-black panthers, each animal in motion as if leaping, slithering, or flying off the person's body.

Ren was fascinated, but no matter how closely she leaned, she couldn't hear their chatter.

Scanning the crowd, her eyes landed on Ah-Puch.

Her heart leaped at the sight of him. He was facing away from her, gripping the stone hearth, but even from this side of death, she could see the roped muscles in his back through his white button-down shirt. She could sense the power radiating from the god like heat rising from summer asphalt.

Gone was the skinny kid with no powers. But how?

Ren pounded on the slick wall, desperate to get back to the land of the living. "A.P.!"

A woman with a fire-breathing dragon inked on her cheeks walked up to him, but Ren could tell by his averted gaze and tense stance that he wasn't interested in anything she was saying.

Suddenly, a hand went around Ren's mouth and a voice whispered in her ear, "Hey, don't freak or scream, okay?"

With a swift back kick to her assailant's knee, Ren broke free and spun, fists raised.

"Edison?"

Standing before her was a boy, tall and lanky with dark eyes and hair, part demon and part something else that no one could confirm. He was loyal, sweet, and funny, and he was not dead. Or at least he didn't look it. Come to think of it, he looked really good. She wasn't sure whether it was the low light, or the dark hoodie and cargo pants.

He gave her a sheepish wave. "Hey."

"Hey?" Ren managed. "I thought..." She grabbed his arms and gave them a shake, as if she needed more tangible proof that he stood right here in the flesh. "Are you real? The Smoking Mirror said... I thought you were dead!"

"I guess, technically, I'm half dead," he joked.

"This is so not funny!"

He forced a frown and nodded. "Right."

Then, unable to be mad at him a second longer, she threw her arms around his neck and hugged him. He was definitely real. "How...? Why are you here?"

Edison pulled back, offering her a tight smile. "I was raised here, remember?"

Right. Xib'alb'a was his home. Or at least the place where he'd been hidden away since birth in order to keep his mixed-blood identity a secret from Ixtab. But then A.P. had found him and whisked him away a couple of months ago.

"But you were... Ezra said she saw you losing a battle. I don't get it." Ren felt a tidal wave of emotion, mostly relief but also confusion. The idea of Edison losing a fight was madness given how powerful the demon was. He had the ability to create energy from different sources, such as light or heat, or even super-intense emotion, like fear. He could use it like a sphere of power that expanded until it hit its target with a blast. So he was pretty much a walking, breathing bomb.

"I did lose," he said flatly, squeezing his hands together. "I had to."

"Had to?"

"I was there when the arrow flew," Edison said, throwing his gaze to the rocky ceiling. "I was their prisoner by then, and when you were hit and everything fell apart, I maybe . . . picked a fight." His eyes flicked back to Ren's. "It's a bummer of a rule, but half demons can't just walk in and out of Xib'alb'a. Especially ones who aren't supposed to exist."

It took Ren a handful of seconds to process exactly what her friend was telling her. "Wait. Did you seriously let them kill you?" *For me?* she added silently.

"*Kill* isn't the right word. I mean, I am part demon, Ren, and we're sort of like . . ." He paused before adding brightly, "Cats. We've got lots of lives. Not nine, exactly. More like . . ."

"Like what?"

"It doesn't matter."

"Edison!"

"There isn't a rule book for halfers, ya know?" He stuffed his hands in his pockets and rocked back and forth on his heels. "I don't really know how many times I can bite the bullet—or is it kick the bucket?—and return to the land of the living. Anyhow, I'm here."

"So you could have been dead for real?"

"But I'm not." He flashed a smile that in no way was going to win Ren over.

"You can't just go around dying! You could have been stuck here for good, and you didn't even know I would end up here. I could have gone to the Aztec underworld of Mictlan, and your sacrifice would have been for nothing! And now what? You're stalking around, sneaking up on people?"

He glanced over his shoulder, then back at Ren. "Maybe you could be a little quieter?"

"Can we just get out of here?"

Edison gestured to Ah-Puch through the translucent wall. "Are you sure you want to do this?"

"This? You mean tell A.P. I'm not dead?" The god must have been sick with grief. All those people at his house were probably demon warriors in disguise or something, ready to launch some massive revenge plot. But then it occurred to Ren that if Edison, a half demon, could sneak his way into the underworld, surely A.P. could have waltzed right in, too, especially given that he had a new condo here. So then why hadn't he?

"You've been gone a month, Ren," Edison said. "Things have changed in the living world."

"A month?! My abuelo!" The last thing he'd heard was that Ren had gone searching for the cinco.

"I sent a note to him that you were working undercover on an important mission and not to worry."

"You can send letters from the underworld?"

"Sure. I mean, stamps are super hard to come by, but we've got a pretty good delivery system."

Ren felt a ball of relief unfold in her gut. "Thanks. I . . . owe you one."

"Nah. If I had a grandpa, I wouldn't want him to worry, either."

Ren chewed her bottom lip, nodding. "How do we get through this wall?" Then she pounded on it again, shouting the god's name. But he didn't turn. As a matter of fact, no one did. Was this like a one-way mirror sort of thing?

"Could you stop doing that?" Edison said.

"What's your deal? I want out of here, and I want to see my best friend!"

Edison rubbed the back of his neck and grimaced. "Ren, he, uh . . . isn't the same."

"Because he's a god again? You think that would scare me away?" She shook her head. "I met him when he was, like, the fully powered god of death, darkness, and destruction."

Ren followed Edison's gaze to Ah-Puch. She called the god's name again. A.P. must have heard her this time, or sensed he was being watched, because he cocked his head and turned slowly.

"Oh man," Edison said, rubbing his forehead and wearing a pained expression that looked a lot like fear. "You really should know, he's like, um . . . way different."

The god's eyes found Ren's. His dark gaze pinned her in place. Okay, he was definitely back in his terrifying godly form. Ren wanted to smile and say, *Hey! Surprise! Back from the dead!* But she couldn't find the words or her footing because Ah-Puch didn't look happy to see her.

Our former king is out for blood.

"This is a really bad idea," Edison muttered.

But Ren was only half listening. She was lost in her thoughts. *Maybe A.P.'s mad because I made him promise to kill me.* Murder was definitely a mood killer.

The god strode toward her, his eyes angry slits. Swirls of black mist rose all around him, snapping like vicious jaws.

The guests' gazes followed the god, and as they did, their inked beasts shifted their gazes, too.

Ren saw it then, in the god's obsidian eyes. There was no recognition in them, only fury. "A.P.?" Ren whispered, shrinking back.

Then, with a violent growl, the god thrust out a hand and ripped Ren from the underworld.

6

Ren had never been in the grip of the god of death and destruction before. She had never been the reason for his wrath.

She had never faced his absolute darkness, and yet here she was dangling at least eight feet in the air, held there by a single finger under her chin, as if she were a mere feather.

A painful frost crawled over her skin.

The crowd was silent.

"The last fool who spied on me," Ah-Puch growled, "lost his head."

"It's me!" Ren cried, trying to wriggle free, but there was no way that was going to happen until the god said so. "If you'll just put me down, I can explain!"

A sinister smile fanned out across his mouth. "I think not. But lucky for you, I like to play with my food a bit before I devour it."

Someone in the crowd laughed, a grating sound that sent a long shiver down Ren's spine. Ah-Puch's stony expression caused a new wave of panic to surge through her veins.

"Why are you acting like this?" she asked. "I'm your best friend. You're being rude!"

The god's dark eyes glittered menacingly. "I have no friends."

Ren, still chilled, looked around quizzically. "But you're

having a party." She saw no sign of Edison and wondered what had happened to him.

"They are not my friends." The god swept a hand in the air, and the crowd vanished as quickly as it had materialized. "They are a necessity."

If Ren lived through this, she was definitely going to ask what he meant by that.

How could A.P. not remember her? So this was what Edison had been trying to warn her about. Fresh anger slammed into her panic like a hammer, smashing it to bits.

"I was *killed*!" she shouted.

"You look very alive to me. But not to worry, that won't be for long."

"And I went to the underworld to some disgusting spider house, faced off with Ixtab, and ate some not very good macarons," she went on, growing more frustrated with each word. "My shadow magic was removed and stuffed into a cage, A.P.! And then I had to cross Scorpion River with a skeleton just to get back here to your ungrateful—"

"Ah, ah, ah," A.P. sang, wagging a finger in her face. "Be very careful about what you say next." Then he frowned deeply. "And what is this A.P. you speak of?"

"It's my nickname for you."

He stared into her eyes with an intensity that could ignite her into a mini bonfire. But the rest of his expression was flat, unmoved. She clearly wasn't getting through to him. She took a deep breath and tried a different tactic. "I saved your life once," she said. "This is your safe house, guarded by mountain spirits Citla and Mina, and I know it was awful to ask you to kill me, but I couldn't be queen, and you did it because...you understood, and because...you love me...." The god had never told her such a thing, but she had sensed it on more than one occasion.

"I know"—when he spoke his next words, they carried a darkness Ren felt down to her bones—"nothing of love and its endless weaknesses."

A freezer-like burning sensation spread though Ren's chest. Tears threatened. And not because she was afraid of being devoured or turned into an ice cube, but because she was staring into the eyes of a being she had learned to love and trust. A being who didn't even remember her.

Ren felt a familiar power rolling off Ah-Puch. Shifting her gaze to his wrists, she saw that he wore a single glowing band on each one. She blinked, took a breath, could barely form the thought, much less believe it. But there it was, a mere six feet from her....

The time rope. Split in two.

"I...I gave you that!" Ren squealed, pointing. She wanted to cheer, to pump her fists, to do a victory lap, but she was still dangling in the air with the god of death on the verge of destroying her, and something told her it would likely be a slow and painful process. "That's my rope!"

But what did it matter? The rules of the rope were simple. It could never be taken, only given away, and there was no way this version of Ah-Puch would give away that sort of power.

"You are a sad, pathetic little creature," the god said. "Foolishly brave, and entirely out of your mind. These cords are mine. They have been since..." He hesitated, and his face clouded over. "Since..."

The cords began to glimmer.

They pulsed once, twice, drawing the god's attention. Ah-Puch let Ren fall to the floor as the ropes uncoiled, one end of each remaining around his wrists and the other ends snaking toward Ren as she got to her feet.

With a growl, Ah-Puch jerked his hands back, but even his godly power wasn't enough to pull the great time rope back to him.

Ren watched as the twin ropes floated in the space between her and the god of death, drawing nearer and nearer to her. She held her breath as they twisted around her wrists with an unimaginable warmth, binding her to Ah-Puch.

Wait! This was all wrong.

"Make it stop!" Ah-Puch demanded.

"I...I can't!"

The air went still. The clock on the mantel stopped ticking; even the gloom froze. But not Ah-Puch—he yanked on the ropes, which only made them grasp tighter.

"Can you just chill out?" Ren insisted, hoping she wouldn't be forever tied to this grouchy, irrational, murderous god.

"Do you know who you're talking to?"

Ren rolled her eyes. "Why do all you gods have to be so infuriating and egotistical?"

"How dare—"

There was a flash of blue light, and then Edison drop-rolled into the room. He jumped to his feet, his hands held out defensively as if he didn't trust the time rope's hold on the god. Ren had forgotten how cool his ability to evaporate and reappear at will was.

"Hey, Ah-Puch," he said. "Good to see you."

"What is this treachery, demon?" the god roared. "You think you can use a portal from the underworld to penetrate my dwelling?"

"I didn't use a portal," Edison said, keeping his distance. "Though it was a lot harder to get in than I thought. But don't worry, I'm here to help jog your memory." He rubbed his jaw and sighed. "I made a solemn oath to you to protect Ren no matter what. And she's going to need you, so like it or not, you're a part of this now."

An oath? Ren frowned. Then she remembered that when she first met Edison he'd said A.P. had hired him to protect her. At the time, she'd found that hilarious, given that she was the daughter of time and a shadow bruja.

"I know every creature that works for me, demon, and you, with your half-breed blood that I can smell from here," the god said, scowling, "are certainly not one of them!"

In the next instant, Ren and Ah-Puch were encircled by a sphere of light so blinding she had to squeeze her eyes shut. As the god bellowed curses and threats, Ren wished she could raise her hands to clap them over her ears, but they were still bound by the ropes.

Her feet began to lift off the floor.

Ren felt a warm hand grab her arm as the light vibrated with a low hum. She knew without looking it was Edison, trying to keep her grounded. A current of cool air brushed her cheeks. Then the light faded, and Ren opened her eyes to see that the safe house was gone.

The trio was now standing within a semicircle of five pyramids that were surrounded by a jungle of metallic trees. Thick cobwebs dangled from the skeletal silver branches, and the dark sky was riddled with cracks, like it was about to shatter.

"Puksik'al," Ren whispered with a sense of awe.

"That's Mayan for *heart*, right?" Edison said, his eyes darting back and forth across the massive pyramids. "How did we get here?"

"The time rope brought us to the heart of the Old World," Ren told him. "It's a place the Maya gods created together, where they could meet, give counsel, pass judgment."

"Not *this* god," A.P. growled, tugging at the time rope. "I demand to be set free from this miserable, wretched place!"

He looked around at the Old World, probably with a bitter taste in his mouth and wicked memories in his mind. After all, Ren knew, this was where he had faced off with the Maya gods who had wanted to keep him locked away, and later Zane Obispo, fellow godborn and son of fire, who had wanted to end him.

But why had the time rope brought them here?

Turning in circles, Edison drew a hand through his thick hair. "This place is amazing—tons of power pulsing everywhere! I've never felt so much energy in one place. Not even in the Maze of Nightmares."

Ren shuddered at the memory of their near-death experience there.

Raising his hand, Edison flexed his fingers, and a blue

sphere of light appeared in his palm. It pulsed like it had breath, casting a pale blue tint across his dark features. It reminded Ren of the vision she'd seen in the maze, the one in which she'd driven a dagger through Edison. She sucked in a sharp breath, willing that prediction to become a pile of dust. *It wasn't real. It could never be real.*

The demon launched the energy ball into the air like a rocket. It met the torn sky, ricocheted, and burned out before it fell to the ground.

"Hmph," Edison snorted. "I guess that sky is stronger than it looks."

Ren said, "This is where the first world was dreamed up. And the second, and the third. The oldest and most powerful magic in the universe was born here." *My mother's time magic.*

A.P. tugged on the rope again. But the harder he jerked, the tighter it gripped.

"It's not going to let you go when you're throwing a big fit," Ren said.

"This blasted rope will NOT hold me!"

"Er, it already is," Edison said kindly, which only made A.P.'s growl deeper.

Ren, too occupied by the majestic beauty and history of this place, ignored the god and told Edison, "This is sacred ground. The whole place is held together by magic."

"I've read about the Old World," Edison said. "How each side of each pyramid has ninety-one steps, making three hundred and sixty-four in total. When you add the step taken to enter the temple at the top, the total comes to three hundred and sixty-five, the number of days in a year."

"How charming. A demon who can count," A.P. said with a roll of his eyes.

"This is how the marking of time came to be. It was invented in this place," Ren said proudly, as if she had been one of its architects.

At the same moment, the sound of metal crashing against metal reverberated through the steel jungle.

Clang. Clang.

Great flashes of light flared in the distance as if lightning were consuming the forest. A cold feeling wrapped itself around Ren. The air seemed to thicken, darken, and shimmer all at once. She felt as if death itself had just arrived.

"What's that?" Edison whispered.

"I think it's the Sparkstriker," Ren said, "banging her axe against the trees."

"The lightning-pounder?" Edison asked.

Ah-Puch groaned. "More like a strange witch-slash-seer who trains orphan girls to be warriors, which is the most preposterous mission I have ever heard of!" He looked down at the time ropes and gave them a shake. "Take us away from here!"

"The rope brought us here for a reason," Ren said. "I think it has to do with the fact that time was created here."

"You know nothing of time or history or magic," A.P. declared in a wicked tone.

Edison's expression tightened. "Actually, Ren knows a lot, and if your memory weren't so . . . faded, you'd know that she's the most powerful godborn and she saved your life."

"I have never needed saving," the god asserted. "And you," he said to Ren, "are a pitiably weak creature without an ounce of magic or power." Black mist floated from the god's mouth, as if each word was wrapped in his darkness.

Ren's face burned hot, her chest caved, and her heart pounded relentlessly against her rib cage. The god was right. She had no powers, no magic. . . . She had nothing but hope and affection. Affection for a god who maybe didn't deserve it, but she knew that somewhere deep inside of this monster, a part of him loved her, too.

She was still a godborn by blood, and that gave her the ability to talk to Ah-Puch in the most private of spaces: their minds.

You told me once that you knew a thing or two about the dark, she said.

His expression was tight with fury as he loomed above her menacingly. *How dare you speak to me like this, uninvited and with such insolence?*

You need to remember me.

The corner of his mouth twitched. *What I need is to do is extricate myself from these bindings, and to destroy them as quickly as I plan to destroy you.*

Ren forced herself to remain still, to not shrink back.

You said that the dark was all-consuming, and that it tricks you into making you think you want it. It makes you believe you'd rather dwell in its depths than seek the light. And that means you know about light, too!

Clang. Clang.

The sound was coming closer, and with each crash, the ropes warmed and glowed brighter.

The god's nose flared and his jaw clenched. *I would never in the longest of eternities express such a feeble, useless thought.*

"I can sort of see why you're not the most popular god," Ren whispered.

Edison said, "I don't think that's going to motivate him."

Ren gripped the rope, closed her eyes, and imagined A.P. as he used to be, as she remembered him. His anger coursed through the ropes just as Ren filled her heart and memory with love for the god. She let the emotion grow and expand like a balloon. The god was silent, too silent. Ren opened her eyes and looked up, expecting his death glare to kill her instantly.

The god's gaze locked on hers, and swirls of darkness clouded his black eyes. "What did you just say?"

Even though she hadn't said a word, she knew the god had felt her love.

And then . . . she saw it. The softening, the remembering.

He blinked, stepped back. The darkness receded completely, and his shoulders slumped. "Ren?"

Edison huffed what sounded like a sigh of relief as tears sprang to Ren's eyes. Without hesitation, she flung herself into A.P.'s arms. The god of death wasn't a hugger . . . ever, but in this moment, in this tiny flicker of existence, he wrapped one arm around her and then another. He held her close, so close she could feel his heart beating with joy. Or maybe it was her own joy. But it didn't matter. He remembered her!

"How . . . ?" he faltered, trembled, then pulled back to create some distance between them—as much as the rope would allow, which was about six feet.

His obsidian eyes searched her face, full of doubt and suspicion, as if he couldn't quite believe Ren stood before him. "I watched you die! You were . . . consumed by the dark!" His gaze flicked to Edison's. "And you . . . Those fiendish lords caught you and . . ."

"When I saw you go from kid to god," the demon said, "I knew it was up to me then . . . to keep my promise to protect her, so I did."

"He let himself get killed!" Ren clarified. "How could you make him take a stupid oath like that?"

"I didn't," the god said. "He volunteered."

Oh.

Ren was lost in a storm of questions and confusion, not only about the past but also the present. She wasn't sure where to begin, so she started with what mattered most: her friends. "Where is everyone else?" she asked Ah-Puch. "Are they okay? And Monty? Where is she? Tell me everything."

At the same moment, a thick red mist rolled through the jungle, twisting and morphing into what looked like giant bony hands as it came closer and closer.

Clang. Clang.

A voice echoed across the Old World. "So the time has finally come."

A.P. scanned the vicinity. "Who goes there?"

"You know who I am," the woman's voice sang out.

"The Sparkstriker!" Ren shouted, thinking this was a pretty dramatic entrance even for the lightning-pounder.

"The great seer," the woman amended. Her voice came from all directions. "The great timekeeper. The great lightning-pounder."

"One *great* would suffice," A.P. muttered.

An enormous crack opened beneath Ren's feet. She spun

to get out of the way and determine where it had originated, and that's when she saw the figure. There, at the edge of the tree line. She wore a long red robe, and her auburn hair was a nest of knotted strands, each woven with a string of tiny silver bells. At her side was a huge stone axe. She lifted it high above her head and slammed it into a tree. A violent blow rang out across the Old World.

Then, with a smile, she said, "*Now* the telling can begin."

7

"I WILL CHOOSE the timing of the tale," Ah-Puch warned.

"You are in my world, god of death," the Sparkstriker said, tossing her hair back so that the bells chimed. "And if you ever hope to leave it, I suggest you follow my rules."

"She has a point," Edison whispered to the god.

The night jungle began to glow a sparkling green that illuminated the darkness. The effect was mesmerizing.

A.P. snarled, jerking on the time rope with clenched fists.

"Please," Ren whispered to the god. "Let's do what she says."

"Excellent plan," Edison said, eyeing the axe. "That lady looks pretty tough."

"I AM A GOD!" A.P. shouted.

The Sparkstriker drew closer. She was short in stature but had an air of dignity that made her imposing. "A god with no real power here," she replied.

"A.P." Ren touched his hand gently. "Deep breaths. It's okay. Just hear her out."

Ah-Puch inhaled long and deep. The red in his cheeks faded, and all too quickly, a sinister smile formed on his mouth. "Of course. But do remember, witch," he said, his gaze locked on the Sparkstriker, "a god's memory is long."

"Actually," the Sparkstriker said, fluffing her cape, "I heard you've had a lot of trouble in that department. . . . But no matter, your faculties seem to have been restored, and—"

"Can't we all get along?" Ren said, thinking they were wasting time fighting over trivial things.

"This place smells like dread," A.P. said. "And truly, how about a renovation? Do you not see the cracks in the sky?"

The Sparkstriker's eyes blazed. She twirled her axe like a baton, never taking her gaze off the god. "Oh, Ah-Puch, that is exactly why you are here."

A.P. laughed, a deep, rumbling laugh that should have terrified the woman, but she didn't even flinch. "I am not fixing your hellhole. In case you don't remember, I am the god of *de*struction, not *con*struction."

"Uh . . . I'm pretty handy," Edison chimed in, raising his hand. "I mean, I've never fixed a broken sky, but—"

The Sparkstriker held up her axe to silence the demon. "Let us begin with the tale."

"Or what?" Ah-Puch growled.

With a way-too-pleasant smile, the Sparkstriker said, "And when you are done, I will perhaps grace you with all the Seeing I have been engaged in." She blew out a puff of breath. "I'm not sure you will like it, god of death, but we can't always choose our destinies, now, can we?"

Please let me incinerate her, Ah-Puch told Ren telepathically.

You know that isn't going to happen.

But it makes me feel better just to imagine it.

Over the next fifteen minutes, Ren learned what had happened in the moments that followed her death. Monty, the Aztec hunter-warrior, escaped. The Lords of Night vanished, taking Ren's godborn friend Marco with them. No one knew where the enchanted bird Zyanya had flown off to, only that she hadn't been seen since. And the Obsidian Blade, the arrowhead that housed the bird and could put the lords to sleep? Also gone. Ren knew that if she wanted to find the bird, she had to find the blade first. Zyanya couldn't stay away from her home for too long—it was like a beacon and would eventually call her back.

"Let's not forget those five detestable, deceptive, miscreant godborns who started all the trouble," A.P. said. "They disappeared. I hope they're all writhing in agony somewhere in the bowels of the underworld."

Ren started listing them. "Let's see. . . . There was Serena, daughter of the moon, Kenji, son of bees, and—"

The Sparkstriker giggled.

"You find this amusing?" A.P. said.

"These names . . ." she said. "I remember pounding lightning into each of them. They're like a litter of pups I raised myself."

"Then you did an abysmal job," the god said, earning a knowing smirk from the woman. Ren could tell that she held secrets.

"Go on," Sparkstriker said impatiently. "You were talking about the miscreant godborns."

"Right," Edison said. "Diamante, daughter of Akan, and Ezra . . ."

Ren's mind tripped on Ezra, the daughter of spells and magic. Ezra had the ability to astral travel and put moments to sleep. She once possessed the orb that had awakened the Lords of Night in the first place.

"Ezra tricked me," Ren said. "She knew the only way to get her hands on the Obsidian Blade was by using me to get to you, A.P."

"Ah, yes," the Sparkstriker said. "I remember her cleverness."

Ren recalled the hateful words Ezra had spewed at her when Ren was in a shadow cage of her own making. *You're not even pure. You're tainted with Mexica blood, a shadow witch, a descendant of dead gods.*

Ren felt a sharp pain in her chest that radiated to her stomach. She'd been so tired of being discounted, of being bullied and pushed around. And she had let that sadness and fear and anger open her up to the darkness.

"You think Ezra is still with the lords?" Ren asked the group.

"Yes," said Edison. "According to a couple of A.P.'s spies, and some ghosts in the underworld."

A.P. rolled his eyes. "How many times have I told you that you cannot trust a ghost? I didn't pluck you from the underworld so you could be gullible."

"Really?" Edison countered. "I've never caught one lying to me."

Clang. Clang.

The Sparkstriker struck a metal tree once more before she adjusted her cape and sighed. "Let us stick to the facts." She sounded a little like one of those judges on TV.

A.P. growled, and if his gaze could shoot fire, Ren was sure the Sparkstriker would be a charred kabob about now.

Edison folded his arms across his chest and added, "All the rogue godborns are with the Lords of Night. Don't know if they're prisoners or not."

"Mmm," the Sparkstriker said. "Yes, well, I could have told you that."

"Then can you tell us where they are?" Ren asked.

"Not the precise location," the woman said, "but I can tell you it has been quite a dismal experience for them."

To Ren's surprise, Ah-Puch began to laugh ... like belly-grabbing, body-shaking hard. Oh, demons, was he losing it?

"What's so funny?" she asked.

A.P. shook his head, sighed, and gathered himself with a few breaths like he was embarrassed about the outburst. Then, in an even and threatening voice, he said, "It's funny as in ironic, as in so incredulous it has to be a jest."

"Which part?"

"That Ezra, a pathetic nothing of a godborn, the daughter of the new and entirely anemic goddess Yohualli, could do all this damage." His expression tensed with anger. "We need to take care of her once and for all."

The Sparkstriker's stone axe came hurtling through the air, curved around the god, and sailed back to her hands.

A.P. dodged, and the time rope still connecting them dragged Ren in the same direction. "I am growing tired of your voice," he told the Sparkstriker. "Not to mention your presence."

"A.P., stop it!" Ren cried. "I'm sure she's just trying to help."

"By throwing her ridiculous little toothpick of an axe at me?" He tried to lunge at the woman, and the time rope pulsed, glowing with a power that stopped him in his tracks. "I AM NOT A DOG ON A LEASH!" he shouted in frustration.

The Sparkstriker smiled a smile that carried the weight

of her clear animosity toward the god. "Woof, woof," she said under her breath, and Ren could only hope A.P. hadn't heard her.

"I don't want to get revenge on or hurt anyone," Ren said, trying to get the conversation back on track.

"Do as you like," Ah-Puch said haughtily. "But when I get my hands on the Lords of Night, they will pay a price greater than blood for what they did to you." With each word, the veins in his neck and forehead expanded, his eyes bulged, his nose flared.

"A.P.," Ren said, patting his arm, "you need to breathe. Find your center, your calm, so we can figure all of this out."

Edison nodded. "Stress is a total killer. You wouldn't believe how many ghosts I've met who in life had keeled over because of it."

"Calm?!" A.P. exploded. "You want me to be calm when those lords suffocated you with darkness? When they crowned you queen against your will? When they forced your death?" The god snarled. "You cannot be serious, godborn! I will rage against the injustice until I bring them down—every last one of them—in an epic show of strength and pain." He gave the rope another futile tug. "And why is this blasted thing still tying us together?!"

Ren looked down at the rope. For the first time, she wondered, "Why is it in two pieces? Did you break it or something?"

"Had I done so, its magic would have been demolished." Ah-Puch adjusted his shirt cuffs. "Besides, why would I do that when, the moment it attached itself to me, it restored me to my godly form? Finally, I was rid of that despicable teen body I was woefully—"

"You owe the rope a debt of gratitude," the Sparkstriker interjected.

He shot a narrowed gaze at the woman. "Why are you still here?"

She sighed. The bells in her hair chimed, and she said, "To record this critical tale." The Sparkstriker turned her eyes to the sky. Its cracks split wider, and more light leaked out to reveal moving images, as if on a screen. There, Ren saw the entire scene of her death play out: Monty releasing the arrow, the shaft flying straight toward her, then stabbing her in the heart.

Edison said to the Sparkstriker, "Does she really have to look at that?"

"There is power in memory," the woman replied.

Ren's mouth went dry, and she felt sick. It was one thing to experience death, but it was an entirely different thing to watch it from an outsider's point of view. But she wouldn't take her eyes off the images above them, from the magical arrow that had taken her life. She saw the godborns being whisked away by the Lords of Night. And then she saw the time rope sailing to Ah-Puch in his teen form, the magic gripping his wrists and exploding in a great flash of light.

She stole a quick glance at A.P. now. The god was as still and silent as a statue, his eyes fixed on the horrific moment. For the first time, Ren realized what it must have cost him to order her death, and it broke her heart.

"Such an epic ending to the beginning of the tale. I can see why you had to forget the girl," the Sparkstriker said to A.P. "The pain was just too great."

A.P. leveled the woman with one of his signature hateful glares. "There is no pain I cannot endure!"

"Or maybe, when you became a god again, it was like someone hit a reset button in your brain," Ren guessed, wishing Ah-Puch and the seer would quit fighting. "Like A.P. defaulted back to the factory settings. Not actually, but you know what I mean."

"Sounds reasonable," Edison put in.

The god's face clouded over. "Your theory is pathetic and, frankly, annoying. I would never show such weakness." He turned to the Sparkstriker. "Is that the limit of your all-seeing magic, witch? Some images sailing across the sky?"

The woman looked at Ren. "I can keep replaying it . . . or you can tell us what happened to you *after* your death."

Ren winced, then swallowed.

Edison—faithful, loyal Edison—said, "She went to the underworld."

"Exactly."

A.P. turned his narrow gaze on Ren; it was as if all the pieces were falling into place in his mind. Dark mist rose off his shoulders.

Uh-oh. Here comes the storm, thought Ren.

"You've left out the most important fragment, godborn." He drew closer. "Ixtab did not release you from death because she has a big heart. So, tell me . . . what did you give her?"

Ren swallowed past the painful, throbbing lump in her throat. The only way out was through the lousy truth. So Ren tipped up her chin, took a deep breath, and said in a single

whoosh of words, "I-promised-to-bring-Ixtab-the-crown-of-
jade-and-shadow-and-if-I-don't-deliver-it-in-the-next-six-days-
I'll-go-back-to-being-dead."

Edison uttered something Ren didn't catch because she was
too focused on A.P.

The god was frozen again, as in not breathing or blinking
or otherwise showing any signs of life.

"That is certainly the truth," the Sparkstriker put in. "But
not *all* of it."

"Never make a deal with a god, Renata!" A.P. snarled. "Have
I taught you nothing?"

"It'll be okay," she reassured him. "I just need to find the
crown and—"

"You don't understand, godborn," A.P. said. "There is no
crown to find . . . because it was destroyed."

8

All Ren heard was *crown* and *destroyed*. Now her heart was in her throat, her spirits were sinking, and a delirious, maniacal laugh was threatening to bubble up inside her because this was NOT her life.

"Are you breathing?" Edison asked Ren, fanning her with his hands.

"Why are you staring at me like that?" A.P. said to her, inching back.

The Sparkstriker said, "Many truths are quite painful and too hard to accept."

Ren blinked, trying to process this new truth, but no matter how she looked at it, the crown, her ticket to being alive, was gone. She had wagered her entire future on something that didn't even exist.

"Are you sure?" she finally said. "Maybe you saw wrong, or it was an illusion, or—"

"I saw it blown apart with my own eyes," the god said, staying very still, as if any sudden movement would send Ren into hysteria. "It was no illusion."

Edison, his face screwed up in an expression that said *eek, your life sucks*, nodded in confirmation. So he had seen it, too.

"I can show you the entire affair," the Sparkstriker said, "if you'd care to see a replay?"

Ren shook her head. "Who . . . who would do that? Can you show us that?"

"I cannot. It seems they remained hidden."

"Does it matter?" the god asked pointedly.

He was right. The crown was no more; it didn't matter who had demolished it or why.

Frustrated tears stung her eyes, but she refused to let them fall.

"I won't let Ixtab steal your life," A.P. said.

"A deal is a deal," Ren countered bitterly. "And you know it."

"I never play by the rules."

Ren felt breathless, like the air was too thin and the world was too big and she was too small for any of this. As grateful as she was to have the god of death in her corner, she knew that even he couldn't undo a godly deal. And Ren wasn't about to remind him that the last time he battled Ixtab, he'd lost . . . his entire kingdom.

"Look," Edison said, placing a hand on Ren's shoulder, "the crown split into two pieces, flying in two directions. So maybe . . ."

Like lightning, Ren spun toward Edison. "*What* did you say?"

"Could you please stop with the sudden movements?" A.P. pleaded. "You're yanking me around!"

"I said the crown split into—" Edison started

"Two pieces!" Ren cried. "That's all? I . . . I can find them, then. I can put the crown back together again!"

Edison was smiling, his whole face beaming with optimism and confidence. "Exactly!"

"Okay, Humpty-Dumpty," A.P. said, rolling his eyes. "Oh, demons, did I really just say that?"

"Yes, and it has been recorded," the Sparkstriker offered with way too much amusement.

Two pieces. Two pieces, Ren thought anxiously. *Way better than blown to smithereens. I can do this.*

And then she remembered Marco and the cinco, all being held captive by the lords. Whether friends or foes, she couldn't let fellow godborns rot away. She took a deep breath and tried to calm her frayed nerves by making a mental to-do list:

1. Locate the crown. (That didn't sound so bad. And she'd never promised to bring it back in one piece....)
2. Rescue Marco and the cinco...if she could find them. (Ren's stomach began to sink.)
3. Drop-kick those awful lords back to dreamland. (Her heart started to spasm. How was she going to do that if she didn't have the Obsidian Blade, which could be anywhere in the entire universe right now?)

Edison said, "You look sorta not good."

Ren covered her face with her hands and held back the *how-can-this-be-happening?* scream she so wanted to let loose.

"She does look rather unwell," A.P. put in.

"Her turmoil will pass," the Sparkstriker said. "All is temporary."

Ren dug deep, scavenging any ounce of optimism she could find. It had always been her magic wand, her go-to trait, the innate ability she had always leaned on. She understood the power of one word: *Believe. Believe. Believe.*

But that was before. Before the world had shown her that high hopes are too quickly dashed and hearts are too easily broken.

"Ren," A.P. said. She hated that tone of voice, his fatherly *this-is-an-unwise-decision* voice.

"No!" Ren held up her hand, shaking her head. It didn't matter how tragically twisted she felt inside, or how impossible it all looked. Her stubborn heart wouldn't allow her to give up. "Don't even try to talk me out of it. Besides, you should want me to find the crown so I don't have to go back to the underworld." Her eyes flicked to Edison's. "No offense to your home. . . . I'm just not ready to be dead . . . again."

"No one is ever truly ready," the Sparkstriker put in.

With a scowl, the god said, "What I was going to say was that I want you to live, and if I have to tear this entire earth apart piece by piece to ensure that your heart continues to beat, then I will."

"Spoken like a true hero," the Sparkstriker said, rolling her eyes.

Ren felt a tremor of emotion that stole her words. In that moment, all she wanted to do was fall into Ah-Puch's arms and cry. *But tears are a luxury,* she thought. One she couldn't afford right now.

"And I'm at your service." Edison raised his hand as if he might salute and then dropped it quickly. "I mean, all my powers are. And we're going to find the crown, and you're not going to die, and—"

Ren couldn't help it. Her heart melted . . . fast, like a pat of butter on a hot tortilla. Her cheeks warmed and her pulse sped up. "Then I guess I . . . *we* have six days to find those pieces."

Ah-Puch stared down at the time rope binding them. "You will have my full godly power. And this time," he said, raising his eyes to meet hers, "I will not fail you."

"I know," she said, trying to reassure him. None of what happened on her last quest had been his fault. The teen A.P. hadn't had an ounce of power. He'd been just an ordinary kid—a dopey, brave regular kid sticking by Ren's side no matter what.

Ren turned to the Sparkstriker. "You're a powerful seer. If you can't show me where the godborns are, can you show me where the crown is, or . . . the Obsidian Blade?"

The woman hesitated, twirled her axe, then said, "I can show you something greater."

The twin ropes hummed. The piece attached to Ren's left wrist dropped to the ground, releasing Ah-Puch's right wrist as well.

"Hey!" Ren said, jumping back.

The god frowned. "What's it doing?"

The freed rope began to snake through the grass. Coiling and uncoiling, winding toward the pyramids.

Unintelligible whispers rose into the air.

"What is this madness?" Ah-Puch demanded.

"It's . . . It's charging," Edison whispered, opening and closing his fist. "I can feel it. It's gathering power."

"Your energy measuring capacity is quite impressive," the Sparkstriker said to Edison as they all followed the rope's zig-zagging course up the center pyramid's steps, blazing like a thread of fire. Ren could also sense its strength expanding. And as the rope covered ground, the tan stairs began to glow a beautiful jade, the color bleeding up the structure until it looked like it had just received a fresh coat of paint.

Within seconds, the entire plaza was pulsing with life, each pyramid glittering in the moonlight with so much vivacity, so much blue and green, Ren could hardly catch her breath.

"Yes," the Sparkstriker whispered. "Yes."

Unexpectedly, the time rope rose and floated back to them. It looped itself around the other length of rope that was still connecting Ren to the god of death. The god tried to wrench himself away, but it was no use.

Ren gulped as she watched the two pieces fuse together. The golden time rope she had once worn around her throat, had wielded as a weapon, was different somehow, not only in its brilliant golden-jade glow, but in the vibration of its magic.

"Whoa," Edison breathed.

Clang. Clang.

The Sparkstriker slammed her axe into the stone steps, sending a wave of green rippling up the sides.

Then came the whispers, loud and insistent and familiar. "You're not dead. I won't let you be dead." It was Marco's voice, clear as a bell. "And seriously?" he said. "Even death is no excuse to leave me rotting here. I won't die a prisoner, Ren!"

"Marco?" Ren cried. Her voice was frantic, skating the edge of absolute panic. "Where are you?"

The god asked, "Who are you talking to?"

She turned to A.P. just as the rope released both of them and fell to the ground. "Did you hear him?" she cried. "It's Marco!"

The god rubbed his wrists where the rope had been. "The son of war?"

The entire Old World began to quake. The rope started to slither away from them.

"Wait!" Ren rushed to retrieve it, but just as her fingertips traced the magic, it slid out of reach. It continued gliding until it was lost in the glow of the metallic forest.

"The rope!" Ren made a run for it, but the Sparkstriker thrust her axe in front of the godborn, stopping her in her tracks.

"All in good time." *Clang.* The woman slammed her axe into the steps again.

Instantly, everything went still. Ren blinked, looking around. There was no more A.P. No Edison. No pyramids. It was only Ren and the Sparkstriker standing at the edge of the shimmering jungle.

Ren whirled to look over her shoulder. "Where are A.P. and Edison?"

"On the other side of this truth."

"Truth?"

"I told you I can show you something greater than what you've asked for."

"But the rope—it's getting away."

The Sparkstriker swept back her cape. "I pounded each and every godborn with lightning. I know their strengths and weaknesses."

Ren didn't want to be rude, but she didn't really see how that was important in this moment. "Sure, okay, but can we get the rope first?"

The Sparkstriker's hair bells began to chime annoyingly.

"Do you remember your own ceremony? When I pounded you with lightning to locate your dominant power?"

Ren nodded, thinking it had been pretty uneventful.

"And you thought you'd traveled to Saturn?"

How did she know that?

"Right." Ren felt a ball of frustration coil tightly in her stomach. Couldn't they have this convo after she got the rope back? And where was it going, anyhow?

"But no dominant power was found," the woman said tersely, "because I couldn't get past those shadows of yours."

Welcome to my life. "Okay . . ."

The Sparkstriker tapped the handle of her axe against her left palm. "And what neither you nor anyone else knows is that I still have the lightning bolts . . . from each godborn."

Now she had Ren's full attention.

The Sparkstriker's eyes glittered with a strange delight. "And those bolts carry secrets."

A pool of water appeared in the ground next to the woman. The pond was filled with glowing silver fish, whizzing back and forth so quickly that Ren could hardly track any one of them.

"If you want to know where your friends are," the Sparkstriker said, "you will have to take a swim with lightning."

Ren snorted, watching the luminous creatures zigzag back and forth, flashing blindingly. "Uh . . . wouldn't that be sort of dangerous? You know, water and electricity . . . ?"

"You said you wanted the truth."

"I do."

"Then this is the only way."

Ren twisted her fingers nervously. "And afterward you'll help me find the time rope?"

"The time rope is on its own journey, child. And you are on yours. Now, what do you choose to do? I have many critical matters to attend to."

"But..."

"No more buts. They are always excuses."

Ren pressed her lips together. "Okay, but on a scale of one to ten, how dangerous would you say this is going to be?"

"Well, the truth is never without its risks. Swimming with lightning fish charged with old magic isn't exactly wise, but it's the only option if you truly want to locate your friends."

"Is that how I heard Marco's voice?" Ren asked, fighting a long shiver that had gripped her spine. "Through his lightning?"

"Perhaps. You know how channels of magic can get crossed and strange messages can get through."

Trembling, Ren began to tug off her boots. She set them aside, pulled in a deep breath, shook out her hands, and, before she could change her mind, jumped into the electrified water.

9

The water was so cold Ren could barely move her limbs.

And it was dark, with none of the flashing of a few moments ago. Worse, there were whispers down here—hair-raising, wicked whispers that gripped Ren so tight she was sure she would implode.

You're nothing. A weakling without magic.

Ren closed her mind to the insults, kicking her legs, grasping at the dark. Hot coils of energy seized her every few seconds, as if a high voltage was burning through her blood.

Zzzzap.

The pain was a searing agony that made her wish for death. Almost.

Waves of fear washed over Ren as every last inch of her was lost to the whispering, freezing dark. The weight of the universe was sitting on her lungs, which were screaming for air.

Zzzzap.

She writhed and grunted and pushed through the water, grasping at the slimy, uncatchable fish.

A black curtain fell over her vision. Panic struck her heart and lungs. With one hard thrust, she pushed herself to the surface, but where she thought was up must have been down, because she hit a wall.

Failed before you've even begun.

With a ceaseless struggle, Ren grasped at the dark, frantically searching for a way out, for air. Her lungs begged for a single breath. But she couldn't, wouldn't, suck in the water. It would mean certain death. Yet...

The pressure mounted. Thick and heavy and all-consuming.

With one last thrash, she caught a lightning fish. It squirmed and wiggled in her grasp. Ren's heart slowed to a pathetic little thump. Slowly, bit by bit, her consciousness began to fade.

Until a familiar voice broke through the despair.

Is this all you have in you?

Pacific?

You really must stop getting into so much trouble.

Save me!

You must save yourself.

Anger, shock, regret, and grief swelled inside the godborn. How could her own mom be so...so cavalier? So heartless?

Zzzzap.

Time is running out, Pacific said. *You really need to breathe.*

Breathe? Was she serious? Ren was drowning in a magical pool of lightning fish, being electrocuted every few seconds, and her mom wanted her to breathe?!

Instantly, a memory pulsed brightly at the edge of her mind. She was six and sitting in a thick patch of grass with her abuelo. He was teaching her about the power of breathing, visualization, and mantras, and how to use her mind and spirit to overcome adversity.

Letting go, Abuelo had told her, *takes the greatest strength of all.*

Now a shattering pain radiated from Ren's center across her entire body.

When you face death a second time, Ixtab had said, *you will realize your full supernatural potential.*

At the same moment, a shapeless shadow moved like a dream across her mind's eye. Heat tore through her, weaving between her ribs.

It felt like magic, and its hugeness terrified Ren even more than the idea of drowning did.

You think your weak little magic can save you? the pool taunted.

Ren squeezed her eyes shut and clenched her fists. Her lungs burned with the need for air.

Focus! Pacific insisted.

Ren concentrated on the stirring power that was . . . trying to break free. But the harder she tried to touch the magic, to command it, the more it slipped through her fingers.

She turned inward and forced her mind elsewhere, to a place of peace where trees swayed and the air was warm. As she visualized the beauty, she felt her muscles relax and her pulse slow, and she heard her heart whisper, *Letting go takes the greatest strength of all.*

An intense power raced through her veins.

Then came an explosion of light, hot and searing, as if electricity flowed through Ren's veins. The force was so great, she threw her arms out, channeling the energy right into the water, as she snatched another lightning fish.

And then she saw it.

Magic bled from the fish and through her fingers in a shimmering stream of jade light. Just before she lost consciousness, Ren heard her mother's voice.

So that's your godborn magic.

10

Ren was in a nice warm bubble of a dream when she opened her eyes to find herself submerged in a shallow pool of water.

Her first thought was *I'm still in the lightning pool.* A logical conclusion, except that there were no fish, no cold, no darkness. And no pain.

Am I dreaming?

Another logical conclusion, considering that she was breathing. Underwater! But no water entered her nose—only clean, warm air that filled her lungs with calm and peace and . . . joy.

Ren watched the sunlight thread through the lily pads floating above her and thought she could stay in this world of blissful silence forever.

The memory of her mother's words edged into the calm. *So that's your godborn magic.*

Which is what, exactly? Breathing underwater? Ren thought as she stood up. She was now waist-deep in a twenty-by-twenty-foot pool blanketed with bright white lilies. Sandstone rock formations loomed above her, stretching toward the cloudless pale blue sky. The air, which she could breathe as normally as before, had the scent of rain clouds in the distance.

At the far end of the narrow stone courtyard was an angular building that blended effortlessly into the landscape of sage, sand, and rock. Stepping out of the pool, Ren wrung her hair and realized that the agony that had radiated through her ribs and down her spine was completely gone. As a matter of fact, she felt energized, and one hundred percent famished.

Her clothes dried instantly, and somehow her boots were parked at the edge of the pool. Quickly, she tugged them on, glancing around, trying to figure out where she was.

In that instant, she sensed she wasn't alone. She could feel it in the tiny hairs that stood up on the back of her neck, and in the minuscule rise in temperature.

Ren turned to find Pacific standing there.

The goddess wore a midnight-blue cape lined with shimmering sequined stars. Her long white-blond hair flowed over her shoulders. She was as beautiful as ever—full lips, high cheekbones, and eyes the color of a calm sea in the sunlight.

"There is much to talk about and little time," Pacific said. "And before you ask, you have only been asleep for a few hours, and I have sent a messenger to collect that dreadful death god and his demon companion. It is against my better judgment to bring them here, but I realize that Ah-Puch would likely start destroying everything in the world until he knew that you're safe." The goddess shook her head. "Him, I can get over, but that demon? Really, Ren. I would expect you to keep better company."

Ren felt a boiling anger erupt in her stomach. "What does being a demon have to do with anything? He's nice and super loyal and...guess what? He might have the biggest heart of anyone I've ever met."

Pacific laughed, a melodious sound that only made Ren's

annoyance flare. "You do have a habit of collecting misfits, don't you?"

Ren had never thought of her friends that way. Sure, they weren't ordinary or typical, and maybe they were unpredictable and challenging and strange, but only in the best possible ways.

"Where am I?" Ren asked. "What happened to the Old World?"

"The Old World served its purpose," the goddess said. "This is my sanctuary. A realm of healing and refuge, a place of silence and renewal." Ren had to admit that her mom had great taste. The place oozed Zen, like that monastic yoga retreat Ren had seen in a travel magazine at her dentist's office.

Pacific studied her with a combination of fascination and concern that confused Ren. Where had that concern been when Ren was drowning? Pacific had just remained in her front-row seat, watching it all play out.

"You didn't save me," Ren said, her tone even but her anger stirring. "I could have died." The words made her feel the sting of betrayal. It was in the heat of her cheeks, the pounding of her pulse, the fire burning in her chest.

"Ah, but you didn't," Pacific said.

"No outbursts, please," said a small voice. "It is not conducive to healing."

"Who's that?" Ren looked all around the vacant space, but they were alone.

"Must you be so loud and insistent?" Pacific said.

"Truly," said the small voice, "she is more trouble than you described."

Ren turned, sensing that the voice was coming from the pool. Following Ren's gaze, Pacific said, "The voice belongs to one of the water lilies."

Ren balked. "The lilies can talk?"

"And you're a talking human," the lily said with a hint of annoyance. "Congratulations."

Pacific sighed, handing Ren a towel from a nearby chair. "The lilies do many important things besides communicate verbally."

"Yeah, like heal your broken body," the lily said.

"Heal?"

Pacific said, "Apparently, you inhaled some of the lightning water, which is very bad for your stomach lining. Never mind how much havoc it wreaks on your skin. But it is the heart it can damage the most."

"That wasn't even the hardest part," the lily went on. "Your mind required the most work. Lots of cobwebs in there. But not to worry—we cleared them all out, and you should feel good as new, or actually better than new. Something like serene and blissful. Am I right?"

Ren nodded as she touched her chest gratefully. "Thanks, but that doesn't explain how I could breathe underwater."

"The pool is infused with great magic," Pacific said.

"Very great," the lily echoed. "But don't get all bigheaded or anything. This was a one-time deal. You aren't a water-breather. Got it?"

Oh. Ren's heart sank. Being able to breathe underwater would have been a supremely awesome power. She was about to ask what her godborn magic was when something stopped her cold. There, around the goddess's throat, tucked beneath her strands of glossy hair, was...

"The time rope!" Ren shouted, dropping the towel. Her voice echoed across the rocky cliffs. "It took me to the Old World, then went kind of wacky. Edison said it was recharging itself. Is that true?"

The goddess offered an unreadable smile. "So, your demon isn't without a brain."

"He isn't *my* demon."

Pacific ignored her. "The Old World, the realm where time was born, is the only place where the rope can recharge, but that isn't the only reason the rope took you there." The goddess paused like some annoying teacher expecting the answer without even asking the question.

But Ren didn't have any answers. "Okay..."

Pacific held the rope gently, studying its new mottled gold-and-green color. "You also needed to see the Sparkstriker, to find your lightning bolt."

Ren stared down at her hands as if she half expected to see a fish still wriggling there. Which made her wonder, where had it vanished to? Had she lost it in the transition between worlds?

Pacific looked up from the rope and met Ren's gaze. The corner of her mouth twitched like she might smile, but she didn't.

Ren felt a sudden desperate longing to touch the rope, the magic she had felt so close to not so long ago. It had responded to her thoughts and feelings, obeyed her commands, made her feel powerful. And now it was lost.

Pacific said, "The rope has told me everything. What it has seen and been through. Your deal with Ixtab was quite foolish."

"I had no choice."

"You *always* have a choice."

"Okay, well, then I chose not to be dead."

"Except in death," Pacific corrected herself under her breath. "I suppose there isn't always a choice in *that* matter."

Ren wasn't in the mood to talk about the philosophies of life and death, not when she was carrying so much weight on her shoulders.

"I have to go," Ren said. Then the dam broke and all the words came rushing out. "Marco needs me, and everything is so messed up, and it's my fault, and I have to find my friends and the crown, and..." She forced herself to take a steadying breath, wishing Pacific wasn't looking at her with such pity in her eyes, a pity that spoke volumes: *You cannot succeed.*

"All in good time, Renata."

Except I don't have any time.

Did Pacific know that, too? That Ren had bet her future on a bit of shadow and jade that must hold amazing power if Ixtab wanted it so bad?

"But I heard Marco," Ren insisted, "and he said...How was that possible, by the way?"

"There is much we need to discuss," Pacific said.

"Like what my magic is? I felt it burning me. I saw it coming out of my fingers—well, out of the lightning fish, in that weird jade-colored light, and if my power isn't breathing underwater, then—"

Rubbing her brow, Pacific said, "Could you please not blurt or blather or otherwise appear to be an anxiety-ridden human? Really, Renata. Show some composure."

The lily's voice said, "Self-possession is a virtue, you know."

"You want me to be composed when I nearly drowned, was electrocuted, saw some weird light coming out of me, and woke up in a pool of water lilies that can talk and heal?"

"She does have a point," the plant said.

Pacific stared at Ren, a cold and unfeeling expression on her face. "At first, I thought I had overestimated you, that perhaps you would fail in discovering your ability."

When you face death a second time, you will realize your full supernatural potential.

Ixtab's words were like a million daggers to the heart. Ren's pulse kicked up. "You mean you knew what it was all this time?" she squeaked.

Pacific leveled her with a shrewd gaze that made Ren's skin itch. It was all the heartbreaking answer Ren needed.

"You seriously let me almost die," she yelled, "just so I could find, or connect to, my godborn—"

"Power never comes without sacrifice," the goddess said. "And do not look at me with such disdain. I could have left you to die in that smelly fish pool. But luckily for you, you are the daughter of time," Pacific said. "And to think you existed under the weight of all those shadows that buried your true worth. It's truly appalling."

"I happened to *like* those shadows," Ren argued, thinking about how much she missed them.

During her SHIHOM training this past summer, Ren had practiced connecting to her Maya power over and over, but it was like she couldn't get past the shadow magic, as if the two magics couldn't coexist in one body. And now she understood why. She would have to make room for something new. She spread out her fingers, sensing the unfamiliar magic pulsating beneath her skin. Unlike the heavy and intense power of her shadows, this magic was light and delicate.

"Don't you see?" Pacific said. "The lightning—*your* lightning— triggered your godborn powers, which were lying dormant."

"And what if my magic *hadn't* gotten triggered?" Ren argued. "What if I had never found my lightning? What if . . . ?" Images of the darkest corners of Xib'alb'a flashed across her mind, and she shuddered.

Pacific held up a hand to silence Ren. "You must get your melodramatic nature from your father."

You're the one in the cape! Ren wanted to say. She longed to give her goddess mom a piece of her mind, tell her that she lacked true loyalty and devotion and all the qualities that Ren prized most, but she needed her too much to spiral into a fight she was sure to lose. And maybe, she told herself, maybe Pacific had done her a favor. Okay, the electric fish experience had been appalling and painful and terrorizing, but ultimately Ren had connected with her godborn magic, and wasn't that a good thing?

"Are you ever going to tell me what my power is?" Ren asked, holding her breath, hoping desperately that it was as good as either her lost shadow magic or the time rope. She needed something truly awesome if she was to succeed in achieving her three goals.

"We'll get to that, but first I believe you owe me a bit of gratitude," Pacific said. "I granted you the great honor of coming to my home and allowed you to sleep alongside my beloved water lilies."

"We are quite potent," the plant said proudly. "Surely you've heard of our powers, given that our mythology dates back to the beginning of time."

Ren remembered something she had learned at SHIHOM about the water lily's significance. "You're the revered flower of the Water Lily Jaguar," Ren said, "a powerful ancient god who's a big mystery because no one's ever seen him."

"Well, *I've* seen him," the plant said smugly.

Ren's curious heart skipped a beat. "So, he exists?"

"Indeed."

"Not now," Pacific warned the lily with a cutting glare.

"One way or another, the truth will come out," the lily said.

In that instant, the air shifted, and Ren sensed something of great magnitude—an idea, or a story she hadn't yet heard. She could feel its vibrating warmth deep in her bones. The sensation was both strange and invigorating, and the more that Ren tuned in to it, the sharper her senses became. It was as if she could smell the truth, taste it on her tongue, feel its breath on her neck. "What truth?" she asked.

Pacific's blue eyes sparkled as her gaze shifted to the top of Ren's head.

"Oh boy," the lily said with a sigh.

"What?" Ren turned to gaze at her reflection in the pool, and there, poking out of the top of her head, were two spotted jaguar ears.

11

"I'M A CAT!" Ren hollered.

She tugged on the rounded furry ears that were rooted firmly in place on top of her head.

"You must stop shouting," Pacific insisted. "I will explain everything."

"Explain?!" Ren's heart was blasting into the atmosphere at supersonic speed with no hope of return. "I'm a freaking cat!"

"Well, jaguar, to be more specific," the lily said.

Ren's hands flew to her human ears. "And I have four ears!"

"Let us go somewhere more private," Pacific said to Ren as she shot a glare at the water lily pool.

"Hey!" the plant groaned. "I want to be a part of this. I want to see her powers. This is mythology in the making!"

Ignoring the lily, Pacific swept back her cape. The tiny stars along the hem twinkled as the air warmed and the sky began to glow a rosy pink. Ren held her breath as the light bent and morphed all around Pacific like a prism, as if the goddess herself was a gateway. In the next exhale, Ren felt a gravitational pull and then found herself standing on a cliff high above the earth.

The world below was like a sand painting of infinite hills, deep canyons, and wide mesas.

Beyond the otherworldly rock formations was an endless

ocean with turquoise water so luminous, it could hardly be real. If Ren weren't spiraling into a puddle of feline shock, she might have appreciated the stark beauty, or the warmth of twin yellow suns, floating side by side, their buttery light glittering off the water's surface.

"What I have to tell you is of great significance," Pacific said. "But it requires you to be calm."

"I don't want to be calm! I want to know...how..." Ren felt hot and clammy as she tried to wrap her head around the fact that she was now in possession of a couple of cat ears.

"*I* am the Water Lily Jaguar deity," Pacific said.

"But he's...She's..." Ren couldn't begin to complete the thought because her mind was drowning in a sea of bewilderment. How could the goddess of time also be the great Water Lily Jaguar? A goddess of myth and maybes. A deity many said never existed.

And then Ren felt a spark of knowledge flare to life. She suddenly remembered how Pacific had first appeared to her godborn friend Zane Obispo in the middle of the ocean. He had called the goddess "a surfer cat" because she'd had jaguar ears.

Zane's description of his first encounter with the goddess swept over her with category-five-hurricane force. According to him, a huge spotted cat at least four times a jaguar's normal size had stepped out of Pacific's body like a feline ghost.

Why had Ren never asked him about that? How had she ignored that detail? "Do you have a jaguar ghost living inside of you?" she managed now, praying she hadn't inherited *that* trait from her mom.

Pacific paused, then said, "Not a ghost, but a spirit of phenomenal strength."

Oh, sure. She said it like it was the most normal thing to house a phenomenal spirit or whatever. "How...how can you be the jaguar god?" Ren asked. "You're the goddess of time and fate."

"The jaguar was my first iteration as a deity, and one I cherished," said Pacific. "But as my powers grew, so did the other gods' fear of me, so I had to change my spots, so to speak. I had to hide my truth. But I am and always will be the Water Lily Jaguar Goddess."

Something like a wall of bricks collapsed inside Ren's mind. In the world of Maya magic, the truth always seemed to be changing faces.

"And in the end, what did it matter?" Pacific sneered. "The gods tried to execute me anyway, and I was forced into hiding. Why do you think I chose the ocean?"

"Because water throws off the gods' senses?" Ren guessed.

"And because I am connected to water in a deep and powerful way."

Ren clutched her stomach. She knew Pacific was telling the truth, not just because Ren could sense it, but because the goddess could absolutely pull off this secret—she was the queen of hide-and-seek. She had stayed hidden for hundreds of years without the gods even knowing she was alive. And she had concealed four hundred boys in a constellation!

"Does this mean...I'm part jaguar?" Ren asked. Her voice wavered with uncertainty and fear, and perhaps a pinch of fascination. Maybe being a giant cat wasn't such a bad thing. Her good friend Brooks had lived her whole life as a shape-shifter and could change into a hawk at will, which had come in super handy loads of times.

"No," Pacific said. "You are not a jaguar. But you do possess its magic, its prowess, its strength."

"Then why do I have these . . . ?" Ren reached up, but the cat ears were gone. "Hey! Where'd they go?"

"The ears appear when your jaguar senses are heightened, Renata."

"Jaguar senses?"

"About fifty times more potent than an actual jaguar's, give or take."

Ren had imagined that her godborn power would have had something to do with time or fate. Never in her wildest imagi-nation had she thought her mom had another earth-shattering secret up her sleeve, one so big it would change the course of Ren's life. "That's my godborn power? Jaguar senses?"

"You say it with such disdain," Pacific said as a warm breeze swept across the cliff. "Perhaps a bit more gratitude is war-ranted. You are gifted with the magic of the jaguar god!"

"But there was an explosion . . . in the water," Ren recalled. "Jaguars don't explode things."

"That was merely your magic coming to the surface."

"So, no to shattering stuff?" Ren asked with a hint of disappointment.

"Truly, Renata? You would rather detonate your enemies than carry the magic of jaguar blood?"

Sort of?

"Is this magic how I heard Marco? Except I didn't have my cat ears yet, so..."

"While you hadn't activated your jaguar magic, that didn't mean it wasn't there, below the surface, trying to emerge." Pacific adjusted her cape. "Plus, you were in a place of extraordinary power that may have allowed him to reach you using some form of communication magic."

"Is that a thing?"

"Only between beings who care about each other," Pacific said. "And let us not forget that he is the son of war. He's exceptionally strategic, and if anyone could find a way..."

"It would be Marco," Ren finished. She turned and gazed at the desert landscape, across the pink-hued mesa that led to the glittering ocean. "So what can I actually do? You know... as a big cat."

Pacific curled the time rope around her wrist. "Only you can know that."

"Me? How should I know?"

"Because you are a natural empath. Because you have extraordinary instincts. Because only you can call up the magic. All you have to do is connect to your inner cat."

With a wince, Ren said, "Please never say that again."

"You cannot shed the truth of who you are," Pacific warned. "The blood that runs through your veins, the Maya magic that is a part of you."

"I just thought..." Ren said, trying to make sense of this new, life-changing feline fact, "that I... I'd have some power over time itself."

"Yes, well, that isn't the case. Now, let us accept what is and get on with this."

Just then, on the tail end of a breeze, Ren caught a whiff of A.P. and Edison. Their scents were unmistakable. The god's was smoky and gritty, while the demon's was earthy with a touch of freshly mown grass. Instinctively, she raised her nose to the air, barely able to contain her grin. "I . . . I can smell my friends."

"They arrived three minutes ago. We will need to work on your timing."

"So, what else can I do besides sniff people out?" Learning to master new skills was never easy, and she had just barely figured out how to control her shadows, but there was something so natural at play here, as if she had always known this feral magic.

Before Pacific could answer, Ren felt a vibration run down her spine. Magic pulsed in her limbs and glowed across her fingertips.

Yes, whispered something inside of her.

At the same moment, the air undulated and Pacific morphed into an enormous spotted jaguar, looming to an impossible height. The beast's glossy coat glistened like a waterfall, and her eyes were the most intense blue Ren had ever seen.

"Whoa!" Ren cried, stumbling back.

Pacific blinked, and then, with the flick of her paw, the day sky transformed into a blanket of blackness. "That's better."

Ren sucked in a sharp breath. "You can talk! Like out loud."

"You too often underestimate the power of a supreme being such as myself."

Ren's head throbbed, and with each blink she expected her cat eyes to adjust to the dark, but they didn't. She could barely make out the shadowy formations in the distance. "I thought cats had great night vision."

"They do—but you cannot select which bit of magic you will inherit," the goddess jaguar said. "You will have to rely on your other senses, on your instincts."

Somewhere in the back of Ren's mind, she thought she should be terrified, but she wasn't. She was too focused on the power pulsing beneath her skin.

Pacific said, "Shall we?"

Ren shot her mom a look of utter confusion. "Shall we what?"

The beautiful cat blinked; her eyes were two blue orbs floating in the dark. She took off down the cliff's sharp descent.

Ren's mind shouted, *DANGER! DO NOT JUMP OFF CLIFFS!* Ignoring the screaming in her head, and as if driven by instinct alone, Ren leaped over the side of the precipice.

Even with limited vision, Ren traversed each rocky outcropping as easily as if she were walking along a flat road, and the thrill of it was almost too much to contain. She picked up her pace and flew over boulders. She sprang across dry riverbeds, and with each breath she felt her magic stirring. Her jaguar ears sprouted, and she could hear the waves pounding the shore miles away as she increased her speed, scaling the rocky hills with stealthy precision.

There are times when it feels like your heart is holding its breath. Like the first time Ren saw a lavender sun set over a glittering sea, or the first time she felt shadow magic sweep through her veins.

But this...

Ren was sure this memory would outlive her, that it would grow wings and soar forever and ever.

The wind swept through her hair as she raced behind the jaguar faster and faster. So fast the world simply whizzed past in a blur.

Dark forms expanded and fluttered in the shadows.

What are those? Ren asked Pacific telepathically.

Distractions. Never allow yourself to be distracted.

They came to a chasm at least fifty feet wide. The jaguar stopped well ahead of the ledge and looked back at Ren with an expression hard as granite.

"No way!" Ren said, coming to a halt. "I can't make that leap."

How do you know unless you try?

Because if I don't make it, I'm going to be splat city.

The cat, with her shining eyes, gave a regal nod, then turned and began to run toward the brink. Her massive paws pounded the earth, and with a single launch, she catapulted herself into the air. Ren watched with fascination as the jag's muscular body stretched out in the moonlight—lithely, poetically, before landing with ease on the other side.

"Fine for you!" Ren shouted glumly. "You're a talking cat goddess! "

Forget what your limited mind is telling you. What does the magic tell you?

Ren looked down at the blue light bleeding from her

fingertips; the warmth of the magic had invaded every crevice of her body. Her muscles twitched with anticipation. And she knew, without a doubt, that she was meant for this.

With a deep breath, she shook out her hands, exhaled, and said, "Here goes nothing." Then she took off running. Her legs turned with lightning speed. *Don't look down,* she told herself as the chasm drew closer. *Don't look down.*

And just as she came to the edge, she hurled herself with every ounce of strength she possessed. Her arms and legs windmilled through the air, bursting with heat and magic.

Then reality came crashing down on her. She was too far away and didn't have enough gas. She wasn't going to make it to the other side.

Her vision tunneled, darkened. Not now! She couldn't go into one of her trances when she was flying a hundred feet above the earth!

A violent shiver grabbed hold of her just as the world stilled. But she didn't black out like all those times before. This time, it was like she was looking through a prism of ice. Beyond the shards, Ren could make out a shadowy figure at the end of the long, dark tunnel. At the same moment, the temperature dropped so fast that Ren gasped, struggling against the bone-numbing cold.

And then a voice broke through the ice.

"Ren?"

"Marco!"

"You . . . have . . . to . . . find . . . us . . . soon." His voice grew weaker, more distant with every word, and the sound of it split Ren's heart open. Tears pricked her eyes.

"Can you hear me?" Ren called out.

"Time...is...running...out."

The tunnel began to fade, two icy hands squeezed Ren's lungs, and her world came back into view.

Slam!

Her body crashed into the rock wall. Pain radiated across her bones while her fingers clung to the ledge.

Well, that wasn't very pretty, Pacific taunted.

"How 'bout some help?" Ren shouted, realizing it was probably a futile request. Her mom was valedictorian of the DIY school.

You have more strength than you think.

With a grunt, Ren repositioned herself. She tugged and she pulled, but her struggling wasn't enough. Her muscles were spent, her fingers were slipping. And her hope was waning.

No! There are too many things I still need to make right. I have to get to Marco. He had sounded so uncharacteristically weak and lost, which told Ren things were dire. In that moment, she decided the crown would have to wait. First, she had to find and save the son of war.

I will NOT break my skull open tonight, she told herself.

A strange pressure built in her chest, thick and heavy and throbbing.

The pressure expanded, rising higher and higher, until Ren trembled with the weight of it, until she couldn't contain the painful burden one more second. It clawed its way up her throat with a scorching heat and forced its way out.

She threw her head back. Her piercing roar shook the earth with so much force it catapulted Ren up and over the cliff. She landed on her hands and knees, panting and shaking with a shock that reverberated through her like thunder.

The jaguar stalked over to her and whispered, "And *that* is where the power of your magic lives."

12

Ren could feel the roar still reverberating through her as she and Pacific (now back in a humanoid goddess form) walked to the shore to meet up with A.P. and Edison.

"My power is in a *growl*?" she asked Pacific.

Pacific continued walking in silence, and just when Ren thought she might not answer, the goddess said, "The jaguar is sacred—a formidable warrior, a cunning creature. Its roar is filled with power. A power fueled even more by your immense determination."

Ren nodded, but a part of her still didn't get it. She wanted to know more but was too twisted up inside to think about it right now, when she was about to face A.P. She tried to imagine how it would play out when she told the god she was a sort of . . . cat.

When Pacific and Ren approached the beach, the god and demon were whispering near a long wicker table stacked high with lobster tails, crab legs, fruit kabobs, and bread.

Ren's cat ears twitched, zooming in on the convo that her human ears would never be able to hear.

"I don't trust any of this." That was A.P.

"Why not?" Edison asked.

"Pacific is cunning, stealthy, always watching. I'm sure she sleeps with one eye open," the god said. "She must have something up her sleeve to bring us all here."

"Oh, A.P., let's not embellish," Pacific said, sweeping her cape back with a flourish and a teasing smile. "I sleep with *both* eyes open. And I didn't want *you* to come here at all."

"Such theatrics, Pacific," A.P. said, adjusting his shirt cuffs. "I would expect something a bit more... intelligent, logical from you."

Pacific sighed through a small chuckle. "I see you are back in your monstrous form, thanks to my magic."

"I believe that magic is Ren's and... mine." Then he flashed a dazzling smile that held a universe of threats.

"This is a really amazing place," Edison put in with a nervous chortle. "And the food looks and smells great."

A.P. shot a glare at the demon. "Let's be a little less lavish with the adjectives, shall we?" His gaze landed on Ren's, and it was like he could see the truth there.

"We should sit down," she said.

"I'd rather stand," the god replied.

"Oh, trust me," Pacific said. "You're going to want to be sitting for this." She gave Ren the floor with a small nod.

And that was how Ren began her tale. With everyone seated around splendid food, under the moonlight of a magical realm, while the waves rolled gently to shore like they wanted to hear the story, too.

"YOU'RE A WHAT?!" A.P. shouted, pounding his fist on the table.

Across from Ren, Edison stared at her with wide eyes like he was trying to see her feral magic.

"Can you just be nice about it, A.P.?" Ren said, stuffing a

bit of cheese bread into her mouth, wishing she hadn't spilled every little detail.

"A cat?" A.P. snarled. "Really, Ren . . . It's . . ."

"What do you want me to do?" Ren shouted, matching the god's ferocity. "Send it back?"

"This is a good thing," Edison insisted way too cheerfully as he snapped open a crab leg. "Your strength will be a big help on the quest." He leaned closer. "But you're sure you won't turn into a jaguar? Or, like, hunt and eat . . . things?"

Ren shook her head. "I don't think it works like that."

"But she can roar," A.P. said with a half-twisted grin. "I heard it from here."

Ren thought about the rush of power she had felt. And the strange tunnel and Marco's voice.

"There is something else that has long eluded me," Pacific said.

"Only one thing?" A.P. smirked.

Ignoring the god, Pacific pinned Ren with a focused gaze. "Your trances."

"What about them?"

"I see now that they always resulted in unconsciousness because the gateway to your godborn power had never had the magic to sustain itself. But now . . . a trance might open a method of communicating across time and space."

"Do you mean I can control my trances? Use them to communicate?"

"Only time will tell."

"That's pretty cool." Edison smiled. "Can I see your ears?"

Ren blushed, a bit shaken from her frustration with A.P., who was now grunting and dragging a hand down his face like her being a cat was the worst fate in existence.

"Do you have something against felines?" Ren asked the god angrily.

But before he could answer, Pacific jumped in with "Ah-Puch, I must call for the oath of gods. You must promise that no one else shall know my true identity."

A.P. observed the goddess with cold black eyes. "Return the time rope to me, its rightful owner, and I will consider your oath."

Ren wanted to sock him one. Couldn't he just be agreeable for once?

Pacific smiled, haughtily amused as she folded her arms across her chest. Silence fell for a heartbeat, two. Waves crept to the shore. "The rope has changed," she rasped. "It has recharged, as you know, and now it will make its own decision as to whom it shall serve."

That statement gripped Ren by the throat like an icy fist. "But I thought it could only be given freely, and I . . . I gave it to Ah-Puch." She and Pacific had been over this, how Ren had done it to prevent the rope from falling into the lords' hands.

"The god of death was a poor choice, Renata," Pacific said. "His dark powers drained the rope of much of its magic. What little it had left was used to reverse the effects of time and return him to his godly form." Her gaze darted to A.P. "So a *thank you* would be most welcome."

Ah-Puch's eyes narrowed to gloomy slits.

Pacific removed the rope from her shoulder and held it

out. It glimmered in the moonlight, gold and green and blue. "Whom do you choose?" she asked softly.

The rope twisted and curled, then floated over the table. Ren felt its warmth, its power and magic, and she found herself leaning toward it, wishing it would choose her. Her spirits sank immediately when the rope drifted back to Pacific.

"How convenient." Ah-Puch fixed the goddess with a piercing stare. "That rope belongs to Ren, and you know it."

Ren loved him for trying to help her, but she could sense where the rope's loyalties lay. With its creator and protector. Still, as much as Ren was relieved to see the magic back where it belonged, she felt a little jab of disappointment.

"What I know," Pacific said, leaning against the table threateningly, "is that magic shifts and adapts as circumstances change, and my rope had to reinvent itself to survive *your* darkness."

Instantly, the air chilled, the waves froze, and jagged ice crystals jutted out of the sand.

"Hey!" Ren said, her breath hanging in the air. "It's all good. No need to fight. Or you know, freeze us out."

Ribbons of blue shimmered across Edison's skin as he rubbed his demon arms.

"Fight?" Pacific laughed. "Even the great and mighty Ah-Puch has no power in my realm, and he knows it."

A.P. stood. His expression was pure hate. "For now, goddess. But do not forget I know your secret."

"I won't tell anyone," Edison swore, saluting the goddess before popping more crab into his mouth. "Ever."

Pacific sighed, her gaze lingering on the god of death. "You clearly have a soft spot for my daughter. Revealing my secret would put her in danger since she carries the feral magic of the jaguar. And something tells me," Pacific cooed, "that you would rather die than injure her."

A.P.'s mouth turned up into a predatory grin. "Something tells me the gods are going to notice her cat ears."

"She was in a great battle with a mystical jaguar," Pacific said. "And when she killed him, she took his magic."

"Oh, but I would never do that," Ren insisted.

Everyone was staring at the godborn now. "Right," she said, shrinking beneath their gazes. "Couldn't we say the great jaguar was dying and I—"

"No!" Pacific insisted.

"We really need to go," A.P. said with so much calm it unnerved Ren.

Edison shot her a side glance, like he didn't trust the god's sudden composure, either. Regardless, A.P. was right. They had to get going, and Ren knew exactly where their first stop needed to be.

Pacific turned to Ren. She plucked a single thread from the time rope. The strand glided between them, glowing the same color of jade as Ren's magic. "A parting gift," the goddess said. Ren reached out to touch the thread, but it recoiled, then flew down to her boot, where it wrapped itself around the ankle.

"What the heck?" she uttered, stepping back to get a better look at the string.

Pacific said, "This will allow you to create a brief gap in time should you ever need one."

"Cool!" Edison said. "So she can stop time?"

"Barely," Pacific said. "The gap will be short—a few minutes, if you're lucky."

"Thanks," Ren said, knowing that this gesture of generosity was a big leap forward for her mom. She thought maybe she should hug her or something, but the goddess was already backing away and spinning the time rope like a lasso. It expanded in front of Pacific until an iridescent pink gateway appeared. "Where would you like to go?"

Ren threw back her shoulders, fighting the quiver that was working its way up her legs, and said, "The scene of the crime."

A.P. snorted. "There are too many of those to count."

Ren met his sharp gaze. "We're going back to the Mirror of the Gods."

13

It's no easy thing to return to the place where you died.

As they stepped out of Pacific's magical gateway, Ren sucked in a sharp breath, repeating the same mantra in her mind. *I can do this. I can do this. I can do this.*

The light of the full moon gleamed across the dark waters of Lake Zirahuén.

"Why would you return us to this vile place?" A.P. grumbled, staring into the darkness of the forested hills.

"Because this is where I last remember seeing the Obsidian Blade," Ren said. "And in case you've forgotten, that's where Zyanya lives, and we're going to need her to save Marco and..." She didn't want to waste her breath on the rest of the sentence, which was this: *to save him I'm going to have to go up against the Lords of Night, and to do that, I need the one weapon that will throw them into an eternal nap.*

"I AM THE GOD OF DEATH!" Ah-Puch boomed, his voice echoing across the trees. "I do not *need* a blade to inflict torment on my enemies."

Edison crossed and uncrossed his arms, shifting his feet like he didn't want to be here, either. Ren wondered if the memories of that "death" day haunted him the way they haunted her.

"But the bird flew away," Edison said.

"She's connected to the blade, and it'll call her back eventually."

"I thought you wanted to find the crown first."

"That has to wait." Ren bit down on her lower lip. "Marco's in trouble, and I need to get to him soon."

"You're in trouble, too," A.P. said in a low voice.

The god was right, but something else was scratching at the edge of Ren's mind. She had another motive for being here. She had to know what the lords were planning, because whatever it was, it was big.

Her mind wandered back to that day in the garden of Black Flowers with the Prince Lord. She had tried guessing the lords' plan. *And once you're all awake, you're going to destroy the Maya gods and take over the world.*

That would be wholly unoriginal, the Prince Lord had said.

Crowning her queen had renewed their magic. If they didn't want to use it for a takeover, then what *did* they want to use it for?

"Marco's the son of war, Renata," A.P. said, shaking her from her reverie. "He can take care of himself."

"Not if he's being held by *five* very powerful Lords of Night." Ren wondered if the lords had found out about Jade Is Her Skirt's wicked little plot to take the crown for herself and use its immense powers. But to what end? And now that the crown was obliterated, what was Jade's plan?

Argh! Nothing made sense!

"And what about your safety?" A.P. barked. "You're just willing to waste the few days you have left to save some... godborn?"

"If I were in his place, you'd stop at nothing to free me."

"She's right," Edison said quietly, his eyes darting between Ren and the god, but there was a shift in his demeanor that unsettled Ren, like he was keeping a secret. "We should separate. I'll take the south hills," he said. "See if I sense the blade's magic."

And then he vanished into a cloud of blue dust.

"While you look for your little dagger," A.P. ground out, "I'm going to set an army to search for the crown's pieces."

"You're just going to . . . leave?"

"No, Ren. I'm going to do something useful!" He turned his dark gaze to the lake, then back to the godborn. "And vengeance will be a part of that plan."

"But I need you here!" Ren felt suddenly uneasy and even vulnerable at the thought of being without the god's protection.

"You can fend for yourself," he said, as if he could read her fears plainly. "But if you wish me to stay, then I will."

Ren knew it was smarter to split up and attack the problem from multiple angles. She gave a small, reluctant nod. "Okay. You can go. But how will you find me again?"

The god chuckled. "It will take me all of five seconds." And then he stalked into the forest, morphing into a thick shadow as he went.

Alone on the shore, Ren felt her heart hammering in her chest. Her pulse pounded in her ears, and she felt like she might drown in the ghastly memory of her death. To get her mind off it, she set her sights on what mattered—finding the blade.

As she paced near the water's edge, the hairs on the back of her arms stood on end, and her cat ears emerged, pricking at the sound of a very sure-footed, stealthy someone she could sense nearby. Ren froze and took a whiff of the cool night air, trying to sniff out the someone, but strangely, they had no scent.

How is that possible? she wondered.

That's when she heard it, the *whoosh* of air. Faster than lightning, Ren spun and caught the glowing blue arrow meant for her back.

Gripping the familiar weapon, she realized who was stalking her. "Monty?"

Her friend stepped into the moonlight. Her hair was a tangled mess, cascading around her dirt-smeared face. And her dark eyes were hungry, feral.

"It's me! Ren!"

"Ren's . . . dead," said Monty. Her gaze traveled upward. "And you're . . . a cat!"

Ren started toward the hunter, but Monty was quick to load another arrow. "Don't move another inch!"

"Monty!" Ren cried. "I'm alive! I went to the underworld, but Ixtab set me free, and . . ." She could see she wasn't even close to penetrating the armor that was Monty. "You and I went on a quest together to stop the Lords of Night, and then everything went bad, and they crowned me queen, and I couldn't live like that, so . . ."

Monty's gaze hardened, and she shook her head. "I . . . I killed you," she whispered.

Tears sprang to Ren's eyes. "You had to! It wasn't your fault. I made you promise, and it was too much to ask, and I'm so, so sorry."

Monty lowered her bow and pushed a matted strand of dark

hair from her face. And then she was running into Ren's arms, squeezing her so tight, the godborn thought the hunter would snap her spine in two. "How...how is this possible?" Monty cried.

Ren gave her friend the abbreviated version, including her newfound powers. The hunter took it all in without a single interruption, like she was committing each word to memory.

When Ren was done, Monty said, "Does that mean you can shift into a giant cat?"

"Not that I know of."

Monty adjusted her quiver. "I guess that makes us both jaguars."

"Are you a full-fledged Jaguar Warrior now?" Ren asked. "I see you still have possession of your magical arrows." Ren handed back the one she had caught.

"Yeah. I guess when I...ended you, the sacrifice was some epic thing. It earned me a place in the Jaguar tribe."

Monty didn't seem too excited about having achieved her lifelong goal. Maybe, Ren figured, the price had just been too high.

"That's fantastic! Congratulations!" Ren pulled her friend into another hug. "Want to celebrate with a swim?"

Monty broke free. "Do I look that dirty?"

"Well, uh, a bath wouldn't hurt..." Ren sniffed politely. "You don't smell, though. Why can't I catch your scent?"

Monty made her way to the lake and splashed her face and arms. "No one can smell a great hunter, not even a godborn with jaguar magic." She dunked her head into the water and scrubbed her hair. Then she stopped and glanced over her shoulder. "You know, after everything, A.P. . . . He . . . kind of went mad."

"And he just left you here?"

Monty shook her head. "I disappeared into the woods for a while, thinking I might go home. But then I knew . . . I couldn't leave this place."

"Why?"

"This . . . This is where . . ." Her voice trembled. "Where I felt closest to you."

"How have you survived?" Ren asked.

Monty smiled for the first time. "I lived off the land. Jaguar, remember?"

"But you're a vegetarian."

Monty's eyes widened. "Oh, I didn't kill any animals!"

Ren smiled back, but she couldn't shake the feeling that something was different about Monty, and it wasn't just her disheveled appearance—it was in her voice and her demeanor. It had only been a month since Ren had seen her, and yet the hunter seemed older, wiser, maybe even harder. "I guess we can start our own jag club now," Ren said.

"Except I don't have ears," Monty pointed out. They both laughed, but it was a hollow sound.

After a moment, Monty got up and walked over to Ren, shaking out her hair. "It's cool that Ixtab let you go and all, but why do you think she wants the crown of jade and shadow so bad? Like, it must be pretty powerful, right?"

Ren nodded. "I don't know what it can do, though."

"So, um . . . I think I can help you find it."

"You can?"

"After the crown went flying, there were two trails of gold dust just kind of suspended in the air, so I sent an arrow to follow the one heading south," she said as she braided her hair over her shoulder. "It took a long time for the arrow to come back to me—like a whole day—but when it did, it told me something that didn't make sense."

Ren's heart was leaping out her chest. "What?"

"It went to Cehualoyan—the fourth level of Mictlan."

With a grimace, Ren squeezed her hands together. A small angry chuckle bubbled up as she considered the irony of it: she'd have to travel to the Aztec underworld to avoid being doomed to the Maya one.

"But that's not the weirdest part," Monty added. "Cehualoyan is also known as the place of snow. It's where a spirit remembers the saddest moments of their life—which sounds really awful and not a great design, but whatever. The point is that the crown also went to Devils Tower in Wyoming."

"Wait . . ." Ren frowned as she grappled with the strangeness of it all. "You mean one piece went to Cehualoyan and the other went to Devils Tower?"

"That's what I thought too at first, but the arrow was super clear: the one piece landed in *two* places. Interesting, right?"

"How is that even possible?"

Monty let out an exasperated sigh. "Because Devils Tower is *also* Cehualoyan. Don't look so confused. I remember my mom telling me that many spots in our world are actually mirrors of enchanted places. Something about access points from the human world . . . But what matters is that one crown piece is at Devils Tower!"

"I need to tell A.P. so he can go get it!"

Monty scrunched up her face. "Yeah, doesn't work that way."

"What do you mean?"

"It's your crown. You're the only one who can retrieve it."

Ren pressed the heels of her palms into her eyes. "Ugggh!"

"It's all good," Monty said, patting Ren's shoulder. "I'll help you, and with Edison and A.P., that's like a gold-medal team right there."

"A.P. is now on some wild-goose chase for a crown he'll never be able to find, and I don't have the blade, and who knows where Z flew off to, and I'm no closer to Marco." The rush of words penetrated Ren's core, whispering things to her like *You're a failure and you haven't even begun.* "Marco sounded awful, Monty, and time's running out. Before anything else, we have to find him."

"He's super tough, Ren. And we'll totally find him. Then we'll slap down those wicked lords and get the crown." Monty waved a hand through the air. "Easy."

"I wish that were true."

At the same moment, Ren's magic began to vibrate, rising to the surface, telling her that they had company. Monty must have felt it, too, because she crept backward and, in one swift movement readied an arrow, pointing it at the water.

Ren gestured for silence as she crept toward the lake.

The dark glassy water rippled as she drew nearer. Her ears pricked and her nose twitched. She caught an unusual scent—something floral. Every muscle in her body was ready to pounce, but she held her magic in check, waiting. . . .

A great light flashed beneath the lake's surface like an exploding star. Was it the blade? Could Ren be that lucky? Maybe Zyanya had sensed her presence and was coming back to her!

Nope.

What rose from the water was most definitely NOT the magical shadow bird.

14

A young woman with shining raven hair par-tially emerged from the lake.

Her naked torso was draped in shimmering white flowers. A scaly tail swished in the water beside her, glowing a deep bronze like her skin. "Who disturbs my rest?"

Ren sucked in a sharp breath. "You're... Eréndira... the mermaid."

"The princess who cried this whole lake?" Monty asked, lowering her bow.

According to the legend Ren had heard, the mermaid had once been a human princess. When she was captured by Spanish conquerors and imprisoned in a forest, Eréndira cried night and day, begging the gods to save her. The deities sent her a flood of tears, which transformed into a beautiful lake. She dove into it to escape and turned into a mermaid.

Eréndira blinked, studying Ren and Monty. "And you are..." She floated closer, peering through the night. "A hunter and..."

Out of the side of her mouth, Monty said to Ren, "How'd she know that?"

"It might have something to do with those arrows."

The mermaid's gaze shifted to the godborn. Then, with a gasp, she said, "My queen... apologies. I didn't recognize you with... those ears."

Ren frowned, cupping one furry ear. "Uh . . . I'm not a queen."

"I saw your coronation," the mermaid argued. "Right here on these waters. And I also saw your . . . assassination." She drew closer, staring at Monty, her eyes widening with every inch. "*You* are the one who shot the queen!"

In an instant, the princess Eréndira morphed from a beautiful lady of the lake to a completely scaled creature with black claws and yellow fangs.

Monty's arrows began to glow blue, a warning that she was in danger. *Kinda late notice,* Ren thought scornfully.

"You don't understand!" Ren said, blocking Monty with her body. "I made her do it! Because I . . . I didn't want to be queen."

"Who *wouldn't* want to be queen?!" the mermaid demanded.

"Who *would*?" Monty muttered, trying to fight her way in front of Ren. But the godborn kept pushing her back, wishing for once the hunter wasn't so zealous with those darn magical arrows that never missed.

"*You* wouldn't," Ren said to Eréndira, who was now at the lake's edge, a mere five feet away. "When those Spaniards forced you into captivity, you cried night and day. You chose a way out, and so did I."

Monty whispered, "That was a lot of tears, by the way. . . ."

The woman's scaly face sagged, and she withdrew her claws. "You are right, mi reina." She shook her head. "So how is it you are alive?"

"A gift from the underworld."

"Is that why you're a cat? Is it some kind of punishment?"

Monty snickered. Ren threw a sidelong glare at her, then said to Eréndira, "I'm not a cat.... I just have ... jaguar senses, or powers, or ..."

"But those are cat ears, are they not?"

Ren inhaled a long, slow breath. "I am not a queen, and I am not a cat, I promise."

Seemingly satisfied, the mermaid said, "I am pleased you are not dead. First, I've never met a queen—my mother died in childbirth. And second ... well, I don't really have a second reason. But I would like to offer you a gift, mi reina."

Monty shifted her feet and whispered, "I love gifts! But only good ones. No itchy sweaters that give you hives."

"What kind of gift?" Ren asked the mermaid.

"My tears were made of pure magic. The lake they created has been called the Mirror of the Gods."

"So the Lords of Night can look at themselves?" Monty guessed.

"So they can spy on me," Eréndira corrected. "But when the moon's reflection fills my waters, like tonight, chances are good that the gods cannot see or hear me."

"What a bunch of snoops," Ren said while Monty threw in a grunt.

"Yes, well, aren't all gods?" said the lake creature.

"Word," Monty said.

"For those I deem worthy, these are wishing waters," Eréndira went on. "And you are worthy by royal decree."

"What do you mean?" Ren asked.

"It means that you are the great queen of the Lords of Night.

Therefore, I must obey your command, and if you insist on making a wish, I must grant it."

Monty rubbed her hands together. "Now we're talking."

Eréndira said, "But it must be simple, benign, nothing that will draw the attention or ire of the lords. Perhaps not uttered while you have cat ears."

"Um..." Ren wasn't in the market for a benign wish. Everything she needed—indeed, her very existence—was for sure going to make the lords mad. She considered wishing for the rotten lords to be thrown back into Sleepville, but she was pretty sure that wasn't benign and would most definitely make them mad. But so would saving Marco or restoring the crown. *Psh.* What good is a wish if it doesn't mean something? "Benign?" she said."

"As in nothing that could be considered hostile."

"So basically, a nothing wish," Monty argued.

Ren shot her a look and said, "I wish for the Obsidian Blade."

The lake creature blinked and dove beneath the water, swishing her tail back and forth.

"Hey!" Ren called. Then to Monty, "Where'd she go?"

"Maybe she's looking for her wish wand."

"Is that a thing?"

"No, but it sounds really good, huh?"

A moment later, the mermaid reappeared in her more beautiful form. Her sweet floral scent permeated the night air. "I wasn't sure I heard you right, so I had to clean out my ears," she said. "Am I to understand that you want the weapon that will put our lords to sleep?" She whispered this last part. "That is treason! Blasphemous. Hardly benign. I could never help you with that! If they found out, they would dry up my lake! They'd skin my scales, remove my teeth..."

Monty scowled. "Your teeth?"

"Yes, a mermaid's teeth are like pearls with loads of magic, and...Oh, never mind. I shouldn't be telling you all this."

"No one has to know you helped me," Ren said with a hint of desperation she hoped the mermaid couldn't detect. "Like, just pretend you don't know what the blade is for. I mean, maybe I just want to see my friend Zyanya." The pesky, annoying bird Ren had a strong affection for.

Eréndira glowered, glanced around, then said, "The risk is too great."

It was time to play hardball, a game Ren hated. But desperate times called for desperate measures and all that. Squaring her shoulders, she said in the most royal voice she could muster, "I am your queen, and I ask this with respect and honor and..." *Wait. Was I supposed to use the word* command?

Ren was cursing herself for not knowing more about royal protocol when Eréndira said, "But, mi reina, the blade will do you no good."

"Why?" Ren said.

The mermaid rolled her eyes. "The bird is no longer in residence. She has flown the coop. Disappeared into the sunset. Left the building."

Ren couldn't imagine where Zyanya could have gone and why she would have abandoned the safety of her home. How was the bird resisting its pull? Ren hoped Zyanya was okay....

"I can use the blade to find her with my arrows," Monty said, reminding Ren that the hunter could get an exact location on someone by using one of their possessions.

Ren studied the mermaid—her beauty and elegance, the way she carried herself like a true princess. "I wish for the blade."

The mermaid's eyes softened as she floated a hand on the surface of the glistening water. "Such a shame you do not wish to wear the crown of jade and shadow, a blend of two magics..."

"*Two* magics?" Ren said.

The mermaid's eyes went wide. "Did I say *two*? I meant a blend of great magic."

Monty snorted. "I can spot a lie a million miles away, and I'm not saying you're lying or anything, but you're for sure hiding something, which is its own sort of lie, I guess, and..."

"Monty..." Ren said between clenched teeth.

Eréndira plucked a flower from the garland around her neck, twisting it nervously. "It's only a story, and probably not even true. You wouldn't believe the echoes of tales I catch beneath my waters."

"Please, my... er, lovely subject." Ren tried not to wince as she took a step closer. "Tell us."

The mermaid sighed, then whispered, "The night you were crowned, there was a symbol on the surface of my lake."

Now that she mentioned it, Ren remembered. It was the same symbol that had appeared in each place a Lord of Night had woken up—a tight spiral made up of dozens of little circles. And in the center, a seven-pointed star. But its meaning, which she learned from A.P., was even more mysterious: *The initiation is near.*

Initiation for what? Ren was killed before she ever got to figure that out.

"Do you know anything about the symbol?" Ren asked.

"I do not," Eréndira said quietly, "but I can tell you this: the crown of jade and shadow is a blend of two ancient magics, neither of this world. Some say the jade carries the magic of old gods. As in way before the lords, even. And the shadow carries the magic of old beings."

"What do you mean by 'old beings'?" Ren's pulse pounded in her ears. "Other gods?"

"Do these beings have a name?" Monty asked.

"The Unknowns."

Ren stopped breathing, wondering how this mermaid could know such a big secret. "What . . . what do you know about them?"

"Only their name," Eréndira said with a disappointed sigh. "Do *you* know something?"

Ren didn't trust her mouth not to betray her, so she merely shook her head. But she did know something. She knew that it was the Unknowns (aka aliens!) who had helped the Maya gods create the "Fifth Sun," or human beings. And that the gods were once friends with the aliens . . . until one of the Unknowns had a kid with a demon and started a new race of very powerful creatures, so powerful that their offspring could overthrow the Maya deities.

So the Maya gods declared war, and the Unknowns vanished, only to return a few hundred years ago, when they created an alliance with the Aztec Lords of Night, put them into a slumber to save them from death, and promised them a new world when they awoke.

The whole thing reeked of bad fish, and Ren had spent plenty of time trying to figure out why the Unknowns would care about the lords in the first place. Why would the aliens promise them anything? And what did "a new world" mean anyhow?

"Are you saying the Unknowns created shadow magic?" Monty asked. "Because that flies in the face of—"

Ren pinched the hunter's arm.

"Ow!"

"Did you poke yourself with another arrow?" Ren shot Monty a warning glare. She didn't know how much they should divulge to the mermaid, and the last thing Ren wanted was for the hunter to blab that it was the Aztec goddess Jade Is Her Skirt who had created shadow magic (or at least that's what she had told Ren). But what if it was all lies?

"Flies in the face of what?" Eréndira asked, one hand on her scaly hip.

"Myth," Monty blurted with a chuckle. "I've heard all kinds of stories about shadow magic. Weird stuff for sure."

"Yes, stories always have holes and gaps and danger zones," the mermaid said. "Now, my queen, your wish is for a dangerous weapon, one that is not supposed to exist, one I cannot just conjure out of thin air. . . ."

Ren's heart folded in on itself.

"So there are limits to your wishes," Monty said.

"There are limits to all magic," the mermaid said. "Even those arrows of yours."

"Not really," Monty countered. "They're deadly accurate, and they return to me after I—"

"And can you hit a target a hundred miles away?"

Monty shifted her feet. "No, but I have to be able to *see* my target, right? That isn't the arrows' fault."

"You're telling me I can't wish for the blade?" Ren asked, circling back to what really mattered.

Eréndira floated a hand over the tranquil water, sending ripples across the lake in great rings that spun and swirled into a massive vortex. "In this case you can, because I know about everything that enters my domain," she said. "I saw the fight you had with that boy on the shore the night you died."

"Marco?" Ren asked as the memory came back to her.

"He was no match for your power, and he knew it. But what *you* didn't know was that, in your desire to win, you got distracted. He swiped the blade from your waistband, whispered a few words, then kicked it into the lake. And since it is now at my fingertips—"

"Yes!" Monty pumped her fist in the air.

Ren felt a storm of emotions. Relief and hope because the blade was so close, but also gratitude that Marco was her friend. Of course he would have protected the one weapon that could put the dark lords back to sleep! He was always one step ahead in any and all battle strategies, and right now, Ren could have kissed him for his brilliance.

"Marco's such a baller," Monty said.

As the vortex continued to spin, a beam of lavender light emerged from the center. And floating inside that beam was a black arrowhead, otherwise known as the Obsidian Blade.

"That's it!" Ren nearly shouted.

"If you want it," Eréndira said, "I must ask for something in return."

"What happened to all that *Your Highness Queen, I must do as you ask* stuff?" Monty asked with a groan.

Ren couldn't take her eyes off the symbol on the arrowhead, even though it had no power in and of itself. It represented Zyanya, the shadow bird who, when present, possessed all the magic. And if the bird was gone, then maybe Monty really could use the blade to find their missing feathered friend.

"What do you want?" Ren asked, wondering what she could possibly give a mermaid.

Eréndira's bronze tail swept through the water. "I want my freedom."

"Freedom?" Monty said. "Are you, like, stuck here or something?"

The mermaid nodded as a golden tear rolled down her cheek like glitter. "The lords condemned me here forever."

"Such jerks!" Monty muttered.

"But how can *I* undo any of that?" Ren asked.

"You still don't understand," Eréndira said. "You are the great queen of the Lords of Night. You hold tremendous power, and if you proclaim that I am free, then I will be."

"But I . . ." *Great queen?*

Monty nudged Ren. "You aren't going to make me start bowing to you or anything, right?"

A cackle flew through the woods. Swift and loud and lingering. Ren froze with terror. Every muscle in her body tensed, ready to fight. She lifted her nose to the air and caught a familiar scent. It was the goddess Jade Is Her Skirt, only about a hundred yards away.

And drawing closer.

15

"**Did I interrupt your little soiree?**" Jade's dark voice echoed through the woods.

Ren spun back to Eréndira. The weapon was still suspended in the vortex of light. "Give me the blade!"

But the mermaid looked too shell-shocked to comply. "She knows," Eréndira whispered as she backed toward deeper waters. "I should have realized. . . . The lake . . . Jade is the goddess of bodies of water, and . . ." She threw her gaze to the sky, where the moon had slipped behind a bank of clouds.

"Uh-oh," Monty mumbled.

Ren stiffened, wondering how much Jade Is Her Skirt had heard. Could she see the blade suspended above the lake, too? This was wrong. ALL WRONG! If Jade knew Ren was alive, then the element of surprise was gone.

"Such treachery," Jade scoffed from wherever she was, "and now you shall pay. Let us begin with the siren."

The mermaid gasped. Her chest spasmed once, twice, as her arms were thrust over her head and held there by some invisible force. Golden tears snaked down her face. Her gaze locked with Ren's in a silent moment of agony, and she mouthed, *Please.*

Jade sighed. "Dear, dear Renata, queen of shadows, and now queen of the Lords of Night. I'm hurt you didn't tell me you escaped death. That I wasn't your first call. You and I had plans."

"Only *you* had plans," Ren shouted. "Let the mermaid go!"

An eerie stillness embraced the woods.

Ren could feel a jaguar roar rising in her throat, clawing its way up and up. Her pulse felt like lightning as her every instinct teetered on the edge of wildness and a longing to fight. But there was no one to battle.

With her bow cocked, Monty turned toward Jade's voice. "Get the blade," she told Ren quietly. "I'll cover you."

A terrible high-pitched buzzing filled the forest. In the next blink, a swarm of darkness swept across the lake. Massive wings hummed and vibrated. Coming closer and closer.

"Dragonflies?" Ren asked, thinking that didn't sound too bad. Not like Kenji's bees, which injected deadly poison into your bloodstream with a single sting.

"They're huge," Monty choked out. Then she grinned. "Easier targets to hit!"

Except that there were thousands and thousands of them, all flying toward the blade, still suspended in the beam of light over the vortex. Which meant that Jade *could* see it. And she wanted it for herself.

Quickly, Ren reached for the thread of time rope around her boot, but the thing wouldn't budge no matter how hard she tugged on it.

Jade laughed.

The dragonflies zoomed closer. They'd have the blade in a matter of twenty seconds.

Glowing arrows flew. The beastly insects plunged into the dark waters. Ren crouched low, ready to launch herself into the air for the Blade when . . .

Monty shrieked. A new horde of insects had encircled the hunter, pinning her arms to her sides. They bit her body, neck, and face.

"NO!" Ren screamed so loud and so insistently that her voice gave way to a feral roar that broke free, shaking the trees and sending waves across the lake. But it wasn't enough to throw off the monsters. Ren leaped onto Monty, covering the hunter with her own body and desperately swiping away the horrible dragonflies.

"Where is all your darkness, Queen?" Jade cooed. "No shadows to help your friend? To strike down my pets? Have you been left with just a little growl? Death is so ugly and so cruel, isn't it?"

Ren continued hurling the insects off Monty, but they only zoomed back with a new vengeance, snapping their jaws, sinking rows and rows of tiny sharp teeth into Ren's hands and arms, breaking open the skin.

She roared with anger, with ferociousness.

Blood oozed from Ren's wounds. She stared in horror—not at the lacerations, but at her blood. It wasn't red. It was a luminescent jade.

She was bleeding magic!

The mermaid screamed. Ren spun to witness a dragonfly grasping the blade in its mouth. Frantic, she jerked at the time rope string on her boot again, with the same dismal results.

A violent blast of energy spread across the lake, sending the dragonflies flying in all directions. Ren jumped to her feet as a wall of blue light emerged at the forest's edge, then curved around the lake, forming a magical barrier against the insects.

Edison!

The blade was falling, tumbling back into the lake, which was...changing. Its waters were now black and thick, glistening like oil. And consuming the mermaid inch by inch.

"Stop!" Ren stomped her boot.

Everything froze. Ren panted, staring down at the time thread around her ankle. Pacific's words echoed across her memory:

The gap will be short—a few minutes, if you're lucky.

Knowing she had no time to waste, Ren glanced around. Monty lay on the shore, curled up in a ball. The dragonflies hovered motionless just beyond the demon's wall of magic. Eréndira's head was thrust back, her mouth open in a silent scream. And the Obsidian Blade floated mere inches above the lake.

Ren backed up, took off running, and launched herself into the air. She sailed across the black waters and snatched up the blade. And then she was in freefall. Down, down, down.

But when she hit, there was no splash.

Instead, there was an ear-splitting *crack*. Shards of glass stabbed Ren's arms, neck, and face as she fell through the Mirror of the Gods.

Instantly, the world was set back into motion.

A cold, slick darkness wrapped around Ren, dragging her under. She fought to stay afloat, to keep her head above water. Buzzing filled the air, louder than before. The insects had gotten through the barrier!

"Ren!" Monty shouted, firing off arrows at anything that moved.

"I don't want to die in this form!" the mermaid choked out. Ren gulped in the cool night air. Then, with all the strength she could muster, she said, "I hereby . . . set . . . you . . . free."

A brilliant green aura surrounded the mermaid just as the lake swallowed her up.

"Eréndira!" Ren cried.

"Come to me, Queen," Jade Is Her Skirt said softly, "and we will change the world together."

"Never!" Ren shouted as four columns of inky water rose, stretching toward the sky. Inch by inch, they closed in around the godborn, and as they did, Ren saw that they weren't made of water after all—they were columns of glass shards haphazardly put together.

"Now that I have your attention," Jade said, "we can talk privately."

Threads of moonlight seeped through the prismed glass that held Ren in a tiny four-by-four-foot prison. But the moon couldn't protect her secrets now—the damage was already done.

Ren felt a roar building in her chest again, rising in her throat, pulsating against her limbs. It was a whopper—way bigger than the last one. And Ren knew that if she channeled her determination and released the power, she could blow the glass chamber to smithereens. Yet her intuition whispered, *Use Jade. Find out what she knows. This might be your only chance to find Marco.*

Ren slipped the blade into her boot while struggling with the violent waves that threw her against the jagged glass structures. Again, she reached for the strand of time rope. She felt its heat, its magic pulsing against her skin. So powerful, so close . . .

What do you want? Ren asked.

You are the queen of the Lords of Night. And you must take your place on the throne. A feast is being prepared as we speak, and a delicious sacrifice in your honor. But you probably don't want to hear about all that, do you, little kitten?

What sacrifice?

Those ghastly things that call themselves godborns.

Ren felt sick. She wanted nothing more than to shatter this glass prison, to face Jade and claw out her eyes. But what good would that do when her objective was to reach Marco? He was likely in some realm that Ren had no hope of accessing unless she somehow got the goddess to give her an admission ticket. Fat chance of that happening!

Jade said, *My queen, you seem upset. But it is not I who ordered their deaths. Although Marco is already so weak . . . using up all his magic to try and communicate with you, a soul he hopes is alive but believes is dead. So tragic, don't you think? But perhaps . . .*

Ren shoved back the tears that had formed instantly. *Perhaps what?*

Jade asked, *What would you trade for your friends who are in my lovely little prison? Your shadow magic, perhaps?*

So Jade didn't know Ren had been stripped of her sombras. That Ixtab had taken them all.

Jade was silent as she waited for an answer Ren wasn't sure she was ready to give. But in the quiet, Ren's heart ached. She found herself missing her shadows. Did that make her a bad person?

Things were getting worse by the minute. "I'm tired of your games. You already know what you want, so just tell me!"

Ignoring Ren's outburst, Jade said, *If you want your friends back, you must marry the Prince Lord.*

Ren's stomach twisted into a thousand knots. *Never!*

How about I sweeten the deal? Jade said. *Once you marry the prince, you will awaken the crown. It will call to you, its rightful owner. This is the only way to recover it, and when we do, you will taste power like no other.*

Ren stopped breathing. It was as if the world's axis had snapped in two and she was hurtling through space. The only way to save her friends and find the crown (and basically save her own life) was to marry the Prince Lord? Was this some kind of sick joke?

And then what? Ren asked, wanting desperately to know what Jade's plan was, what she would be getting out of all this. Why did the crown matter so much to her? And to Ixtab?

Ah, ah, ah. Let us not get ahead of ourselves. You must align with the lords. You must take your place as queen.

Ren had pretty much had enough of the lords telling her what to do. But she needed that crown, and she needed to find Marco. This sham wedding was the ticket to both.

There was a sudden flash of bright blue light. The glass columns exploded and shards flew in all directions. The lake began to evaporate in huge clouds of steam that blocked Ren's view of anything else.

I am going to kill that demon, Jade said so evenly that ice ran through Ren's veins.

Ren heard Edison howl in pain, which shook her to the core. Hot anger seized her.

If you hurt him, Ren shouted, *I will never serve as queen, and you'll never get your hands on the crown!*

Edison's howls stopped. Ren hoped he was still alive.

There is a universe outside of your control, Jade said, *and one within your control. Should you not make this promise, I will kill this demon and every last one of your friends. Now, tell me you promise to marry the Prince Lord and we can conclude our business.*

Ren inhaled. Exhaled. Her mind swirled. The magic in her blood churned. And then she spoke the only words she could: "I promise."

Instantly, the steam rose and the lake evaporated. Ren found herself standing in a muddy ravine, bleeding her magic and trying to hold her shattered heart together with nothing more than hope.

Tomorrow. Jade Is Her Skirt's voice echoed across the forest. *You will enter the realm of the Lords of Night.* In the next breath, Ren felt the goddess touch her palm. *A guide to your future.*

And then Jade was gone.

Tears burned Ren's eyes as she stared down at the tiny glass vial of purple liquid Jade had just given her. How could this concoction guide her anywhere, and what was she supposed to do with it? Drink it? Crush it?

With an aching body, Ren made her way through the vapors. As the mist parted, she saw a beleaguered Edison, illuminated by the blue light of his magic. Ren could feel the power pulsing all around them, shielding her, Edison, Monty, and . . .

Her gaze landed on Eréndira, now standing on two legs,

wearing a short white dress decorated with white flowers. Ren's command had worked!

Ren felt dizzy. She stared down at her insect bites, at the magic still seeping out of her.

"You look terrible," Monty cried. "What happened out there? Did you get the blade?"

Ren nodded and pointed down at her boot. Edison placed a hand on her arm, covering a wound that burned like fire. "Are you okay?" she asked him.

A hopeful but shaky grin turned up one corner of his mouth. "I've been better."

Ren scanned his body from head to toe. "I...I heard you screaming, but I don't see any injuries."

"I think...maybe my demon magic protected me. Like, it could have been way worse."

"Go, demons!" Monty cheered.

Ren's arm felt warm where Edison was touching it. She could feel his magic vibrating against her own, sending pulses of electricity through her. When he removed his hand, she blinked. Her injuries were healed, leaving not even a scratch. She gasped. "You...You're a healer?"

"Not exactly. I...I can only feed magic back into someone," he said sheepishly. "Your magic did the rest."

"Pretty killer, yeah?" Monty said, wiping her arrows with a small cloth. "Except that now he's running on empty."

"What does she mean, *empty*?" Ren asked the demon.

Eréndira pressed her lips together in a straight, worried line.

Edison said, "Doing this sort of depletes my energy, but only for a little while, depending how much I have to use."

Gripping her quiver, Monty said, "Can we have this convo somewhere else?"

"The blade," Edison said to Ren. "Is Z in there?"

Ren shook her head, remembering what both he and the mermaid told her about the bird flying away. But just to be sure, she tugged the arrowhead from her boot and rubbed the engraved bird symbol on the back of it. "Zyanya," she whispered. If there was ever a time that she needed the god enslumberer, it was now.

But the symbol didn't glimmer silver, nor did the wings shift or expand like before.

"We have to go," Edison said, glancing around. "The lords could come back any second."

Ren nodded. "We need a gateway and—"

"Some sleep," Monty said, yawning.

"You gave me my freedom," Eréndira said to Ren, "and now I will give you yours." She dipped her head and began to cry a flood of tears that glowed light green.

"Whoa!" Edison said, inching back. "It's not that bad. I mean . . . you don't need to cry, unless you really need to." He shook his head. "What I meant is—"

"You should stop talking," Monty whispered.

Ren was struck by how fast the mermaid's tears flowed, and how quickly they pooled into a small pond not more than five feet wide.

Eréndira said, "This will transport us away from here."

"You want us to jump into a puddle of tears?" Edison asked.

"If you want to leave this place," the mermaid said, "then yes."

"Where will it take us?" Ren said.

"To a place of rest," Eréndira said. "Are you ready?"

How would Ah-Puch reunite with them? Ren wondered. Then she remembered his claim that he could find her in five seconds flat. Still, she worried he was overinflating his abilities. Gods did it all the time. But she had no choice but to trust his word.

Monty grabbed hold of Ren's arm. "Like I told you, sketchy. How do we know she isn't working for the lords and planning to drown us and—"

"Fine," Eréndira sniffed. "Stay here in these woods and wait for the monster dragonflies to come back and eat you alive."

Edison sighed. "She's right. We need to get out of here." Then, to the mermaid, "Just remember, I'm a demon with a demon's heart and demon's mind, and if this is a trick..." He let his voice trail off with the weight of his threat.

"Not to worry," Eréndira said. "I have only one intention, and that is to enjoy my freedom." She offered a wisp of a smile. "When I say go..." And then she leaped into the pond.

"Hey," Monty said. "She never said go!"

Edison took Ren's hand and then Monty's. "Together."

With a nod, Ren echoed, "Together."

And they all plunged into the mermaid's tears.

16

Ren heard the pounding techno music first.

Boom. Boom. Boom.

With a swift double kick through the water, she surfaced in a warm, brightly lit pool under a starry sky. The pool was filled with little kids who were laughing, splashing, and shouting. The deck was just as busy, with adults on lounge chairs and multiple stewards dressed in white uniforms shuttling about with trays of beverages and food.

"You're in your clothes!" a little girl in floaties shouted at Ren, who now stood in the shallow end. The girl narrowed her hazel eyes. "Where'd you come from, anyhow? You weren't there before, and then—poof!—you were. Like magic."

If you only knew.

"I swam," Ren said. "From the . . . deep end."

As Ren glanced around for her friends, her eyes landed on a bouncy DJ. The banner above his station read: ENCHANTED PRINCESS CRUISE.

Eréndira had transported them to a cruise ship?

The girl wiped a wet mop of red hair from her forehead. Then, peering down into the water, she said, "You have boots on! My mom says no swimming in clothes or shoes. You could drown."

"I'm okay. See? I can stand here."

"You can drown in two inches of water—did you know that?"

Ren gave a half chuckle. "You're really smart."

With a scowl, the girl said, "And you're kinda weird."

"Ren!" Edison waved to her from the pool's edge. He flicked a wave of wet hair out of his face. Ren stared, thinking there was something different about him. He seemed taller, with darker skin and brighter eyes . . .

Get a grip, Ren!

The mermaid hunter stood next to him—Eréndira was trying to fluff her dress's soggy flowers while Monty toweled off. A few gray-haired gawkers peered at them suspiciously over the rims of their fruity drinks.

Ren waded over to the demon, ducking a flying beach ball before he reached down and hoisted her out of the water with one hand.

"Why are we on a cruise ship?" she asked, tugging off her boots and pouring water out of them. The time rope thread glowed greenish-blue, and in a blink, her boots were dry and as good as new.

"It was a mistake!" Eréndira cried. "When I made the gateway, I was thinking about my home, a hacienda named the Enchanted Princess, and the magic must have gotten confused."

"I think it's pretty cool you can cry your way out of anywhere," Monty said.

"That *was* seriously awesome," Ren agreed. If there was one thing she had learned in the world of gods and monsters and magic, it was to expect the unexpected. Like having to jump into a gateway made of mermaid tears while clinging to Jade's vial of darkness and a hope so deep Ren wasn't sure she'd ever see the end of it.

"Where exactly is this ship, though?" she asked.

"Off the coast of Italy," Monty said. "Mind-blowing, right? I've never been on a cruise—or anywhere, really.... I mean, other than Mexico, and you know, a couple of magical realms, but...Do you think we have time to, like, check it out?"

"Italy?" Ren asked incredulously, drawing the attention of a few glaring adults.

"Off the Island of Capri, to be exact," Eréndira said. "Did you know that this is the place where seductive sirens called to Odysseus's sailors? The men resisted by putting wax in their ears."

"You know about Odysseus?" Edison asked with a fascinated expression that made Ren's skin prickle.

"The hero from the epic poem *The Odyssey*." The mermaid beamed. "I've read it countless times. So much adventure and intrigue!"

Prickle. Prickle.

Ren scowled. "Great! Odysseus escaped with waxy ears. Now, shouldn't we be talking about how *we're* going to get out of here, and what to do next, and—"

"Or maybe you should tell us what *that* is," Monty said, eyeing the vial still in Ren's grasp.

The godborn looked around at the crowd. "Not here."

A minute later, they'd found their way to an empty upper deck that overlooked the Mediterranean Sea. Above the dark horizon, a bright moon illuminated the rugged cliffs of the famous island. Ren had read that the Island of Sirens was so beautiful, it could put anyone under a spell.

"Well?" Monty said.

Ren opened her palm to reveal the vial of liquid that was now a shadowy purple. She told her friends what had happened with Jade Is Her Skirt, leaving out the whole promise to marry the Prince Lord and Jade's threat to kill Edison. Just thinking the thoughts made Ren feel nauseated.

"What did Jade mean by *a guide to your future?*" Edison asked.

Monty made a face. "Do you have to drink that stuff? Because it looks kinda poisonous and nasty."

Eréndira said, "I've seen one of these before. If you pour it onto the ground, it will open to a precise place."

"Which is where?" Monty asked.

"Wherever Marco is," Ren said, finally understanding. Jade had given her access to the location where her friend was imprisoned. But that meant the Prince Lord would be there, too. Ren's insides felt like they were shrinking, compressing so tightly she'd soon be nothing more than a tightly coiled ball of anxiety and dread.

"Why would Jade do that?" Edison narrowed his eyes. "Why would she give you the key to their location?"

"You promised her something," Eréndira guessed.

"Uh-oh," Monty muttered.

Ren swallowed. "I . . . I kind of told her that I would . . ." The words refused to cross her lips.

"Would what?" Monty said, leaning closer.

Ren blurted, "Marry the Prince Lord."

"WHAT?!" the demon, mermaid, and hunter said in unison just as someone shouted "BINGO!" from the deck below.

"Look," Ren said, trying to shake off her own doubts. "Jade

said that once I'm married to the prince, the crown will call to me. Then I can find it and . . . It was the only way to save Marco, and . . ."

"And you believed her?" Eréndira asked with a wince.

A cool sea breeze swept across the deck, chilling Ren to her bones. "The deal is binding."

"Well," the mermaid said, "gods are master deceivers. They can take words and promises and cut them into tiny unrecognizable bits so you think you're agreeing to one thing and yet—"

"You're really being duped," Edison put in.

Ren felt hot, foolish, and buzzy all over. "Then I'll beat her at her own game. I'll find Marco myself."

"But you still need the crown," Monty said with a puckered face like just uttering the words hurt her.

Ren's head wasn't just swimming, it was drowning in all the possibilities, none of which would get her out of tying the knot with Mr. Sunshine. "I'll figure something out."

"*We* will," Monty said.

Edison's gaze found Ren's. His dark eyes held hers for a moment before he said, "We should get some sleep, and then we'll head out as soon as the sun comes up."

Just the idea of rest filled Ren with an exhaustion that gripped every inch of her mind and body. But would she even be able to fall asleep, knowing what was ahead of her? Knowing she would need all her energy to save Marco? But at least she knew how to get to him now. And that was progress, wasn't it? Then why did she feel so hollow and like an utter failure?

Monty rolled her eyes. "How can we rest when we have so much to do?"

"You'll need your strength," Ren said. "We all will."

"I wish you luck," Eréndira said as she stared out at the glittering Mediterranean. "But it's time for me to go."

"Go where?" Ren asked.

"There are other mermaids down there, calling to me." Eréndira lifted a single shoulder. "Maybe my gateway wasn't a mistake after all. Maybe this is my destiny."

"I thought you wanted to be free," Edison said.

"Free of my prison," Eréndira said softly. "Not of who I am, not of being a mermaid."

"Will you be okay?" Ren asked.

The mermaid smiled. "Thank you for your help, and your concern. Here's one last piece of advice: Don't trust the Lords of Night, no matter how good their promises sound." Then she climbed onto the railing and sang "Freedom!" before she dove into the ocean with a quiet splash.

After indulging in an all-you-can-eat burger bar, Ren and her friends slept on cushioned loungers beneath the wide starry sky. If it wasn't for the fact that Ren was on an impossible quest, she would have called it peaceful. But her gut was churning, her mind was racing, and her blood was pounding.

And when she finally did fall asleep, her dreams were far away, wispy, barely there things, except for Jade's voice reminding her: *Once you marry the prince, you will awaken the crown. It will call to you, its rightful owner. This is the only way to recover it, and when we do, you will taste power like no other.*

"Ren?"

Ren startled awake to find Edison looming over her. He sat on the edge of her lounger, whispering, "Are you okay? You were talking in your sleep."

She sat up groggily, wishing she could shake Jade's voice from her memory. "I was? What did I say?"

"Uh . . . you were calling my name."

Heat crawled up Ren's neck. "Oh. I . . . um . . . I don't remember that."

"So," he said, his mouth curving into a teasing grin, "I guess you were having a nightmare."

A quiet laugh escaped Ren. Maybe she had called his name out of guilt, she thought, the kind that was buried deep in her dark, traitorous soul for not telling him about Jade's threat.

Edison rubbed the back of his neck. His gaze drifted toward the endless sea while Monty, a few feet away, snored like a giant.

"What's wrong?" Ren asked, worried that maybe she'd said more in her sleep than he let on.

In the dim deck lighting, the demon looked like a human boy with a strong jaw and kind eyes who deserved a lot more than the lie Ren was feeding him. "I don't think you should marry the prince," he said.

Oh.

"I have to. It's the fastest way to—"

"Ah-Puch will find the crown," he insisted. "We know where the first piece is already, and maybe Monty can use that to find the other one."

Ren shook her head, remembering what Jade had said about

the crown calling to its rightful owner. And Monty herself had said that only Ren could retrieve it, a fact that the godborn relayed to Edison now.

"That makes things trickier."

"Plus, you know a deal with a god is binding."

He angled his body to face her. "I know why you made the promise. You cut the deal to save us."

"Edison..."

"And I don't need saving. I'm a demon, Ren. I'm the stuff of nightmares and darkness. I can take care of myself."

"You're not made of that stuff," Ren argued, opening and closing her fists. "I think you're super nice and... It all happened so fast, and I had to decide, and it's just a vow. Like a quick *I do*, and then the crown will call to me, and we'll put the lords to sleep—I mean, once we find Zyanya and—"

After a long breath, the demon said, "It's—uh—not as easy as all that."

"Why?"

He stood, paced, looked back at Ren. "Once you marry him, you won't be able to leave his side. You'll always be tied to him."

Ren froze, unable to blink or breathe, much less process the demon's words. No. Edison was wrong. He had to be. "No way! That's, like... prison! How do you know?"

"Because a marriage of magic is always forever."

Ren felt sick. And even sicker when she imagined what A.P. was going to do when he found out. There would be no end to his fury, and it was all because she hadn't asked Jade the right questions. She hadn't read the fine print.

Sitting taller, Ren said, "Then Prince Lord will be the first one we put back to sleep."

"Except we have no idea where Zyanya is."

Wretched reality!

Ren pulled the Obsidian Blade from her boot and rubbed its sides, wishing for an impossibility, realizing with a heavy heart that everyone has their own prison: a lake, a blade, a promise.

"We can't tell Ah-Puch," Edison whispered, as if he could read her mind.

Ren stood and wrapped her arms around herself. She knew Edison was in this because of his own promise to the god of death, but protecting her didn't mean he had to keep her secrets. "Thank you," she said so softly she wasn't sure he'd heard her.

"For what?"

"For being a really good friend."

The demon's mouth spread into a lopsided smile. "Thank me when we get out of this alive."

In the next breath, gold wisps of light bled across the dark canvas of night.

"It's too early for the sun," Edison said.

A cold shiver gripped Ren. Her cat ears sprouted, twitching in anticipation.

"What is it?" Edison whispered.

Ren crept to the railing. "Something's coming . . . across the water." She could feel it. *Heat.* She could hear it. *Humming.* She could smell it. *Vanilla.*

And then Monty's arrows began to glow blue.

17

A violent wind stormed across the glassy sea.

Colossal waves formed, swelling and surging with a magic so...

Familiar. Ren shuddered with dread. *No! It can't be.*

"What the...?" Edison raised his hands defensively; tiny bolts of electricity radiated from his fingertips.

Not *what*, Ren thought. She knew *who* was coming, and the last thing she needed was some unnecessary battle that would only ignite more hate and suspicion and death.

With intense focus, she stamped her boot, bringing Edison, the storm, and the sea to an abrupt halt.

Silence fell all around, dark and eerie and unnatural.

Ren shook out her hands, took a breath, and stepped closer to the railing as she peered across the sea, wondering if the reach of her time gap was wide enough to have slowed down the prince, too. Would it even work on him at all? The crevices across the sky continued to split, bleeding more golden light, as if the sun itself were trying to break through Ren's magic.

And then came his voice—that soothing, hypnotic, bedtime-story voice. "So, you really are alive."

Ren's eyes darted back and forth furiously, trying to locate the Prince Lord. Okay, so the time gap hadn't affected him.

"And you're... a cat," he added.

"Why are you here?" Ren asked, realizing Jade must have reported back to him. Which meant he knew Ren had promised to marry him. Which meant... *Ugh! This is so messed up.*

A bright light blazed at the other end of the deck, forcing Ren to shield her eyes.

"Pardon me," the prince said. "I forget how high my wattage is. I'll turn it down."

Ren rolled her eyes. *Whatever, Mr. Sunshine.* She forced herself to face the golden sun prince. He stood fifteen feet away with a halo surrounding him like he was some kind of angel. He for sure wasn't.

But he did look exactly the same as the last time she had seen him: sixteen-ish, black hair that hung to his shoulders, and dark eyes that looked as if they were made from beams of sunlight. And like before, he wore faded jeans and a white T-shirt. You'd think a god would have a bigger wardrobe.

Ren squared her shoulders. "If you're here to drag me to... your kingdom or wherever, Jade already gave me an admission ticket, and she said I have until tomorrow."

The prince smiled, and Ren was surer than sure that the halo around his big head burned even brighter. "I do not drag or force or coerce, mi reina."

Ren cringed. "You *forced* me to be queen."

"I did no such thing. I offered you a choice, and you *chose* to save your friends." His eyes flicked to Monty, who was frozen in mid-snore while her arrows still glowed blue. "And besides, even if I wanted to, I cannot give you access to your new realm. You must come of your own accord."

New realm? Anger burned through Ren like hot acid. *Own*

accord? Was he joking? She hated how the gods twisted words to suit their own objectives. Without knowing exactly what Jade had told him about their agreement, Ren thought it would be wise to keep her cards close to her chest. A small voice inside her whispered: *What would Marco do?*

After he threw the first blows? she thought as the answer flew into her mind. *The son of war would think like the gods—twisted and complicated and treacherous.*

The Prince Lord's gaze dropped to the string around Ren's boot, then went back to her face. "So that is how you stopped time. Quite valuable."

"I can't stop time," Ren corrected. "It's just a time gap, and it'll probably end soon." She hated playing small, but she didn't want him thinking that her powers or the piece of rope could be used for his own gain.

His mouth trembled on the verge of an annoying smirk. "And the ears? What do those do?"

Ren inched closer. "Why are you here?" she asked again.

But before he could answer, a tingle crawled up Ren's spine and her ears pricked with the sound of gnashing teeth.

Every cell in her body froze in terror. The god of death was seconds away.

"You need to go!" she said to the prince.

He merely grinned a toothy grin and crossed his arms over his chest. "I'd rather not."

Ren wanted to rip out her hair in frustration . . . Or his.

In the next blink, A.P. appeared beside her, his eyes narrowed to obsidian slits. Black mist curled around him like a blanket of darkness.

Ren's pulse thundered in her ears. This was bad. It was so, so bad!

"A.P. . . ." she said, but that's as far as she got because the god of death was already walking toward the prince.

"Well, well, well, if it isn't the great and mighty Ah-Puch, mastermind of evil and eternal soul-ripper," said Prince Lord. "It's been what . . . five hundred years?"

"He's not evil," Ren insisted, racing to catch the god of death. "He's my best friend and . . ."

"And you," A.P. said evenly to the prince, "are the pathetic sun boy who tricked Renata into becoming a queen."

"You guys know each other?" Ren said, astonished that their Aztec and Maya worlds had somehow collided.

Ah-Puch flicked his wrist, and a cape of darkness pinned Ren in place. Okay, so he was mad, but truly, he was handling this much more calmly than she had expected, which might have looked something like him breaking the prince in two . . . or three or four pieces. And if that happened, Ren's plans would go up in smoke. Marco would die in captivity, the crown's pieces would stay hidden, and Ren would be scrolling through Xib'alb'a's Zillow listings.

"We can talk this through nice and chill," she said while her runaway heart jumped ship.

A.P. spoke to Ren telepathically. *I have good news and bad news.*

"You seem angry, Ah-Puch," the prince said. "Perhaps we should dial things back a bit?"

"Of course," A.P. said. "After I destroy you."

"So violent," the prince replied mockingly.

I'll take the good news, Ren said to the god, trying to distract him. If A.P. found out now what she had promised, the prince would be crushed under the weight of the god's fury.

I have information about the crown, A.P. said.

What?!

"You should look the other way, Ren. You don't want to see this," A.P. warned aloud before casting a net of darkness around the prince that instantly extinguished his light and drove him to his knees.

"Stop!" Ren screamed.

A.P. glanced over his shoulder at her with murderous eyes and a wicked expression. "Stop? Stop what? I haven't even begun."

Tell me what you learned about the crown, Ren told the god.

Only that the pieces cannot be found.

Did that mean Jade had spoken the truth? That only Ren could find the pieces, and only once she was married to the prince?

"Can you let me go now?" she called to A.P., whose entire attention was focused on the dark lord.

"After I am done with *him!*"

A deep and ferocious roar thrashed inside of Ren, begging to escape. She struggled, fought against its power until there was no containing it.

ROARRRR!

She broke free of A.P.'s spell and lunged toward the prince, throwing herself between him and the god of death.

A.P.'s gaze landed on her, filled with bewilderment and then revulsion and then rage as the black mist around him thickened and pulsated. "What are you doing?"

In the moment of diversion, the prince's light blazed and burned, slicing through A.P.'s darkness like it was butter.

"I told you," the prince said to A.P. as he stood. "I do not like violence. But I especially don't like it waged against me." A hot and powerful gale flew across the deck, knocking over empty chairs and crashing them into the walls and railing.

"I care not what you do or don't like," A.P. growled. "You are going to pay for what you've done."

"Do you mean saving your little hunter's life? Or giving Ren her rightful destiny?"

"Can't we all just talk about this without violence?" Ren pleaded.

A.P.'s nostrils flared and heat rolled off him in waves as he walked closer, never taking his eyes off the prince's. "Move out of the way, Ren."

"She won't choose you," the prince said calmly.

"Be quiet!" Ren shouted. Every muscle in her body twitched with doubt and fear.

"He must be told the truth," the prince insisted.

A.P. growled, throwing his glare at Ren. "Truth?"

Ren shrank back. In half a blink, the time gap dissolved. Everything happened at once.

The wind swelled with velocity and fury.

"Ren!" Edison shouted from the other end of the deck, where Monty bolted upright.

The sky split, and the god of death collided with the night

lord in an explosion of light and dark so powerful it pitched the ship violently.

A ship alarm sounded. Screams erupted from somewhere below.

Then, out of nowhere, a roar gripped Ren, rising, rising, rising. She threw her head back and released the jaguar magic. Power surged through her blood. Great waves crashed over the deck.

"Stop!" she shouted, taking hold of A.P., trying to pull him away.

But he was too strong, too enraged, too far gone in his quest to destroy the Prince Lord.

Ren had one choice, an awful, regrettable choice that would cost her dearly later on. She rushed back to Monty. "Shoot A.P.!"

Monty's face went rigid with shock.

"Just paralyze him!" Ren cried.

"No way!"

Edison shook his head. "He'll never forgive you!"

Ren swallowed the fear and doubt like it was poison. "He'll *never* let me marry the prince, and if I don't, I'll never be able to find the crown and save the godborns."

Monty puffed up her cheeks and blew out a long stream of air. "He's going to rip out my spine!"

"I'll take all the blame," Ren promised as the alarms continued to blare, the battling gods raged, and the night exploded all around them.

Monty looked to Edison, who gave her the barest of nods. She positioned herself, nocked the bow, drew it back steadily, and let the arrow fly. It whizzed across the space, and A.P.

whirled to catch it. . . . But he was too late, and the arrow stabbed him in the side of his neck. He clutched it with both hands, staggered, and collapsed to his knees, his stunned gaze landing on Ren. She had to keep reminding herself that it wasn't a lethal strike.

"I'm sorry!" she cried.

The Prince Lord laughed hollowly, cruelly. "I told you she would choose me." He stood over Ah-Puch, smiling. "Such a pathetic god. But no matter. Soon there will be a new pantheon, a new, stronger god of death, and you will be a mere sentence in the annals of history."

A new pantheon? A new god of death? Ugh! Weren't the Maya and Aztec deities enough for one universe?

A.P. glared at him viciously, unable to speak, to move, to do anything but watch in horror as the Prince Lord vanished into the night, his voice trailing on the wind. "See you tomorrow, Reina. . . ."

Ren rushed over to A.P., dropping down to take his cold hand in her own. "I know you hate me right now," she said as tears flowed down her cheeks. "I know you don't understand."

The ship began to quake with his rage.

"The arrow isn't enough to hold him," Monty shouted as the shaft circled back to her.

Ren looked back at the god. "I had to do this. Maybe someday you'll understand."

Shakily, she got to her feet, backed away, and removed the vial from her pocket. As Eréndira had instructed, Ren emptied its contents onto the deck. A thread of purple smoke rose into the air, sizzling like it contained tiny bolts of electricity. And with each flash, the cloud expanded until it transformed into a winding staircase.

Edison and Monty raced toward the stairs.

"Ren!" Edison shouted. "Hurry! The energy is dying!"

With forced determination, Ren left the god and hurried toward her friends. The moment her boot touched the first step, the staircase began to flicker and fade.

She turned back to A.P. His face contorted into a painful expression as he began to stir. "Don't do this!" he pleaded.

"I'm sorry," Ren whispered, and then the ship, the storm, and A.P. vanished into smoke.

18

The staircase, wrapped in a blanket of gray mist, went up and up and up.

The smell of sewer odor hung in the air, churning Ren's stomach. She plugged her nose, hoping it wasn't worse to breathe through her mouth and inhale whatever was making that stench. "Anyone have a gas mask?" she asked with a groan.

"Yeah, I'm about to puke," Monty said.

With a puzzled expression, Edison said, "Is it really that bad?"

Monty spun to face the demon. "You can't smell it? Is that, like, a demon thing?"

"Let's just keep going," Ren said, wondering where the staircase would lead. Wondering how close they were. Fighting the voice inside her head telling her she was the worst traitor in the universe to have left A.P. like that.

Edison stopped on the step and turned to look down at her. "That was pretty brutal back there. You okay?"

Ren couldn't get lost in a sea of emotion over something she couldn't change. She had to keep marching forward, even if her heart was in pieces over her betrayal of A.P. Even if she couldn't stop seeing the hurt in his eyes. "I will be."

Edison bobbed his head gently, an affirmation that maybe

she really would be okay. "I was wrong," he said. "He'll forgive you."

"I don't think so." Underneath it all, she knew A.P. was still the god of death, darkness, and destruction, and that there were limits to his loyalty and his understanding.

"He will . . ." The demon began to climb again.

"How do you know?"

"Because he loves you like a—"

"Don't say *daughter*, because the gods aren't exactly model parents."

"Good point, but the truth is he really cares, and that means he'll have to forgive you."

Ren's heart plummeted. If only. If only the word *forgiveness* were in A.P.'s vocabulary.

Just as she planted her boot on another step, the staircase swayed and groaned, forcing her to grip the cold railing tighter as she found a new foothold.

"Whoa!" Monty called out.

In the next instant, the metal steps began to liquefy.

Drip. Drip.

A girl's giggle echoed across the space. "Can you walk a little more to the left? I am quite ticklish in the center."

Ren gaped down at the melting stairs. "You're alive?"

"Why wouldn't I be?"

"Uh . . . you're a staircase," Monty said. "And you kinda reek. No offense or anything."

"You're rude," the staircase barked. "And discriminatory, and—"

"Hey." Edison clapped once. "It's all good, and we're really glad you're letting us, um . . . walk on you. What Monty meant was—"

"I have no choice," the stairs blurted. "When I am called upon, I must offer myself up to ungrateful souls who don't care if I suffer under their weight. Or needling shoes that tickle me to death. And if you think laughing until you're sick is fun, it's absolutely not."

"Is that why you're melting?" Ren said.

With a sigh, the staircase said, "I'm melting because you have reached your destination."

"Oh!" Monty squealed like she couldn't wait to get to this mysterious place. "Where exactly *is* that?"

"You'll see."

In the next breath, the mist parted.

The staircase dissolved, depositing the crew onto the edge of a waterway shaded by ancient trees. They were wild-looking things with hollowed-out trunks and gnarled roots that protruded from the muddy earth. At the center of the canal was a small, flat boat painted in vivid pink, orange, and yellow with bench seats and a canopy of woven leaves. A white-and-gold floral arch decorated its front, spelling out the words VIVA LA REINA.

"Long live the queen," Monty said.

A groan escaped Ren's mouth.

"Well," Monty put in, "*Long live the queen* is better than *Kill the queen.*"

"That's true," Ren said with a smile she hoped would make her look light and easy rather than too tightly wound. After all, as the leader of this quest, she didn't have the luxury of falling apart.

"We've got company," Edison said, like some kind of TV detective.

Ren followed his gaze to a woman standing at the stern. She was short and wore a straw hat and a red off-the-shoulder dress embroidered with purple flowers.

"Welcome," the woman said, navigating the watercraft with a long pole. Her face was weathered, like she had spent too much time in the sun, but her eyes were bright and youthful, and the most enchanting silver Ren had ever seen. "I am Zulema."

Monty said, "Cool boat."

"This is not a boat, or a canoe, kayak, or gondola," Zulema said. "It is a trajinera. Do you understand me? It is imperative that we use the right words to describe things. None of this loosey-goosey language." She offered a pleasant but trained smile, then turned her gaze to Ren. With a gentle bow, she teetered, nearly falling before catching herself on her pole. "Oh, forgive me, my queen. The bones aren't what they used to be."

Ren blew out a long breath of frustration. "Please don't call me that."

The woman raised her silvery eyebrows. "Oh, but it is required. And we all fought over who would transport you."

"We?" Edison said.

"Those of us who pilot the trajineras through the canals," Zulema said. "It is much harder than it looks. Takes years of training, and only the most talented are chosen."

Edison inched closer to the woman. "Where exactly are we?"

Zulema said, "The original floating islands of Xochimilco, not the man-made ones built by those vile Spaniards on the ruins of *our* Aztec capital, Tenochtitlan."

Monty said, "*Xochimilco* means *place where flowers grow*, right?"

Zulema eyed the hunter and her arrows with approval. "Indeed, young warrior. A place outside of time, infinite and beautiful, don't you agree?"

Monty grinned, puffing out her chest.

"Let me get this straight," Ren said. "This place is also a real place in—"

"Your world, yes," Zulema confirmed. "Mirrors are critical, each *espejo* feeding the other."

It was then that Ren remembered what Monty had told her about the crown's pieces. That one had landed in *two* places. Devils Tower in Wyoming, which apparently was a mirror for Cehualoyan, the place of snow.

"They're access points," Monty said.

"I've heard of them," Edison said with a firm nod, making Ren feel like the only person in the group *not* in the know. Still, she thought it was cool how Edison's mind held on to things— the guy was a walking, talking Wikipedia page.

The demon rubbed his chin and added, "These access points are really just a transfer of energy that goes back and forth, keeping both places alive. Super amazing. Tons of magic and completely unpredictable."

Zulema said, "Yes, okay, muy bien. Now, come aboard. If I'm late delivering you, my queen, my heart will certainly be carved from my chest."

Monty hopped onto the boat first, followed by Edison and Ren. A moment later, they were gliding through the canal, which was bracketed by thick plots of land that looked like tiny islands. Bright pink salamanders swam at the water's edge where thick clusters of colorful flowers grew at least three feet high.

"Whoa!" Edison said. "Those salamanders are, like, huge."

"Yes, well, the magic of this world ensures that living things reach their full potential," said Zulema. "Unlike *your* world, which stifles everything!"

"How long is the trip?" Ren asked, wishing she weren't so entranced with this beautiful place.

"One hundred blinks," Zulema said. "Más o menos. Oh, so much to do. Preparation for the wedding feast, and your dress, and ay, ay, ay!"

"When is the wedding?" Monty asked, digging her fingers into a bowl of chocolate bits that was sitting on a bench.

"Tomorrow."

"Tomorrow?!" Ren jumped off her bench.

"Exactly!" Zulema said. "Much to do. ¡Vámanos!"

Edison cast a remorseful gaze at Ren, one that said, *You sure you want to hop onto this madness train?*

No, Ren wasn't sure, not at all, but she had to get the crown's pieces and deliver them to Ixtab, and if marrying the prince was the only way to do that, then so be it. Plus, she had another motivation: Marco. She didn't trust Jade Is Her Skirt to keep her word, deal or not, and Ren had to find a way to get him out of this strange realm.

And then there were the other rogue godborns. Even though they had betrayed her in their quest for power, Ren couldn't just let them languish here. Sure, it was their fault that the Lords of Night were wide awake, their fault she was in this mess, but she wouldn't fight anger with anger, revenge with revenge. It wasn't in her nature. After expelling all the darkness that had crowded her heart, she was more determined than ever to be true to her real self.

Tiny red feathers hovered, dipped, and swirled around the flowers. "What are those?" Monty asked.

Zulema blinked. "Oh, those are bird-feather criaturas. Warriors who died in battle. Beautiful, yes?"

Monty screwed up her face. "Why would a warrior want to become a . . . a feather?"

"It is a great honor!" Zulema cried.

Monty frowned, then turned to her friends and whispered, "I don't want to become a feather!"

"There are way worse ways to spend eternity," Edison said, biting back a smile.

"No truer words have ever been spoken," Zulema said, shifting her pole as they drifted around a small bend. "Think of the horrors of the nine levels of Mictlan," she went on. "Those long journeys a poor soul must make through violent winds, and impossible mountains, and a truly treacherous river. Ay!"

Sounds as bad as the houses of Xib'alb'a, Ren thought.

"I think the worst is the sixth level," Zulema added.

Edison said, "Is that the place where invisible hands throw arrows at the souls and each arrow represents a person who had some kind of influence over the dead?"

Ren's insides clenched. She was pretty clueless about the Aztec part of her heritage, and it rankled her that this Maya demon knew more than she did. "That sounds really awful, and kind of twisted," she said.

"It is the nature of things," Zulema offered. "A perfect cosmic plan. And there's no need to worry as long you're faster than the arrows." She busted up laughing.

Monty scowled at her. "You mean to tell me my old fourth-grade teacher is going to try to shoot me in the afterlife? That's messed up!"

"Definitely seems unfair," Edison agreed before patting Monty on the back. "But you're a Jaguar Warrior, so you've got nothing to worry about."

Monty nodded, looking up at the demon confidently. "I *am* fast, aren't I?"

"The fastest."

As they came around the curve, Ren saw that the waterway was actually a network of channels, giving them half a dozen routes to choose from. And they all looked exactly the same.

"HEY!" Monty screamed.

Ren spun to find a horde of bird-feather criaturas flying around Monty like flies on watermelon at a picnic.

"Get them off of me!" Monty cried, swatting at the little beings.

Edison was about to help Monty when Zulema whipped her pole out of the water and pointed it at the demon. "Do not touch those sacred creatures! One swipe, one injury, and your soul will dry up and blow away like a handful of sand. They are only saying hello to a fellow warrior—they are offering their blessings."

"Blessings?" Monty eked out as she went very still.

Ren watched with fascination as the tiny beings flitted around Monty, a full-fledged member of the Jaguar tribe.

In half a second, Monty's scowl melted. "I can hear them whispering!" she said with a ginormous smile.

Ren inched closer. "What are they saying?"

Monty tilted her head to listen to the little feathers. She nodded. "Mm-hmm...okay..." Then her eyes went big.

"Well?" Ren said as Zulema navigated the little boat around another bend, where an arched stone tunnel came into view.

The warrior cleared her throat. "Nothing. Just chitchat about the weather, and welcome, and viva la reina, and stuff like that."

But Ren was sure the criaturas had said something more important. Edison raised a single eyebrow and studied Monty with suspicion.

"Would you look at that?" Zulema announced. "Already here!"

The boat floated into the tunnel and toward a small dock, where Zulema moored the craft. Everyone disembarked.

As they made their way down a shadowy, torchlit corridor, Monty tugged on Ren's arm.

Ren stopped and turned. "What did the feathers really say?" she whispered.

"They said there is only one way out of here."

"Okay..." Ren wasn't sure where the hunter was going with this.

"There'll be one window of opportunity during a blood moon tomorrow night, and..." Monty blew out a puff of air, leaning closer. "And if we don't get out then, we'll be trapped here forever."

19

Get out. Trapped.

The words ricocheted in Ren's mind with each step through the subterranean chamber. Every instinct told her to flee while she could, but she had taken a sacred oath to not only one god, but two!

And now she had a little over twenty-four hours to get hitched, rescue Marco, and get the heck out of here with everyone's heads still attached to their necks.

"So what's the plan?" Monty whispered to Ren as they followed Zulema through the dank tunnel.

"I'm thinking."

Monty harrumphed. "Well, we aren't a bunch of chickens who're going to run just because some feathers said so."

Ren smiled at Monty, the young warrior-hunter A.P. had found, the girl who wasn't afraid of anything, whose heart was made of something more valuable than gold. Ren felt a swell of gratitude, not only to have her on the team but also to call her friend. "No, we're not chickens," she said quietly while Zulema went on and on about the wedding and the food and the flowers. "But if the feathers told you we have to leave during the blood moon, then we have a lot to do in the next twenty-four hours."

Edison, leaning closer to the convo, whispered, "I can gather some intel tonight."

"Good thinking," Monty said, nodding at the demon, "since you can get in and out of all the rooms with your woo-woo disappearing mist act."

Edison grunted out a laugh, then hooked an arm around Monty's neck, pulled her closer, and rubbed her head with his knuckles.

"Hey!" She ducked out of his grasp. "Watch the arrows."

Zulema spun on her heel. "Well? Are you going to answer me?"

Ren froze. She hadn't even heard the question.

With a sigh, Zulema asked, "Do you prefer quail or lamb for the wedding feast?"

Ren shuddered. No way could she ever eat either one. Had Zulema never seen how adorable lambs and baby quail were? "I'm vegetarian," Ren squeaked out.

Zulema's face fell. "Oh. That's dreadful. I'll speak to the chef. Perhaps he can make venison."

"Isn't venison deer?" Monty whispered.

"And your wedding cake?" Zulema said brightly. "We have the best baker in the universe, a true confectionary king. You should see what he can do with icing. Do you have a favorite?"

"Uh, I guess chocolate is fine."

"Fine will not do, my queen," Zulema said, gesticulating wildly with her hands. "We need oomph, panache, decadence!"

"Wow," Edison whispered out of the side of his mouth. "She takes her cakes seriously."

Monty said to Zulema, "How about a confetti cake?"

"It is up to the queen."

Ren nodded. "Everyone loves confetti."

With a huff, the woman turned and continued to lead the way, tugging a small gadget like a mini walkie-talkie from her pocket. "Javi," she said, speaking into the device at a low volume that Ren could still hear, "the queen is vegetarian. Yes, I know. Mm-hmm...And what is a confetti cake?"

While Zulema changed the menu from meat to other meat, a plan began to unfold in Ren's mind. "We should split up," she said to her companions, deliberately falling a few paces behind their guide. "I don't trust Jade, so I'll look for Marco. Monty, you need to get exact instructions from the feathers so we'll be ready, and Edison—see if you can figure out what the Lords of Night are up to and if it has to do with this new pantheon the prince told me about."

Edison gave a firm salute, earning an eye roll from Monty. "She's a queen, not a general," said the hunter.

"Same thing," the demon said.

While Edison and Monty argued the point, they reached a stairwell and began to climb.

Ren's cat ears protruded, stirring with jaguar magic. She heard voices above, far away. But there were too many to isolate any one conversation. She trained her senses, pressing through the chaos, searching for a single voice: Marco's. But there was nothing.

She would search another way. Lifting her nose, she sniffed the air, hunting for his scent.

Hunting.

Her blood warmed.

Hunting.

Her bones vibrated.

Hunting.

There it was. Marco!

He smelled of ash and leather. And he was close. Was Serena with him? And the other rogue godborns?

What about Ezra? Was she a prisoner, or had she gotten into the lords' good graces by helping to wake them? Not that the gods ever felt any kind of loyalty to anyone. Knowing them, the daughter of spells and magic had been tossed into some dungeon, too.

An unexpected hope stirred within Ren. It sparked her nerve and steeled her heart. She could...*would* do this wedding thing. How hard could it be? It was just a few words spoken in public. She'd do it to retrieve the crown, and once she did, she'd find a way to undo her bond to this...prince. She'd be as sneaky and conniving as they were.

Reaching the top step, they came to a wide, round chamber with a circular opening in the ceiling that let in the daylight. A crew of men and women were busy painting images on the walls with strokes of brilliant blues and reds and gold.

"This is the chamber of new history," Zulema said. "But come along so I can show you the entire palace."

New history?

The crew turned at the sound of Zulema's voice and immediately bowed to Ren. This time she didn't balk. If she was going to pull this off, she needed to play her role to perfection.

Ren blinked, looked closer at the murals. They were painting scenes of the lords waking up. The first wall depicted Xiuhtecuhtli, the Fire Lord, rising from flames that scorched the earth.

"Back to work," Zulema ordered them.

"Who are these people?" Monty asked as the workers immediately fell back in line.

"The dead," Edison said quietly.

"Souls from the underworld," Zulema corrected, her silver eyes sparkling. "Given a second chance. They are happy to be here, and to be of such service to our five dark lords." She paused, stared intently at Ren before dropping the bomb. "Soon to be nine."

Ren's heart seized. "Nine?" Is that what the Prince Lord had meant when he mentioned the new pantheon? And could only one pantheon exist at a time? Was part of their plan to go to war with the Maya gods?

Zulema smiled, a small, wicked-looking thing that transformed her entire face from pleasant to fierce. "Of course," she said. "You didn't think that the five who awoke were going to leave their brothers and sisters in limbo, did you?"

Ren had to swallow the astonishment climbing up her throat. A god was a god was a god. Power-hungry and in it for themself. Which meant that the five awakened lords weren't just being benevolent by planning to rouse the other four. No— the lords needed their compadres, but for what? And if that were true, they also needed Ezra and her magical orb to awaken the rest. Okay, so maybe she wasn't in a dungeon.

"Once you are married to our Prince Lord," Zulema added, "your image will also grace these walls."

Ren managed a smile, regal and agreeable, even though all she could think was *No thanks!*

As they were leaving, Ren's gaze fell on another painted

scene: great bolts of lightning shredded the night sky as the second Lord of Night, the Smoking Mirror, awoke.

Ren stopped to examine it.

The likeness was creepy—bronze skin, ebony hair, chiseled features. She first met the god of war and strife in a department store in LA. He had told her then that she didn't have what it took to be queen. *No composure, no grace.*

You're wrong, Ren thought now.

And as she passed his portrait, his glittering obsidian eyes followed her out of the chamber.

20

Turned out the stone palace consisted of high
walls, enormous courtyards, countless rooms, and impressive
halls, all painted in bright, daring colors.

After Zulema took Edison and Monty to their respective
rooms, she led Ren down a long hall to the queen's suite, a large,
sumptuous space with a golden chandelier, wide open windows,
and a massive mahogany bed draped in silk bedding. There was
also a full-length mirror, a few pieces of furniture, and lush
rugs. Ren peered into the adjoining room.

"That is your private bathhouse," Zulema said.

"Bathhouse?" At the center of the chamber was a four-foot-
high altar piled with stones and a clay pitcher.

"Volcanic rock walls keep the heat in," Zulema said, "and
those stones are enchanted with tranquility. Once you pour
water over them, they will create steam to cleanse and calm
you. It is no small thing to wed the great Prince Lord."

"Why do you think he wants to marry me?" Ren didn't
really care what Mr. Sunny-Side Up wanted, but she thought
the question might get Zulema to open up a little, leak some
good intel.

Zulema studied the godborn, a small grin spreading across
her lips. "You have magic in your blood. A rare sangre, a blend
of old and new."

Old and new.

The words reminded Ren of what she had thought was a dream, but now she wasn't so sure. She allowed her memory to wander back to the day she died, to the moments just before the arrow plunged into her heart, when the Smoking Mirror had said, *Her blood is ageless. Worthy of being joined to the gods. To the Prince Lord.*

"Ageless," Ren whispered. *And with jaguar magic!*

Zulema sniffed. "We haven't had a wedding here in eons. *More* than eons."

Ren saw her opening and dove right in. "Before the wedding, I'd like to see the whole palace. Maybe a tour...?"

"That can come later. For now, you must rest. Take a bath. Make sure to pour the water onto the rocks."

What was with this lady and baths?

Zulema added, "Your attendants will be here at dawn to help you into your dress."

Attendants? So not going to happen. "Oh, that's okay. I can do it myself."

Zulema's eyes darted about as if she were looking for something or someone. Then she walked over to the far wall. "I think you'll enjoy your bath—it was made specifically for you. But make sure to get the steam nice and thick." Then, strangely, she patted the volcanic rock. "So many stories in these walls."

And just when Ren thought the woman would say more, Zulema made her way to the exit through the bedchamber. "Please rest now. Tomorrow is going to be a sacred, magical day, and you will need your sleep. And do not try to leave this suite. The halls are patrolled by the souls of Mictlan. They don't like anyone slinking around, and if they find you, they might mistake you for food."

Food? Was this lady serious?

"But...no one would dare eat the queen!"

Zulema said in all seriousness, "A dead queen is even more powerful than a living one."

Ren was struck silent. Zulema started to laugh, but there was an emptiness to it, a note that told Ren she wasn't entirely joking.

Yeah, except I've already done the dead thing, and it for sure isn't my jam.

"Something amusing?" came a voice from the doorway.

Ren turned to find the Smoking Mirror standing there, blocking the entrance to the suite.

Zulema stiffened at the sight of the dark lord, then bowed and averted her gaze as the Smoking Mirror stepped into the bedroom. "That will be all," he told Zulema, who quickly shuffled out like a timid mouse.

Ren squared her shoulders, standing taller as she waited for the god to speak first. Mostly because she didn't think *hey* or *what's up* was the royal thing to say. And he'd already pronounced that she wasn't good enough to be queen.

But the god only studied her, circling Ren as if he were sizing her up. He smelled of power and magic, and freshly turned graves.

Finally, he came to a stop, facing the godborn. "Are your rooms to your liking?"

Ren felt like nodding but that didn't feel too queenly, either, so she said, "Yes, very."

The god's stare was a powerful thing. "You're still afraid."

Ren bit back the terror rising inside her as she recalled his disembodied words from the day she had ventured into the Maze of Nightmares: *Your fear is the gateway. You can never be rid of me because you will always be afraid.*

Of all the lords Ren had met, this one got under her skin the most. There was something about his very presence, like he was made of mist and shadow, of untouchable and unseeable things, and that made him dangerous. "I'm not afraid of you," Ren managed, holding her chin higher. And before he could challenge her, she added, "Why are you here?"

The god folded his arms across his chest and grinned, but Ren wasn't fooled. There was nothing friendly or amusing about his expression—it was just another mask to hide the truth of his intentions, whatever they were. "I was wrong," he said—three simple words that floored Ren because gods never think they're wrong, and they for sure never admit it. "I told you that you didn't have what it takes to be queen."

"No composure. No grace," Ren said, echoing his own words, wishing she wasn't shaking like a stupid leaf right now.

The god leaned casually against a writing desk. "Do you know who I am?"

Ren frowned. "Is this another one of your games?"

Ignoring the question, he said, "I am Tezcatlipoca, the Smoking Mirror, god of war and strife, associated with the night sky, the north, obsidian, and sorcery."

Where in the heck was he going with this? "I already know all that."

"I am also associated with . . ." He let his words hang in the air dramatically before finishing, "Jaguars."

Ren's breath hitched in her throat. Not because of his long list of godly titles, but because of the way his obsidian eyes soaked her up, because of the way he'd said *jaguars*. So Jade Is Her Skirt had told him about Ren's newfound magic. Which meant the two lords were likely allies.

The god inched closer. "I know a thing or two about the night beast. So, tell me, how is it that you came to have such . . . powers?"

Ren wanted to walk away and never look back, but the guy would only keep digging. She knew she had to cut him off at the pass so as not to arouse any more suspicion. She had to protect Pacific's secret.

"I was in a great battle with a mystical jaguar," she said. "And when I killed him, I took his magic."

The Smoking Mirror burst out laughing. His entire body shook with the force of it. Ren's skin prickled with heat. When he finally gained his composure, he cleared his throat and said, "You can't expect me to believe that you killed a great beast of the night."

Ren wasn't sure where the lies came from, but they flowed like water: "When I was in the underworld," she said, feeling her groove as she went, "I was still lost in the shadow magic. I was trapped in Jaguar House, and I killed a mighty beast."

The god came over, his black eyes narrowed. "I sense the

greatest, most ancient of powers in you. That jaguar must have been quite formidable."

Ren felt the pressure of a low growl making its way up her throat, a strange sensation that both frightened and empowered her. "He was no match for my shadow magic."

"A magic you no longer possess."

Wow. This guy was really quick on his feet. Ren tried to tamp down a shrug, because it was so unroyal, but her shoulders betrayed what her heart couldn't admit.

"Why are you telling me all this?" Ren asked.

"Because you are about to be married to the Prince Lord," he said, his tone shifting briefly. "You will then be able to locate the crown of jade and shadow. And then you will possess unimaginable powers."

Blah, blah, blah, Ren thought. Jade, the liar, had already told her all this.

"And while your jaguar magic is quite impressive," the lord went on, "it is a mere pittance without your shadows. But I can help you harness all of it. I can show you how to be the great night creature, the jaguar of darkness that you are."

Jaguar of darkness?

"What's in it for you?" Ren asked, sure there was no way he or Jade would let her keep the crown once she found it.

"You don't have to decide now," he said, evading the question. "Tomorrow, after the ceremony, you can give me your answer."

"I can give you my answer now."

His dark eyebrows shot up with a surprise that bolstered

her confidence. Ren gave a small nod, doing her best to keep up the act. "I don't want or need your help with my magic."

The Smoking Mirror bared a tight grin, one that teetered on the edge of either anger or amusement—Ren couldn't tell which.

Claws erupted from the lord's fingers, and in half a blink, he slashed Ren's arm open. She cried out, gripping the wound that was now bleeding an iridescent jade.

Ren sensed the familiar darkness encroaching, seeping into the edges of her vision. She felt the roar clawing its way up her throat. She was about to drop into an absence seizure.

But this time, this time she let the growl emerge. It was low but powerful, and it vibrated the air around them. The Smoking Mirror flinched and screwed up his face like he was fighting a migraine. A moment later, he whispered, "So it's true."

"What's true?" she snarled, her voice not her own as she clutched her arm.

"Just remember," he said, never taking his eyes from hers, *"there is only a chance."* And then he was gone, faded into the darkness as if he had never been there at all.

21

Ren found a towel in the cabinet and wrapped
it around her wound. Her mind was racing so fast she could
barely make sense of anything that had just happened, starting with the Smoking Mirror's weird reaction to her roar. As
if he was in pain.

She remembered Pacific's spirit jaguar's words: *And* that *is
where the power of your magic lives.*

Ren definitely felt the power every time she roared. She
felt how it vibrated deeper than her bones, how it fed her with
a strange energy and strength. But what did that have to do
with being a night creature? Isn't that what the Smoking Mirror
had called her?

*I can show you how to be the great night creature, the jaguar
of darkness that you are.*

As Ren removed the towel, she saw that her wound was
smaller than it had felt, now only a scratch, one that was closing before her very eyes.

Her heart pounded as she looked at the jade stains on the
towel. *Ageless blood. A blend of old and new.*

Wait. Hadn't Eréndira said that the crown was a blend of
two magics?

*The jade carries the magic of old gods. And the shadow car-
ries the magic of old beings.*

Ren blew out an exasperated breath, wondering if Edison and Monty were having any more luck than she was in figuring things out. Had they been able to bypass the hungry ghosts patrolling the halls? For sure Edison would be able to. But Monty? Was she stuck in her room, too?

Ren walked around the suite looking for a hidden door—didn't all old palaces have them? Yet there was nothing here but stone walls that seemed impenetrable. She might have considered the window, except there were three ghosts congregated below, smoking cigarettes and throwing dice.

Ren's memory turned to Zulema's weird behavior in the bathing chamber, how she had patted the wall and said, *So many stories in these walls.*

Ren hurried back into the bathhouse and poured the jug of water over the hot stones. Zulema had said they were enchanted with tranquility.

The black stones hissed. Plumes of steam rose. The scent of eucalyptus and lavender filled the air.

She hated to admit it, but the scent was sort of pleasant.

Suddenly, Ren froze. Her cat ears surfaced, twitching with the awareness that she wasn't alone.

A second later, a shadow flitted above her, shapeless and small.

Ren blinked, wondering if she was hallucinating. But then . . .

"This place smells wretched," a familiar voice said.

"Zyanya?!"

The magical bird swept out of a thin trail of steam and perched on the edge of a stone bench near Ren. "How did I know you would be in worse trouble now than when you got yourself killed? The lords' realm? Really? Are you dense, or just dense?"

"Did you come from the steam?"

"Are you unwell? Do you think I need steam to arrive in this place?"

Then why had Zulema given that mysterious message to Ren?

"Where have you been?" Ren cried. "How did you get here? And why are you talking to me out loud—like, not telepathically?"

"Could someone turn off this steam? It's matting my beautiful feathers."

Ren waved her arms wildly. "Is that better?"

Zyanya glared. "And you're a cat? I hate cats!"

Ren wiped her bangs from her face. "Zyanya! Where have you been?" she asked again. "Please, tell me everything!"

The shadow bird shook her head. "Not that it is any of your business, but I needed to spread my wings, to see the world, and I like the sound of my voice, okay? Why should a beautiful bird like me be limited by the silence of telepathy? Nope! I was born to sing. SING!" Zyanya threw her wings out wide, holding them there for what seemed to be a minute for dramatic effect. "And all was going well—I was learning operatic notes when your magic had the nerve to call to me! I could hardly believe it. The girl who escaped death."

Ren blinked. "Er . . . I didn't call you."

"Of course you did. You were my last . . . How should I put it? You were my last . . . controller, so we are connected. Sick, I know, but it is what it is. I tried to ignore you, but your magic is growing louder by the day. Like a beacon. It's quite irritating." Then with a sniff, the bird added, "Could you please put those cat ears away?"

Ren tried to hold back her anger and frustration. "I was worried about you, and you were . . . cruising the world? Singing opera? Seriously?"

"You were *not* worried," Zyanya said with an air of exasperation. "To you I am merely a means to an end."

"Look," Ren said, her heart softening, "you're right that I still need you to put those lords to sleep, but I—I don't think you're just a means to an end. Believe it or not, I missed you."

"Hmph. Why should I risk myself, my feathers, my wings to help you?"

"Because we had a deal, and you left me in that forest!"

"I didn't leave you," Zyanya said quietly, looking away. "When I saw . . . When I saw what they did to you, I thought you were gone, as in forever, so . . ." The bird shrugged. "I flew away."

When Ren reached out to pat her friend's head, Zyanya took flight and landed on a tiny stone outcropping above. "No touchy-touching. Now tell me how *you* ended up *here*."

Ren quickly explained everything.

Zyanya's beak fell open. "Let me get this straight. You're going to marry this prince guy so the crown will call to you so you can find it so you can deliver it to Ixtab so you can remain in the land of the living."

"Right. And to save my friends. Oh, and I only have a few days left to do it."

"Do you know how much can go wrong in between all those so's?"

"Look, Marco sounded desperate, and I need positive vibes right now. No negative thinking."

"You do realize you are in the lords' own realm? And that they are stronger here, surrounded by their own magic? All of this is far too dangerous."

Ren's eyes pricked with frustrated tears. Zyanya was too big a part of the plan to lose. Ren had to try something to keep her from flying off again. "Does that mean you're not powerful enough to put them to sleep in this realm?"

Zyanya balked, gasped, glared. "I am the great enslumberer! Do you not understand my value? Do you truly believe I cannot get around a few gods' magic? Puh-lease."

Ren felt a tiny tug of hope (and satisfaction) in her chest. "So you'll help me?"

"On one condition."

"Okay."

"You don't even know the terms yet."

"Well, they can't be worse than those lords cruising around very awake doing who knows what, building some new pantheon, wanting the crown for its powers but no one has told me what those are, and—"

"You are really, really dense."

Ren scoffed. "That's rude."

"It's not rude if it's true," Zyanya said. "Hellooooo! It's obvious that the lords need the crown for this new pantheon you speak of. They want to reinvent themselves as better versions of their godly forms. Pathetic, if you ask me. But I've been around for ages, and I've seen it before."

"Better versions?"

"Gods do that sometimes—go all in for a massive make-over. They shed their skin, morph, modify, amend, et cetera, et cetera. The point is, they want a fresh start, a new beginning. And this crown must be the fast track to their two-point-oh editions."

Ren thought about how her own mother had reinvented herself, how she had gone from the Water Lily Jaguar god to the goddess of time. But that had been for the purpose of self-preservation. "Why would they do that?"

"Long sleeps can wreak havoc on magic," Zyanya said, waving a wing back and forth. "This steam is truly unbearable."

"They want to be stronger," Ren concluded.

"Yes. Now can we get out of this place?"

Ren began to pace. "So they need me to get the crown for its power to do this reinvention." *That must be why Ixtab wants it, too,* Ren thought. *She's always renovating.*

"A crown that *your* shadow magic activated when you chose to be queen."

A painful heat spread across Ren's chest, radiating down to her gut. She knew Zyanya was right, or at the very least, the bird was onto something that felt a whole lot like Truth with a capital *T*. "This is all my fault."

"Yep."

And then what? Ren wondered. *Are the lords going to kill me once I deliver the crown? A crown some mystery person tried to destroy? And one I need to deliver to Ixtab if I want to keep breathing?*

"Gods really are masters of twisted plots," Ren uttered, feeling the growing impossibility of it all.

Zyanya sighed. "Now, can we get back to the most important matter at hand? Me?"

More than ever, Ren knew she had to fix her mistake, and the first and most important step was to have Zyanya put the lords back into a deep slumber. But that would have to wait until she married Mr. Prince. "Fine. What do you want?"

"You must destroy the Obsidian Blade so I can be free."

"I don't get it. You *are* free. Aren't you?"

"It's all temporary." The bird's wings slumped. "The blade will draw me back sooner or later."

Ren understood—Zyanya was as much a prisoner as Eréndira had been. "Okay. I don't need it now that you're here. How do I destroy it?"

"You must obliterate it with powerful dark magic." The bird tucked her wings tightly against her body. "Which you don't have anymore."

"You mean my shadow magic?" Ren swallowed. "How... did you know?"

"I *am* a shadow bird. I know sombras when I see them, and you, well, you no longer possess such powers. Actually, even your shadow magic wouldn't have been enough."

"I—"

Zyanya held up a wing. "You don't have to explain to me. I saw the darkness that stole your heart and turned you into something else. I gathered it had to do with the shadow magic. But who am I to judge?"

The words felt like a crushing blow, a truth that would forever be a part of Ren's history. With a nod, she said, "I'll find a way to destroy the blade, I promise." She patted the side of her boot. "And until then, I'll keep it close."

Zyanya sighed. "Do you know how many people have made that same empty promise to me? Dozens. All lies, and very believable ones, I might add."

Ren's heart squeezed. "Please . . . you have to trust me." Everything was riding on Zyanya's magic, and Ren *would* find a way to destroy the bird's prison, no matter what it took.

The bird averted her gaze, blinking and sighing.

"Listen," Ren said, "I'll do it whether you help me or not. No one should be trapped somewhere they don't want to be."

Zyanya's head snapped up. "Truly?"

Ren nodded.

"Then we have a deal. Just know that if you fail me, I can put you into a forever sleep with the added bonus of nightmares. I can do that, you know. Nightmares, dreams, you name it."

"I won't fail you," Ren said. "Want to shake on it?"

"I'd rather not."

Ren felt a flood of relief but had no time to enjoy it before she heard a soft, familiar voice.

"Ren, can you hear me?"

Peering through the mist, Ren locked her gaze on the outline of what looked like a ghost. "Ezra?"

Zyanya flapped her wings furiously. "Want me to gouge out the traitor's eyes?"

Ezra, the daughter of spells and magic, *was* a traitor. She was the one who had awakened the lords.

"We need you," Ezra said, her voice faint and faraway. "Please help..."

Zyanya barked out an icy laugh. "You're a conspirator, a turncoat, a—"

"I've changed!" Ezra insisted. "And I don't have time. Marco's here, and—our magic—it's being drained."

"Drained?" Ren's entire being buzzed with anticipation.

"The wall," Ezra said. "Hurry! No time! They're coming."

And then she was gone, faded into the mist.

"Please tell me you don't trust that fink," Zyanya cried. "It's a trap. I can smell it."

"What if it's not?" Ren spun toward the wall. As she drew closer, she saw words that hadn't been there before, painted in red: BLOOD FOR BLOOD.

"You cannot be serious!" Zyanya squawked.

"I think the steam activated the message."

With a sigh, Zyanya shook her head. "It's an enchanted wall."

Instantly, Ren's blood warmed. Her bones tingled and her jaguar ears twitched. "Does that mean we can open it? The godborns might be just behind it!"

"Beats me," said Zyanya. "Try spitting on it. Or saying *open sesame*? Ooh—I've got a grand idea: leave it closed!"

"Blood for blood," Ren whispered.

Without another thought, she pressed her nearly healed wound against a jagged stone, slicing her skin open again. She winced at the burning pain.

"What are you doing?" Zyanya shouted before an enormous

gasp escaped her beak. "Why...why...are you bleeding...that jade color?"

"I'll explain later." Ren wiped her blood on the wall.

The stones began to shift back and forth, across and over like a sliding puzzle game.

Zyanya squeaked. "I do not like this. Any of it!"

Ren watched with utter fascination, her eyes scanning, trying to find the pattern of the stones' movements. A second later, the wall opened with a groan and a grumble. A cloud of dust plumed from inside.

Coughing, Ren stared into the blacker-than-night corridor, sensing that something was in there. She crept closer and closer, sniffing the musty air. But it wasn't freedom that she smelled. It was Marco. His scent was everywhere. In that instant, she decided it was now or never.

"I'm not going in there," Zyanya insisted. "No way, no how."

But it was too late.

Ren swept the bird into her hand and stepped into the darkness.

22

The moment Ren stepped into the darkness,
the wall closed behind her with a frightening thud.

"How dare you force me into this . . . this wretched darkness?" Zyanya hissed, wiggling free of Ren's grasp and hopping
onto her shoulder. "Get me out of here this instant!"

Ren's heart hammered so loudly it nearly echoed off the
walls. "I can't see anything, either," she admitted, wondering
if Ezra the master schemer had set a trap for her, a trap she'd
walked right into.

"But you're a cat!" Zyanya cried. "Aren't you supposed to
have super-duper night vision?"

"I didn't exactly get that gift." Ren took in a long breath and
exhaled forcefully, shaking out her hands as if she could drain
the fear and worry out of her fingertips.

"Why are you heaving like that?" Zyanya asked.

"Okay, I have an idea," Ren said. "Hold on tight and don't
let go."

"That sounds ominous. And terrible. And risky."

Ren stomped her boot, and just as she'd hoped, the time
thread shone green and started pulsing.

"A cat with a glow stick," Zyanya said with a tone of disdain.
"Nifty."

"It won't last long, so we have to hurry."

The corridor was narrow and winding, maybe three feet wide, with headroom of only a few inches, leaving zero room for error. Ren rushed through the tunnel, toward Marco's scent. Toward the hope that maybe Ezra really had changed. But even if she had, could Ren ever forgive her for waking the Night Lords?

A few more turns and the godborn and bird came to a dead end, a chamber with a ceiling so high she couldn't see it.

"I told you this was a trap!" Zyanya said.

Ren stared up the craggy wall that seemed to go on forever. "Marco is up there—I can smell him. And if his magic is being drained . . . If Ezra is right . . ."

"How is that your problem?"

"Because he's my friend. Because he would've come for me!" She took a deep breath to calm herself. "This wall leads somewhere. Can you fly up and check it out? Give me the lay of the land?"

"For what purpose? You can't get up there anyhow. No wings. No night vision. *Psh*, some jaguar you are. And no, I cannot carry you."

Ren patted the wall as she stared up, looking for crevices and ledges. "I can climb it," she said, wishing she sounded more confident.

"In those boots? Impossible."

"Listen, Ezra made it clear that time was running out, and that means I have to free them tonight."

"Don't you think the lords are going to notice their little prisoners are missing? They'll know it was you!"

"By the time they find out, it'll be too late," Ren said, studying the wall and trying to map her course.

"But not too late to throw you into the sun . . . face-first."

Ren swallowed. "They can't do that until after I marry the Prince Lord and find their precious crown." It was just a matter of which ticking bomb to defuse first. She'd worry about face-planting into the sun later.

Zyanya took off with a grumble, the bird's lean shadow expanding across the wall as she vanished into the darkness above.

Alone, Ren waited, pacing. *I can do this. I can do this.*

An insistent whisper stopped her in her tracks. It was Ezra again. "Hurry."

"You led me to a dead end!" Ren said with a growl.

"Just go faster. Figure it out! I can't hold this much longer."

"Hold what?"

Ezra's voice faded with two last words that echoed across the cavern. "The magic."

Zyanya swooped back down, fluttering madly. "We have to go back! Return to the palace. Even that steamy, smelly room is better than—"

"Zyanya! What did you find? Did you see Marco?"

"You do not want to know the nightmare that awaits up there."

Actually, Ren *did* want to know, but there was no time to talk about it. "Fine. I'll do this alone."

"Cuauhcalli!" the bird whimpered with a shiver. "Oh, dread! My precious life is ending. My magic is going to be stolen, my wings ripped from my—"

"What's Cuauhcalli?"

"Death Row! Do you know nothing? And if you think I'm going back up there—"

"We have to find Marco! To get him and the others out of here, or they'll be killed tomorrow."

"Did you not hear me? DEATH ROW!" The bird folded her wings tightly around her body. "I'll wait here."

"You're the great enslumberer!" Ren reminded the magical bird. "You're not afraid of some prison, are you?"

"I am absolutely afraid. This prison isn't like what you see on TV. Nope, this one is very, VERY much alive. Do you get what I'm telling you?" the bird said, waving a wing in front of Ren's face.

"Well, if it's alive, you can knock it out, right?"

The bird twitched all over and then tilted her head, thinking. "I suppose that is accurate in theory. . . . And *theory* could lead to my demise. I have never put an entire place to sleep. It would likely take all my power, or it might not work at all."

Desperation spread across Ren's entire body. "I need you, Zyanya," she said quietly. "The godborns need you."

The bird harrumphed.

Ren placed a hand on the wall, determined to find a way to the top no matter how impossible it looked. "Fine. I'll do it alone."

"I can't believe I'm going to say this," Zyanya grumbled, "but there's a lever at the top. It might open the wall. Or maybe activate buckets of hot acid that swallow us up."

"A lever?" Ren's pulse pounded in her ears.

"Did you not hear the hot acid part?"

"Look, I'm going to climb this wall right now, or you could make it easier and pull the lever. Either way, I'm getting into Death Row."

"Fine! But if you perish, don't come crying to me." The bird snorted, then flew back to the top of the wall. The sound of metal grinding on metal filled the chamber, along with a few birdly grunts. And then Zyanya winged her way back to Ren, panting like she had just circled the globe.

"No hot acid," Ren teased.

"Yet!"

A moment later, the wall began to shift like a giant Jenga puzzle. Ledges and footholds protruded only to disappear again with the sound of more groaning gears.

"That lever is worthless," the bird proclaimed. "It didn't even open the wall!"

"At least it's giving me a path." Ren set a hand on a newly extended step and hauled herself up.

"I cannot catch you if you fall!" Zyanya said, flitting about.

"Can you please be quiet? I need to concentrate."

Instantly, the shelf retracted. Ren hurried to find another. But just as she did, her foothold slid back into the wall, leaving her hanging from a skinny ridge.

A fast maneuver earned Ren another foothold, and then another and another.

Her muscles burned as she quickly scaled the wall, cutting horizontal and vertical moves, struggling against gravity's tug and the ever-shifting pegs.

"Quite impressive," Zyanya said, flying beside Ren. "Just don't look down. Oh! New ledge up to your right. Never mind, it's gone now."

Ren dangled thirty feet above the ground, spent and scrambling for purchase, but there was none. She was so close she could smell it! Blood pounded in her brain and every muscle ached. Her fingers throbbed; they began to slip from the ledge.

"I told you not to come here!" Zyanya scolded. "But nooo, you had to listen to that defector."

Desperate, Ren searched for her next move, but there was nothing within reach. The nearest outcropping was a good ten feet away.

The ledge she was clinging to trembled and started gliding back into the wall one inch at a time. Ren clenched her jaw. "I won't fall." Another inch. "I can do this," she whispered. It was then that she felt a spark of magic inside her chest. Her jaguar magic. She let it expand. The power crawled up her chest, climbed up her throat.

It was time.

She threw back her head and roared.

Then she sprang.

Her magic reverberated against the walls and carried her up until she grasped another shelf. She leaped again and again with the grace and agility of a cat with wings.

The magic felt impossible. Astounding. Mighty.

A moment later, Ren thrust herself over the final edge.

And into Death Row.

23

The world was made of smoke.

Thick and ashy, it billowed out from subterranean fires that smoldered orange and gold, casting an eerie auburn glow across the night as if the sky were on fire, too.

Beyond the wide barren terrain, a charred path led to a tangled forest. Its trees weren't lush or green—they were soaring and black, their gnarled branches reaching toward the doomed sky like witch hands.

Zyanya hovered, glancing around. "See? Terrible. A hellish place. Hot and horrid."

"*This* is Death Row?" Ren's boots sank into the ashy ground. "I don't see a prison or Marco."

"This is more like the entryway," the bird said quietly, perching on Ren's shoulder. "A warning without words."

Ren lifted her face to the scant breeze. Even through the smoke and fire, she could sense that Marco was close. Her heart sank at the thought of her friend being trapped in this awful place. "So we take the road."

Zyanya groaned as Ren made her way toward the woods. "Your roar . . ." the bird said. "I've never heard anything like it. The sound shook the whole place. Nearly shattered my bones— well, if I had any."

"Sorry." Ren would never want to hurt Zyanya, but that

didn't mean she wasn't thrilled about her jaguar magic. Her strength and speed and agility, yes. And her growl? A thousand times yes! Which made her wonder. "Did it . . . hurt?"

"What kind of a question is that?" Zyanya said. "Yes, it hurt! Did you not hear the part about shattering my bones?"

So that's why the Smoking Mirror winced, Ren thought. Her roar had caused him pain, which meant . . . *I'm a walking, talking weapon.*

Ren shuddered. She didn't *want* to be a weapon. Did she?

Just as Ren came to the edge of the twisted jungle, she heard Ezra's voice again, distant and frightened. *Ren!*

I'm here.

Time's up.

No! I'm close!

Ren picked up her pace, breaking into a leaping sort of sprint. But she needed to be faster, stronger. As her feet pounded the earth, she connected to the jaguar within, a reflex that was now easier than blinking.

Instantly, magic rippled through her. Her legs turned with extraordinary speed. Her feet flew over the ground. She pressed harder, faster into the jungle with all its shadows and darkness and mystery. She leaped over protruding roots and fallen branches with a swiftness that was both exhilarating and startling.

"Could you slow down a bit?" Zyanya cried, flying behind her.

But Ren didn't slow her pace. She kept on.

With each step the air grew colder, the night darker.

Marco was close. So close.

And then . . .

Ren halted.

"What's wrong?" Zyanya whispered.

Ren pressed a finger to her lips, shushing the bird as she began to prowl soundlessly, instinctively through the tall leafless trees. She felt one with the night, moving gracefully, stealthily.

I can show you how to be a great night creature.

The jaguar of darkness that you are.

The Smoking Mirror's words were true; Ren knew it deep down. But there was something more to it, the flip side of the coin that he hadn't shown her, a missing piece she couldn't quite figure out yet.

Ren's cat ears twitched. Her senses intensified.

Something or someone was here, watching. Waiting.

"I don't like this one bit," Zyanya whispered as they reached a narrow tunnel made of entangled branches.

An eerie green glow pulsed at the far end, about fifty yards away, giving off enough light that Ren could see dozens of strings hanging from the branches.

Something was tied to each one.

"Do you smell that?" Zyanya said. "It smells like a litter box!"

Ren shushed the bird again. *Someone's here,* she communicated telepathically.

By the smell of things, it's probably a feline beast, unless YOU are the source of the litter box odor, which is entirely possible given that—

Zyanya!

The branches above shifted, groaning with each twist. The

already-narrow tunnel contracted as if it were breathing in and out, out and in.

Do you see what I see?! Zyanya cried, clinging to Ren's shoulder. *Those hanging things . . . They're heads, Renata! BIRD heads!*

In the green glow, Ren saw now that tiny skulls dangled above. She felt a sudden suffocating feeling of panic. It started in her knees and wormed its way up to her heart, which was thudding violently.

Just calm down! she told the bird.

Calm?! You cannot be serious. I am not equipped for this kind of terror and torment!

The branches twisted and moaned as they crawled over one another like snakes.

We must go! Zyanya squawked.

Not until I find Marco.

Marco, Marco, Marco, the bird sang angrily, beating her wings against Ren's neck and shoulder. *What does he matter when our heads could be next?*

Can you put this place to sleep?

I already told you—

There was another loud groan, like the grinding of giant gears. Ren spun to find the entrance to the tunnel now completely blocked by dead branches.

"Well, isn't that just perfect," Zyanya complained. "Now there is only one way out."

But the second the words left the bird's mouth, the other end of the tunnel closed, too.

Zyanya swooped into motion, flitting about with her sleep magic. "It's not working! This place isn't falling asleep."

Ren stomped her boot, hoping to stop the moment and buy enough time to think her way out of this, but the magic thread did nothing. The branches kept twisting, the tunnel continued to constrict, and the tiny skulls didn't stop spinning.

"Why isn't it working?" Ren said.

"Can't you do something useful, like grow some fangs or claws and slash us out of this place?"

"Your parlor-trick magic won't work here," a boy's voice said from above.

Ren jumped, scanning the dim tunnel for the voice's owner. "Who are you?"

"The name's Sean Garrett, but everyone calls me Sgarit— sort of sounds like *scare it*, right?"

"Seems an odd name for these parts," Zyanya whispered to Ren.

"I have many names," Sgarit said, "but that's the one I like the most. I stole it off a business card some prisoner was carrying. The guy was crying up a storm, something about not wanting to die without leaving a legacy." He chortled. "So I told him I'd give him one. And what better way than to make sure his name continues?"

Ren hadn't even laid eyes on Sgarit yet, and already she didn't like him or his hollow heart. "What do you want?"

"It's you who wants something. You're the ones who are trespassing."

"He has a point," Zyanya murmured.

"You trapped us here!" Ren insisted. "And what do you mean *parlor-trick magic?*"

She didn't know why she asked the question. This guy, who wouldn't even show his face, didn't seem like he was going to show his hand.

Sgarit laughed, a bored, sullen sort of sound. "Tricks as in sleight of hand, not magic of the sangre. Tricks with objects and foreign magic." He said the word *foreign* like it was barbed wire in his mouth. Ren knew what he meant: her Maya magic.

But if that were true, how had Ezra or Marco spoken to her from here?

"I am not an object," Zyanya spat.

"In the *Aztec Encyclopedia of Magic, Mysteries, and Monsters,* you are categorized as an object," said Sgarit. "Sucks to know the truth, doesn't it?"

Zyanya's voice roared across Ren's mind: *I am going to shove this kid into the deepest, darkest slumber with his worst nightmares looping over and over for all eternity.*

"If you don't believe me," Sgarit said, "try your sleep magic on me. Won't work. Why? Because you're an object . . . ha-ha . . . and *object* magic doesn't work here."

"You're bluffing," Zyanya said.

"Try it." Sgarit's voice turned cold. "I'll steal your wings and stuff your body so you can hang over my bed with all the other *objects* that thought they could defeat me."

We can't risk it, Ren told Zyanya. She sensed there was truth to Sgarit's words, woven in with some lies. But right now, she couldn't determine which was which.

PLEASE let me risk it, Zyanya said. *Oh, it would be so worth it to see the look of horror on his face, his utter defeat when I consume him with my wings!*

With a scowl, Ren thrust out her chin. It was time to put this kid in his place. "I am the queen of the Lords of Night."

"Yeah, I know who you are."

Sgarit materialized in front of Ren. He wasn't a boy at all. Well, not really. The lower half of his body was all goat, and the upper half was human. His silver-streaked red hair was slicked back, making his large ears poke out even more, and he had too many freckles to count. "If we're going to brag about titles," he said, "then you should know that I'm the warden. The keeper. The guardian of Cuauhcalli."

"So you decide who stays and who goes," Ren said.

"Goes? This is Death Row," Sgarit grunted. "That's Death with a capital *D*, as in no one escapes here. . . . At least not alive."

"I'm going to marry the Prince Lord tomorrow," Ren insisted. "And I'm pretty sure he'll be mad if I'm dead."

"I already told you," Sgarit said. "It isn't up to me. IT decides. And IT doesn't like snoops, spies, and uninvited souls."

Ren's skin prickled. She fought a long shiver as a strange magnetic force seemed to pull her closer to the trees, which were shifting and swaying. Suddenly, she wanted to reach out and touch their charred bark, their scars, and their darkness. She sensed the shadows that lived within each branch. She could taste and smell and feel them. Ash. Cold and empty.

Fighting the urge, she demanded, "Where's Marco?"

"Why would I tell you that?" the boy said.

"Because I want to talk to him. Just once. I mean, isn't he allowed visitors?"

"No. You want to save him." Sgarit drew closer. "He must have done something really awful, like those he came with. And that means a slow sort of demise—first a draining of magic, then a walk through his worst memories, and after that, a dance with shadows, and finally..." He made a paper-slicing sort of sound to indicate *lights out*.

So Ezra had told the truth. "Draining of magic?" she asked, hoping to get more intel.

Zyanya let out a yelp.

"What do you think feeds this place?" Sgarit said.

Ren swallowed past the hard lump throbbing in her throat. A pair of shadow chains instantly appeared around her ankles and wrists. "Hey!" she shouted.

Zyanya tried to zip away, but a long shadow chain caught the bird around her legs, too.

It was then that Ren felt the shadows moving beneath her skin, exploring. She heard Sgarit talking, but his voice was a muffled, faraway thing.

We know you, the sombras whispered. *You have ancient blood. We know you, Jaguar of Darkness.*

The shadow chains lurched, forcing Ren to walk, one foot in front of the other, toward the tunnel's dead end.

"Where are you taking us?" Ren said, struggling in vain against the restraints.

"You'll see."

When they arrived at the end, Ren realized it wasn't so dead after all. There was a giant hole in the ground, a chasm of about fifty feet across and twenty feet deep. The space was bathed in a fiery glow from torches attached to its walls.

Zyanya, uncharacteristically silent, tucked her head beneath a wing while Ren's jaguar instincts flared. She could sense Marco and the other godborns down there. She could feel their pain. She could taste their fear.

Her body vibrated with their longing to be free.

Use your shadow magic, Ezra whispered telepathically.

It's gone!

I can feel...the night is still within you. Ezra's voice was weaker when she said, *Stop being so scared....*

In that moment, Ren realized she *was* afraid. She was terrified of the prospect of feeling darkness move through her again, of letting it steal her heart and mind and spirit. It was true she no longer had shadow magic, but she had something else—her godborn gift. But what did Ezra mean that the night was still in her? Was she really a night beast, like the Smoking Mirror had said?

The great cat stirred within her.

Get inside the blade, Ren instructed Zyanya, *or this might hurt.*

The bird had enough chain to follow Ren's instructions. Just as Zyanya flew into the Obsidian Blade, still tucked inside Ren's boot, the godborn took a giant breath, then opened her mouth and released a ferocious roar.

Sgarit's shock registered in his wide, terrified eyes as he collapsed, covering his ears.

A vicious wind raged through the tunnel. The dead trees bent and writhed.

The chasm quaked. Rocks and forest debris fell into it.

Ren roared viciously. Her blood rushed with power and

magic as she broke free of her chains and leaped down into the gorge.

As she landed with stealthy precision. As she sped down a corridor toward the smells of fear and magic. Toward the sound of beating hearts.

And as Ren ran, she felt the cat within thrashing wildly until she couldn't hold its power. Until...

The air sparked green and blue and gold.

And in the next breath, Ren's world shifted. It didn't happen slowly or methodically or even in pieces. No, it happened fast, like she was in some kind of fever dream.

With a single growl, Ren transformed into a jaguar.

24

Ren gasped as the shock twisted through her system.

The Obsidian Blade twirled through the air, tumbling down. Zyanya emerged and flew in circles above, batting away bits of falling debris before catching the arrowhead on an outstretched wing and tucking it away in her breast feathers. *That's the kind of magic I'm talking about! Big and fuerte and— Are you going to pass out?*

Heart pounding, Ren glared up at the shadow bird. *I'm a cat!*

Have you not been listening?

Zyanya! I have paws and— Ren turned her thick neck to look over her shoulder—*and a tail! How did this happen?!*

Well, it's called magic, and it couldn't have come at a better time. Look at the size of your claws!

The cavern's quaking was now a mere tremble. Ren's mind flooded with possibilities and impossibilities. *I didn't know if it would work. . . . I mean, he said no foreign magic.*

Yeah, well, you're not foreign, are you?

What if I stay like this? Ren was drowning in panic.

Doubtful. Now, have your identity crisis later, because that goat kid is likely on his way to fink on us or do whatever it is that goat kids do, which in this case can't mean anything good.

You're right.

Of course I am!

No time to go bananas, Ren said, giving herself a pep talk. *I need to save Marco, and if I have to do it as a big-pawed, long-tailed gato, then so be it.*

"Excellent attitude." The bird's gaze dropped to Ren's front right paw. "Hey, check it out."

Ren glanced down to see the time thread still secured around her leg, pulsing with a golden-jade light. Its warmth and magic spread through her with a strange sort of comfort, like a well-worn blanket that was made especially for her.

You should perch on me, Ren told the bird breathlessly.

You're not going to roar again, are you?

I'm going to buy us some time. Hopefully.

Zyanya landed on Ren's back. In the next breath, the god-born lifted her paw, praying *Please let this work,* then stamped it back down.

At first nothing happened.

Try again, Zyanya urged.

Ren swished her tail, then lifted her head and, with a determined, regal growl, pressed her paw into the ground again.

The falling rocks slowed, shivering in mid-flight.

"They're struggling against your magic," Zyanya whispered.

Ren could feel her power, the combination of both jaguar and time magic, vibrating through her. She channeled it into the cavern.

A terrible moan reverberated down the tunnel. And then the world came to a stop.

YES! Zyanya cheered, dancing in little circles before she took flight.

Don't celebrate yet, Ren said as she raced down the torchlit corridor. The flames were eerily still.

Every muscle in her cat body shook with power. Her senses registered the smallest of details, like the fact that she could smell the scent of the boy goat who had walked here precisely . . . eleven minutes before.

With each step, Ren could taste the memories of this prison, the sorrow and fear of long-ago captives. She thought, for a moment, that she could even hear their distant whispers, as if they were traveling to her across time and space.

The path grew colder and colder, branching right and left in a labyrinth that took them deeper into the prison. The walls, now solid ice, pulsed with a magic Ren couldn't name. It was dark and old.

The torches didn't emit enough heat to warm Ren and Zyanya, but they did illuminate shadows beyond the ice. Still, like corpses.

Did you see that? Ren gasped.

The bird, now clinging to her back, said, *Unfortunately, yes.*

Keeping her eye on the sombras inside the walls, the jaguar passed another intersection, guided by instinct and Marco's scent. But with every inch she gained, she could feel the time magic waning.

Are you sure you're going the right way? Zyanya asked. *Because that other path looked cleaner, nicer, safer.*

He's this way. I can smell it.

A few moments later, they came to an archway.

Above it, carved into the ice, were the words WHERE THE DEAD LIVE.

Well, that's cheerful. Zyanya snorted. *I think that's our signal to turn back.*

Head slung low, muscles tense, eyes alert, Ren stalked silently toward the entryway. *I'm not leaving here without Marco.*

The bird groaned as the pair walked into Death Row.

Inside, the entire space was made of ice—the floor, the walls, the ceiling, and the massive bridge that was suspended over what seemed like a mile-deep chasm.

Ren's eyes followed the hundred or so yards over the bridge to a row of cells. But from here she couldn't tell if the cages were occupied due to the bars, which were made not of ice or steel, but of thick black vines.

Would her roar shred them? And if it did, would it bring the whole place down around them? She needed more practice, more time!

A chorus of incoherent whispers drifted across the space.

Pulse thudding, Ren turned her head to the side, listening, sensing. The whispers fell away until all she heard was the buzzing of bees (Kenji), the clang of metal (Marco), and the warm vibration of magic (Serena and Ezra).

She set one paw on the bridge.

WAIT! Zyanya shouted in Ren's mind.

Ren halted mid-stride.

Cuauhcalli, the bird whispered, glancing around. *It knows we're here. And if you cross this bridge, there may be no turning back.*

Ren had guessed as much. But that wasn't going to stop her. *You don't have to believe Sgarit. You're not just an object, and that means . . . you can put this place to sleep.*

That's a big if, and look how enormous this place is, how powerful and . . . Zyanya shook her head.

Ren understood the sheer power of belief, of confidence and trust in oneself. *I know you can do this. You're the great enslumberer!*

But how do I do that without knocking out you and the godborns? Zyanya mused more to herself than Ren. *I could try a loop. I used it once at a wedding to keep the bride awake while I put everyone else to sleep. It could work, but . . .*

But what?

The effort alone will drain me. It will likely take all my strength, and that means that I . . . I won't be able to put the lords to sleep anytime soon.

A cruel frustration dug its claws into Ren's ribs. *How long will you be without your powers?*

The last time I performed this feat, my magic was gone for eight days, three hours, and six minutes. But this is different. I've never put an entire prison to sleep!

Which meant Ren had to choose. Save the godborns' magic, or throw the dark lords back into their eternal slumber. She stared out across the bridge toward the cells. She thought about Serena and Kenji and Diamante, how their powers had done so much damage, and yet . . . Marco was innocent. He didn't deserve to be stripped of his magic. Ren knew all too well how terrible that felt.

Suddenly, shadows writhed behind the ice—long, lean, misshapen things begging to get out.

Looks like the time gap is all closed up, Zyanya squeaked.

A sandpaper voice reverberated across the void. "Yesss. Come clossser. I cannot wait to posssesss your dark powersss."

Ren set another paw onto the bridge. *Put it to sleep NOW!*

Zyanya flew up and away. The bird's wings expanded until their darkness swallowed the entire chamber. She flapped her wings with dance-like movement, creating tiny circles as she soared through the air.

"You cannot win," the voice said. "You will die here."

With a snarl, Ren broke into a run.

The shadows behind the ice grew darker.

She caught the scent of something monstrous, hateful, and very dead. It smelled so familiar, so . . .

Ren's memory tripped the moment she heard the cracking of ice. The bridge quaked. She ran faster, harder as the ground beneath her ruptured, split down the center. As the walls splintered and cracked.

As something crawled out of the walls.

Zyanya! she yelled.

I'm trying!

Ren leaped over the fissures, dashing across the quaking bridge with total speed and precision.

Her heart beat thunderously. She was close. So close to the end. To Marco. To—

The voice laughed cruelly. Black smoke rose from the ice beneath her feet.

No, not smoke. Demons. Their scent so like Maya demons, their appearance so *unlike* them.

Four towering translucent monsters with enormous heads, and tentacles that hung from their jelly, bag-like bodies. Their wide mouths were filled with gray fangs that dripped with a milky fluid.

Ren stumbled to a stop.

The demons took a step closer, sniffing the air and snapping their jaws open and closed.

Crouching low, she could feel the roar building inside her body, but if she let it out, she would likely bring down the entire prison. And everyone in it.

Waves of fear and hopelessness began to wash over her.

The demons' movements were awkward, stiff. Their tentacles shot out, searching.

They can't see me, Ren guessed as the world continued to shake violently.

Just then, she felt the ominous rush of enormous flapping wings.

Zyanya's magic pulsed all around her. Ren could sense its power . . . and its struggle as it drained from her friend.

The demons inched closer. Their tongues snapped at the air. Their tentacles stretched toward her.

Desperate, Ren tried the time thread, but the bridge still shook. The walls still cracked. The demons still came. And then . . .

The monsters lunged at her.

Ren sprang.

She slashed through the gut of one demon. The beast wailed as a steaming milky fluid poured out of him. A tentacle grabbed hold of Ren's throat. Hot stinging pain shot through her entire body.

The tentacle squeezed tighter.

"Such power in you," Cuauhcalli moaned. "But it's not enough to defeat me."

Small black dots danced in Ren's waning vision. Her entire
body buzzed with panic and what felt like dying magic.

She thrashed and writhed with desperation—a deep desire
to free her friends, to finish this quest, to live.

Then, in the space of three heartbeats, everything shifted.

Ren heard and *felt* the buzzing of bees, the clanging of
metal, the vibrations of magic.

Zyanya released a painful trill.

Cuauhcalli screamed, "NOOOO!"

The demons vanished. And the fragmented world came to
a standstill.

Ren collapsed to the ground as Zyanya swept back, "I...I...
did it." The bird fell to the ground, along with the blade. Gasp-
ing for air, Ren grimaced at the pain lancing across her throat
where the tentacle had pierced her skin. Her magic bled onto
the ice, sizzling on contact as she transformed into her human
form, clothes and all.

Trembling, Ren put the arrowhead back into her boot for
safekeeping. Then she scooped the little hero into her hands.
"Zyanya?"

There was no answer. Only an angry voice echoing across
the cavern.

"Well, well, well," Ah-Puch said, "if it isn't the most treacherous godborn to have ever lived."

25

Ren was engulfed by the dark.

She was awake but not awake, conscious but floating in a strange dreamlike state.

"A.P.?" she whispered. "How...how are you here?"

"Did you really think there was anywhere you could go that I would not find you?"

Ren squeezed her eyes closed and found herself wishing. Wishing she hadn't had to betray the god of death, wishing she had her shadow magic, wishing she was strong enough to free Marco and the others.

But maybe now everything would be okay. She had the god of death at her side again, and that meant... "You're here to save us," she whispered.

"No." The god's voice sounded strange—maybe angrier than usual, or more scornful. Or worse...indifferent. "I am not going to save you this time."

Ren bit back tears. Naturally, he was still furious that she had betrayed him. She would never forget the look on his face when she'd left him on that ship with an arrow piercing his neck. Or his last words, begging her not to go.

"I'm sorry," she said. "I know you hate me, but I had to—"

"I do not care for your apology. Or your sniveling. Now you are bleeding magic, and your so-called friends are in even worse shape after using the last of their powers to assist that shadow bird in putting Cuauhcalli to sleep. But it wasn't enough, and the prison will awaken soon. You have mere minutes."

Last of their powers? Was Ren too late?

"How... how do I get them out of here?" she asked.

"I would tell you to save yourself, but I know that would be futile."

Ren felt herself fading from this dark place, away from the god she loved like a father. But there was no way she could leave without answers.

"When the time comes," A.P. said, "let only Serena tie the knot. Do you hear me? Only Serena."

Seriously? The god of death was here just to tell her to let Serena marry the Prince Lord?

Before she could ask another question, she was sucked through a vortex of spinning shadows.

Only Serena, the god's voice echoed.

And then Ren opened her eyes.

26

Ren found herself curled in a ball on an icy floor.

Her body felt like a giant block of wood, stiff and unmovable. She blinked, coming to her senses. Zyanya stirred in her grasp, then vanished into the blade in Ren's boot. The arrowhead pulsed with the bird's presence.

Had A.P. really just been here, or had it been a dream?

Your friends are in even worse shape after using the last of their powers to assist that shadow bird in putting Cuauhcalli to sleep.

"Is she dead?" That was Diamante's voice.

"She's our only hope out of here, so she better not be," Serena said with a groan.

"Anyone got a stick to poke her with?" Kenji asked.

"Come on, Ren," Marco whispered, "get up."

Ren touched the wound on her neck. Like before, it was already healing.

"Woot! She's moving!" Kenji said as Ren rolled to her feet.

"About time," Ezra said.

All the godborns were still locked in cells that had thorny black vines for bars. Ren sought out Marco first. There was no fight in his eyes, no sign of his do-or-die attitude. Though his cheeks were sunken and pale, they twitched with an almost smile that told her he was happy to see her. But it wasn't his weak demeanor that stole Ren's breath. It was his hair—now completely silver instead of his recent blue. Ren saw that the same thing had happened to the other godborns.

"You're alive!" Marco rasped. "And you've got cat ears?"

"Your hair . . ." Ren muttered.

Marco sighed. "A wicked side effect."

"Of what?"

"Could you have your little reunion some other time?" Serena spat. "The sleep spell isn't going to hold much longer."

In the next minute, Ren got Serena to confirm what A.P. had told her about the godborns banding together and using their magic to enhance Zyanya's.

I wondered where that big jolt came from, the bird said telepathically to Ren from inside the blade.

"It was only possible because Ezra shared her power and strength," Serena insisted, pushing a tangled white lock out of her worn face.

Ren scowled at Serena. "Why should I believe anything you say? We're here because of you *and* Ezra!"

Marco reached between the barbed vines and took hold of Ren's arm. "Hey, we're one team now, okay?"

Ren searched his green eyes and saw that he believed what he was saying. But that wasn't enough to calm the anger she had been carrying for so long. Serena had plotted to awaken the Lords of Night. She had set off this awful chain of events with her friends' help, and Ren had died because of it.

"I'll never be on her team," Ren said with a growl. And then she remembered A.P.'s words. *When the time comes, let only*

Serena tie the knot. She could feel her body resisting his command, her muscles screaming, *No!*

"Ezra used up all her power to communicate with you," Diamante snapped. "To save us."

"Yeah," Kenji put in. "These vicious vines were sucking up our magic. Man, it was brutal."

Ren turned to Marco, her gaze asking the question he answered with "It's true. None of us have any magic left."

"Which is why we have old-people hair." Diamante wiped a hand across her dirty face.

Ren felt like her heart was going to split in two.

"We don't have time for this," Ezra commanded. "We can review everything later, but right now, this prison is a ticking time bomb, and when it wakes..." Her voice trailed off before she could say the words everyone was thinking: *We'll all be Goners with a capital G.*

Marco said, "Ren, can you use your magic to cut through the vines?"

Excellent idea, Zyanya said, flitting about nervously.

"We tried ourselves," Ezra interjected, casting a warning glare at Serena, "but we couldn't do it. Even together."

Ren remembered the time she and Zane and their friends had combined their magic to create a gateway to the past. She could practically feel the warmth of that memory. Their bond had been built on trust and friendship. Ren shared these things with Marco, but not the four traitors. And yet, all five godborns had sacrificed their magic for one another, and even her, in the hope of escape...

"Ren," Marco said calmly, "you gotta let it go."

Was the son of war, the captain of fury, actually telling *her*
to let go of her anger? She never imagined she'd live to see *that*
day. Regardless, he was right. She knew holding on to resent-
ment was like drinking poison.

The walls quivered. Ren thought she saw a shadow flicker
behind the ice. Her pulse quickened.

Bouncing on the balls of his feet, Kenji groaned, "This is
so messed up, man."

Ren's eyes narrowed as she drew herself up. She felt the
jaguar magic pulsing inside her like a second heartbeat.

Thump-thump. Thump-thump.

She didn't know if it was adrenaline or the desperate need
to get everyone out of here alive, but with a single thought, the
air sparked gold and jade, and Ren shifted into a jaguar. Zyanya
flew out from where Ren's boot had been.

Whispers floated down from somewhere above. Ren could
sense the prison awakening. She could taste its wrath.

A supernatural calm fell over her, like a soft ocean breeze,
and in the next second, she raised a claw. She didn't allow doubt
or fear to consume her with what-ifs. She saw only one outcome: success.

And then she slashed through the vines with razor-sharp
precision.

Horrific wails rose into the air.

A flood of white light spilled from the open vines as she
sliced through the rest of them, freeing the godborns from their
cages.

The light buzzed with magic, coursing through the space
like torrents searching for the blood it had come from. It swept

into each godborn with blinding flashes. The godborns seized up and fell to their knees as their magic bonded to them. For a blink, they were columns of pure light.

And when the magic was back where it belonged, each godborn stood, looking not grungy and spent, but strong, formidable, and determined, a bit like a . . . god? With their shiny, young-people hair restored.

"Can we go now?" Zyanya cried.

The walls shook with a rage Ren could feel down to her bones. She spun toward the ice bridge . . . and saw that it was fracturing.

Crrraaaccckkk.

"Is there another way out?" Serena cried as the bridge split apart and great hunks of ice tumbled into the dark abyss.

Ezra, daughter of spells and magic, lifted her hands and twisted them in midair.

"You'll never escape!" Cuauhcalli raged.

Demons spilled from the walls—hundreds, thousands of them, like an army of ants. Kenji opened his mouth to release a mass of bees that buzzed through the air, attacking the demons, consuming them with their power. Ren shuddered as she remembered once being on the receiving end of those horrific bees.

But as lethal as they were, the bees didn't stop more demons from emerging.

Diamante, daughter of wine and art, swept her hands in front of herself, and streaks of black and silver paint ran down an invisible canvas in front of her, forming a picture of . . . Ren didn't have time to watch.

Marco threw himself into the center of the battle, while Ren lunged, growling and slashing, all the while fighting her voracious longing to roar. She knew that if she let loose, she'd bring down the entire place and everyone in it.

Diamante had painted a stone wall, a crude barrier that merely slowed some of the demons.

Nothing seemed to be enough. Not their power, strength, or magic. The beasts were everywhere, climbing the walls, crawling across the ceiling. Clusters and clusters of them making a stand.

Zyanya soared above, flapping her massive wings futilely, as she was still without power.

Cuauhcalli began to laugh, a low, venomous sound that chilled Ren. "I can do this all day. You are no match for me."

Bolts of electricity flew from Ezra's hands, creating a wooden bridge suspended by ropes. "This way!" she commanded.

Everyone raced across the bridge, struggling to find their balance as it swung wildly. The demons were close behind. Ren could feel their hatred, their darkness—their single-minded desire to kill.

Blistering heat blasted from the walls—instantly melting the ice. Black water rose from the abyss. Violent waves crashed across the passage, sideswiping Kenji. He slid off the bridge with a howl and clung to its edge. One of the beasts sprang at him. In a flash, Ren backtracked, grabbed the demon in her jaws, and heaved it into the water. Then she tugged Kenji back up by the collar like he was a wayward kitten.

"I can't hold it much longer!" Ezra shouted from the other side of the bridge.

"Hurry, Ren!" Marco hollered over his shoulder as he and the others crossed over.

The entire world felt as if it was being held together by a mere thread, a thread that was about to snap.

Through the battering waves, Ren and Kenji raced toward the other side. The second they arrived, Ezra exploded the bridge, sending the pursuing demons spiraling into the vicious tide.

The godborn crew bolted, following Ren's lead through the labyrinth. But it wasn't a retracing of steps. She hadn't been down these passages before, and if she hadn't known any better, she would've thought the cave was leading her somewhere.

"You sure you know where you're going?" Kenji asked.

Zyanya said, "This doesn't look familiar."

"Trust her, okay?" Marco commanded. Then, leaning closer to Ren, he whispered in her ear, "You know where you're going, right?"

In the next moment, light bled through a crevice ahead.

The group emerged onto a bluff. Waves crashed below. To the right was a grassy cliff that followed the contours of the ocean. The sky was painted with streaks of purple and pink as a pale jade sun crept over the horizon. How was it morning already? Ren wondered. Had she really been in Death Row that long?

Ren returned to her human form while the others caught their breath and threw some high fives. All Ren could think was *That escape was way too easy.*

Just then, she caught the scent of . . .

"It's about time," Zulema said, appearing from behind a large rock.

Ezra ran to the woman and hugged her. "You did it! You led us out."

Ren was gripped by a terrible confusion. Ezra and Zulema knew each other? "What's going on?"

Ezra said, "Zulema is a friend. She's been helping us ever since we were thrown into that place."

The woman turned to Ren. "We cannot let the lords create a new pantheon. The devastation would be epic."

"So you know about that."

"I will prevent that devastation," Zyanya sang. "As soon as I get my powers back. For now, I must rest." And then the bird vanished into the blade in Ren's boot.

Zulema sighed. "All will be explained later. For now, I must return to the palace."

"Which is where, exactly?" Marco asked.

Ren sniffed the air. "About a mile away, down that grassy path."

"Handy skill," Kenji muttered.

Zulema said, "I'll give you all a few moments to recover, but please hurry. There is much to prepare."

"For the lords' deaths?" Serena asked with a sinister grin.

Zulema shook her head, then pinned her gaze on Ren. "We must prepare for a wedding."

27

"COULD EVERYONE PLEASE QUIT CALLING IT A WEDDING?" Ren shouted into the sea wind. Her voice echoed off the white cliffs, slamming into her ears ruthlessly.

It was enough to bring the group to instant silence.

Zulema cleared her throat. "It *is* a wedding."

"It's just a ceremony! With no meaning. And how . . . how is it today?" The words flew from Ren's mouth like daggers. She had only been in that hellish prison a few hours.

Kenji grimaced. "She looks like she's going to puke."

Marco muttered something, then came over and took hold of Ren's shoulders, forcing her to look him in the eye. "You know how you're always telling me to breathe, to visualize, or whatever that woo-woo stuff is?"

Ren nodded.

"Yeah, so, uh . . . do that."

"I'm trying," she said after a few not-so-cleansing breaths. "Wait! Why aren't *you* blowing a gasket? Or asking a million questions, or—" Then she realized. "How did you know about the *ceremony*?"

"Zulema told Ezra, and Ezra told us," Marco said, "And yeah, I couldn't believe it. Like, no way would you do something so stupid. But, sitting in that hellhole, I had a lot of time to think, and I decided you had to have a really good reason."

"Or maybe I don't." Ren thought now she should have never struck the deal with Jade Is Her Skirt. Instead, she should've just built a cozy little nest in Xib'alb'a and taken up knitting or something.

Marco squeezed her shoulders once before letting go. "You always have a good reason. So tell us."

All eyes were on Ren, waiting, wondering.

She didn't see any purpose in keeping her motivation a secret—the godborns would find out eventually. Besides, she might need their powers along the way. And if Marco, the king of strategy, trusted them, maybe she could, too. So she spilled it all. Well, except for the whole being-bonded-to-the-prince-forever part.

When she was done, Kenji said, "Reasonable."

With a shrug, Diamante added, "I mean, it's like a vow in exchange for your life. It's a total no-brainer."

"Heck," Marco said, rubbing the scar on his chin, "*I* would even marry the guy if it meant staying alive."

"Really?" Ren asked.

"Nah. I'd rather rot in Xib'alb'a, but if it'll keep you alive, I'm all in. It's not like it's a forever thing."

Ren's stomach twisted.

"So this is about you," Serena said to Ren.

Ren threw her gaze toward the godborn. "This is about fixing what *you* broke!"

"You're the one who went all dark and wrecked Marco!" Serena said with a growl.

"I wouldn't exactly call it a *wrecking* . . ." he put in.

Ezra held up her hand. "Ren's right." The words earned a

scathing scowl from Serena. "And she saved us from that stink hole. What's past is past. People can change, so . . . can we agree to work together?"

"I can." Kenji came over and, in an awkward, hesitant motion, patted Ren on the back. "You . . . uh, you gave us back our magic and . . . we owe you."

"For sure," Diamante added.

"Don't you have a *wedding* to get to?" Serena asked Ren.

Ezra drew in a long breath. "Serena, do you agree to work together?"

The godborn rolled her eyes and snorted. "Do I have a choice?"

"We need to talk next steps," Marco said, popping his knuckles. "Like what happens after the whole wedding nightmare."

"You guys have to leave now," Ren said.

"Leave?" Serena barked out a laugh. "No way!"

"Yeah," Kenji said. "We got your back, Ren."

Serena muttered, "I wasn't thinking about *her*. I was thinking about punishing those evil lords for putting us in that prison."

"Once they know you're free," Ren asserted, "they'll throw you back into Death Row. You have to hide until tonight." She went on to tell them about the plan to escape with the help of Monty and the feather warriors.

The godborns erupted into a million different versions of *NO WAY*.

Marco released a piercing whistle, getting everyone's attention. "Ren is spot-on," he said. "There's no battle to be won here. She needs to do her"—he swallowed—"*thing,* and then we can all escape."

There was silence as darting eyes searched everyone else's expressions for agreement or possible rebellion.

"But what about the lords?" Serena asked, smashing a fist into her palm. "Aren't they going to pay?"

"When Zyanya put the prison to sleep," Ren said, "she lost her magic for a little while, which means that we need a plan B on how to deal with the lords."

"I vote for annihilation," Serena said.

Ezra, strangely calm, said, "We can't go head-to-head with them. Not until the bird is good to go again. Even our combined magic can't put them to sleep."

Ren said, "We'll take care of them after I find the crown."

To her surprise, no one argued. How could they? The shadow bird had sacrificed her magic to save them. Ren only hoped that the bird's recovery would be quick.

"We'll hide out until dark," Marco agreed. "But, Ren, I don't like this. Not any of it. If you get into trouble . . ."

"I won't. The lords need me."

As the godborns turned to leave, Ren remembered A.P.'s words and blurted, "Serena has to stay."

A look of surprise flashed across Serena's eyes. "Me?"

"I need your help . . . with the wedding." Ren didn't want to reveal too much too soon, and truly, what did she know? Only that A.P. had come a long way to tell her *Let only Serena tie the knot.* But even as much as she didn't like the godborn, she couldn't see herself forcing Serena into some marriage bond just because A.P. had said so.

"What kind of help?" Serena asked.

"To, uh . . . be an attendant."

"You want *me* to attend YOU?!"

"In disguise." Ren offered half a grin, knowing that Serena was the queen of illusions, illusions so powerful they could fool the greatest of gods.

They'd never know the godborn was right under their noses. Or at least she hoped so.

"No thanks," Serena said.

"Serena—"

"*I* was supposed to be queen and now you want me to be your attendant?" she scoffed. "Doesn't sound like a great deal."

Ren burned with frustration. Serena was still just as selfish as ever. "Being queen isn't all it's cracked up to be."

Serena scowled. Then, a few seconds later, she broke out laughing.

"What's so funny?"

Regaining control, Serena said, "The fact that I ever wanted to be queen. What a joke! Seems like a terrible gig with too much responsibility and not enough benefits." She threw a long gaze at Ren before adding, "You can definitely have the crown."

Ren let go of a tightly held breath. "Does that mean you'll help me?"

"You can look at it that way, but I really just want to punish those wicked lords."

Back at the palace, there was a flurry of activity.

Ren kept looking over her shoulder, half expecting Jade Is Her Skirt or the Smoking Mirror or the Prince Lord himself to charge into her room in a rage over the Death Row escapees. But perhaps word hadn't reached them yet? Maybe Cuauhcalli was still groggy, or confused, or... entirely humiliated that a bunch of godborns had gotten the best of it.

"She has to wear *that*?!" Serena said, wrinkling her nose as Zulema pulled out a cream-colored long-sleeved shirt and a matching floor-length skirt. When put together, the outfit looked sort of like a grocery sack.

Ren had already bathed and rubbed a bunch of rose-and-lemon-scented oils all over herself, which made her feel like she was about to be thrown into a frying pan.

Zulema handed the clothes to Ren, and after she'd slipped them on (over her ninja outfit) in the other room, she slid on her boots and returned. "This outfit's, uh... kinda... big."

"And hideous," Serena put in.

"It has to be loose," Zulema said. "We must tie the shirt's hem to the prince's shirt in a knot."

Ren went stone-still.

Serena chuckled. "Ha-ha! Is that where *tie the knot* comes from?"

"It is a long tradition, and one that is very important," Zulema said with a frown. "Without the knot there is no marriage. And believe me, the lords will inspect it."

A.P.'s words crashed into Ren's memory: *Let only Serena tie the knot.*

But why?

Zulema, busy decorating Ren's arms and legs with red feathers, said, "Please hold still. And must you wear those boots?"

"Absolutely," Ren said.

Serena clucked judgmentally.

Zulema wiped her brow with the back of her arm and

sighed. "Serena, can you help? Maybe do something other than just standing there looking angry?"

The air around Serena sizzled and popped, and an instant later, she had cast an illusion that made her look like a clown with a painted-on smile. "Is this better?"

"Can you be serious?" Ren said.

Zulema shook her head. "Why would you choose this impertinent child to attend you?" She smacked her forehead. "Oh! I forgot the paste. Be right back."

Paste?

After the woman was gone, Serena cast more glamours so the room changed from a jungle setting to a beach and then a carwash. She zipped through illusions so fast it was like watching cards being shuffled.

Ren sucked in a gulp of air. She understood now. A.P. wanted Serena to make the lords see what wasn't there. If the knot was never actually tied, Ren wouldn't be stuck with Mr. Sunshine forever and ever. Ren mentally kicked up her heels and shouted, *Yippee-ki-yay!*

"How about this one?" Serena said as her face morphed into the Smoking Mirror's.

Ren's breath hitched, but she hid it, not wanting to give Serena the satisfaction of seeing her discomfort. "The eyebrows are a little off," Ren managed. "And the nose is maybe too far to the right."

"My illusions are perfect," Serena said in the Mirror's voice, which made Ren's heart squeeze. "And that's why I'm here, isn't it? It's not to be your attendant. You need me for something bigger. I think it's high time you let me in on your little plan."

"I'll tell you, but first, could you get rid of that face?"

With a half sigh, half snort, Serena reappeared as herself. Ren quickly unfolded what had happened with A.P. When Ren was done, Serena flung herself onto a chair, propping her legs over the side. "So you want me to make the knot look real? That's it? And here I thought this was going to be violent or fun." She smiled evilly. "Or both."

"Will you do it?"

At the same moment, Zulema swept into the room with a wooden bowl. "Hold still for the finishing touches."

She patted some gooey, honey-smelling substance onto Ren's face and neck, and when she was through, Ren checked out the effects in the mirror. Her skin shimmered with thousands of tiny crystals, and when she turned, her face glowed.

A bump and an "ouch" got her attention. She spun to see Edison tripping over a stool.

"How about a warning, demon?" Serena growled.

But Edison paid her no attention. He was too busy righting himself and rubbing his knee, his eyes fixed on Ren's in the mirror. "Hey, you're like moonlight or something."

Heat rushed into Ren's face and neck.

"Oh my god, I'm going to be sick," Serena said. "You really think that line is going to work?"

Edison gave Ren a confused look. "What's *she* doing here?"

Zulema sniffed at Serena. "Come. It is time to decide on your face and"—her eyes roved over the skinny godborn—"dress."

"Dress?" Serena howled. "I'm not wearing some potato sack like hers."

After the bickering pair left, Ren turned to Edison and told him all about reuniting with Zyanya, turning into a jaguar, and breaking the godborns out of Death Row. "Marco and the others are hiding out for now," she concluded. "And you? Did you and Monty find out anything important?"

"You trust the rogues?"

"If Marco does, then I do. Can you send Monty to find them, just so I know where they are?"

Edison nodded, then said, "So, you want the good news or the bad news first?"

Ren, clinging to her optimistic self, said, "Good."

"Okay—you were right. The lords are for sure planning the birth of a new pantheon. And yeah, they need the crown to do it. I guess it has ancient magic in it . . . But we already know all that, so . . ." His eyes darted around the room like he was registering its opulence for the first time.

"How is that good news?" Ren asked.

"Excellent point, but it's better than the other thing I found out."

Ren groaned. "What?"

"Whoever destroyed the crown is super powerful."

"And . . . ?"

"And it, uh . . . can only be destroyed by a god."

"What?!" Ren's body vibrated from head to toe. If only a god could destroy the crown, that meant . . . "So one of the lords did it? But why? They need its power for their new pantheon!"

Ren heard the demon's breathing, but there was another sound in the room—a *thump, thump, thumping* that she realized was his heart.

"Yeah, I thought it was strange, too." He sighed and rubbed

the back of his neck. "But these dark lords—they're not exactly predictable."

"So one of them is a traitor," Ren said, thinking aloud. "There are only five, so it shouldn't be too hard to figure it out."

"I bet it's someone we wouldn't think of."

"Jade's too obvious. Maybe Centeotl."

"Was he that teeth-clicker guy?"

"No, he's the Fire Lord. Xiuhtecuhtli's the Maize Lord—he's the teeth-clicker. But we never see or hear from those lords, and it's always the silent ones you have to worry about."

Edison folded his arms over his chest and dropped his gaze to the floor, processing, thinking. He glanced up and a strand of dark hair fell over his right eye. For a split second, Ren could forget that underneath his skin was a demon. "Sorry I wasn't able to find out more about the lords' plans," he said.

"Are you kidding? Just knowing there's a traitor other than Jade among them is worth a lot. If they're not united, they'll be easier to break." She patted his arm. "Things are looking up." She really wanted to believe that. But her spirit started to dip the second she thought about all that still lay ahead: tying the knot, getting out of this realm with her friends in one piece, finding the crown, putting the lords to sleep.

"Really?" Edison's eyebrows lifted with a hope Ren wished she possessed. The kind of hope she'd had on her first quest before she saw dark and terrible things, before she understood that sometimes evil wins.

"I mean, Marco and the others are free," she said, "and I've even found a way out of this whole marriage mess." She explained her plan with the knot.

Edison's expression went from uncertain to elated in the blink of an eye. "That's brilliant! But are you sure Serena won't double-cross you?"

"I have to trust her." Ren shook out her hands and began to pace, thinking that trust was so much simpler when you had a choice in the matter.

"Hey, are you sure you want to do this?" Edison said. "We can take off right now. Forget all of it."

"That won't get me closer to the crown."

"We'll negotiate with Ixtab. We'll tell her the crown's not worth having. I mean, it *is* busted."

Ren deadpanned, "She'd never go for it."

"Fine. Okay. Then all we have to do is get through this last part," Edison said. "Meet us at the dock below the Hall of History. The criaturas will help us from there."

Ren nodded. She felt the sudden weight of all her decisions, her new magic, her betrayal of A.P. "I'll be there."

From down the hall, Ren heard indecipherable voices. A rush of movement.

"Hey!" Edison said. "Are you okay?" He tugged a handkerchief out of his pocket. It was the same one he had offered her the first day they met.

Ren's hadn't even realized her eyes were misty.

Just as she took the handkerchief, her cat ears pricked. She sniffed the air, sensing something . . . dark.

At the same moment, Edison began to shake, to struggle as if some invisible force had taken hold of him.

"Edison!" Ren reached out, but her hands went through him like sand.

His face twisted in agony, morphed. His skin split open to reveal the face of a monster.

He fell to his knees. He snarled, baring long fangs.

"Say good-bye," a voice said.

And then the demon vanished.

28

"Edison!" Ren screamed. She turned in circles, searching the suite.

Ren used all her jaguar senses to listen, to hunt, but she couldn't catch even a whiff of the demon's scent. It was like he'd never been in the room.

Zulema burst in. "Come! It is time."

"No!" Ren said. "I have to find Edison. He was here and then he wasn't and someone stole him but who and why?" And before her pulse skyrocketed another inch, she realized with a certainty that made her entire body ache that this was the work of Jade Is Her Skirt. It had to be.

A hunched old woman with long, startlingly white hair stepped out from behind Zulema. "You need to hold it together," the woman said. "Just like I do in this ridiculous getup. Did you know the knot-tier has to be old and wise? Like, what kind of a stupid rule is that?"

"Serena?" Ren said.

"My illusion is so good it fooled you," the godborn said, grinning with a mouthful of chipped grayish teeth.

"Who cares?" Ren snapped. "Didn't you hear what I said about Edison?"

"The demon?" Serena puckered up her old face. "So? He can take care of himself."

Ren was going to throttle this godborn in about three... two...

"Ladies!" Zulema said, now standing between the two. "There is a royal wedding scheduled for today, and that must take precedence over everything else."

Ren managed a nod, but the second Zulema turned around, the would-be bride bolted for the door. Too bad a couple of lanky ghosts in gray capes were waiting for her. One shoved her back. "Going somewhere?"

A warning growl erupted from Ren's throat. Claws emerged from her fingers.

The ghosts burst out laughing. The taller one said, "Hey, kitty, kitty, you can't kill us. You know that, right?"

Zulema shouted, "Reina!"

With a snarl, Ren stomped her boot, bringing the moment to a standstill. She lifted her nose to the air, trying to catch Edison's scent, but she picked up another one instead. She raced past the frozen specters, following her nose down the corridor, then to the right, and then...

She came to an abrupt halt. *Monty should be right here, in this very spot!* But Ren couldn't see her.

Then the hunter stepped out from a hidden crevice. Her face was flushed, and her arrows were glowing blue. "I know," she gasped out. "I heard him screaming. And now they're coming for me."

"You need to get out of here!"

"Not without you or Edison." Monty shook her head. "I'll find him. The plan stays the same."

And before Ren could argue, Monty took off down the hall in a single flash of blue.

Why couldn't the hunter ever listen? Or stop being brave? Ren could sense pockets of magic in the air as she rushed back to her chamber; time had started again, but the ghosts weren't the wiser.

"Fine," she said as they looked around like they could tell something was off but they weren't sure what.

Zulema was there in a blink, taking hold of Ren's arm. She smiled at the ghosts, a tight, closed-mouth grin. "The queen is ready," she said.

The ghosts led the way.

The entire dreadful walk was overshadowed by Ren's racing mind, her worried heart. She couldn't let anyone hurt Edison or Monty.

"This thing is so itchy I'm getting hives," Serena said, tugging on her sand-colored tunic. It had a crooked, floor-length hem and a dark strip of leather for a belt.

"Please try to fit in," Zulema whispered out of earshot of the ghosts. "One wrong move and the lords will smell your treachery. Do you remember how to *tie* the knot?"

Serena grunted, "That's insulting."

"I know you can do it," Ren whispered.

As they entered the small room, Ren nearly stumbled. The domed ceiling was filled with a dozen hanging cages, each occupied by a red bird-feather criatura. Ren's heart thudded once—*BOOM!*—then felt like it might have stopped.

Surely, these imprisoned feathers weren't the very same

warriors who were supposed to lead her and her friends out of this realm. Right?

The feathers began to sing—a gentle, sad sort of song that made Ren ache all over. She shifted her gaze, and her eyes landed on the Prince Lord. He sat on the floor, on a woven wedding mat, with his back to her. His ridiculous halo shimmered all around him like he was the sun itself. Standing above him was the Smoking Mirror. He wore an emotionless expression as he watched her every move. The Maize Lord and Fire Lord stood off to the side of the Mirror. Each of the gods was draped in a deep blue robe that reached their feet.

How much did they know? Which one had taken Edison? Ren hated being in the dark, hated that they seemed to have the upper hand—still.

This isn't a wedding, she thought. More like a tangled web of lies and secrets.

As the feathers sang, Ren put one foot in front of the other until she was sitting on the mat next to the prince, as Zulema had instructed.

A tremble snaked down Ren's spine, leaving her cold. She clung to the sliver of hope that Monty was safe and had found Edison.

In the next blink, Jade Is Her Skirt materialized before them, wearing a shimmering white gown with green and pink feathers sewn into the hem and neckline.

Instantly, the criaturas stopped their song. The room fell into a hush, like it was holding its breath waiting for the goddess to speak.

Jade, too wicked to be so beautiful, smiled. "We will make this short," she said with a dark, penetrating gaze. "For the outcome is more important than the event."

Short was good.

The prince traced his fingers across Ren's, and she was about to pull away when he whispered telepathically, *I don't want to do this, either.*

Keeping her eyes on the blank stone wall, Ren frowned, unsure why he was telling her this now. *Then why are you?*

It's my duty.

Jade's eyes fixed on Serena, who stood behind Ren, still fidgeting with her tunic. "You are the chosen attendant?"

"I am."

"You don't look familiar."

Ren's whole body went rigid. *Please don't blow this. Please don't blow this. Or say anything rude or vicious or both.*

"I was promoted from the kitchens," Serena said, like she had been practicing the line. "I am honored by the queen's request."

Ren nearly whipped her neck around to make sure the person behind her was actually surly Serena. Not only was the godborn quick-thinking, but also her tone sounded deferential. Enough that Jade turned her attention back to Ren and the prince. She raised a hand over the two of them and said some words in a language Ren didn't understand.

The goddess glared at Serena. "That is your cue, woman."

With a hiccup, or maybe a grunt, Serena bent down and touched the back hems of Ren's and the prince's shirts. She must have been tying them into a knot the way Zulema had shown her. There was a spark, a channel of warmth that snaked through Ren, and if she didn't know any better, she would have thought that Serena had actually tied her to the prince.

But no way would Serena betray her again. Not when her own freedom was on the line. And then Ren realized how hard this must be for the daughter of the moon, whose desire to become queen had driven all her terrible decisions up until now.

Had she really changed?

Serena stepped in front of the couple and . . . bowed. It looked so genuine, so wholehearted, that Ren thought, *This girl could become a sensation in Hollywood.*

The prince sighed. "Are we done now?"

"Not yet," the Smoking Mirror said, coming over to inspect the knot. He stood there for so long, Ren was sure he had seen beyond the godborn's illusion.

Out of the corner of her eye, Ren saw Zulema slip out. Where was she going?

"Well?" Jade finally asked.

There was a suffocating moment of silence until the Smoking Mirror said, "It is done."

Ren looked up at Serena.

And the godborn's mouth curved into the smallest of smiles.

29

Ren clenched her jaw. What did that smile mean? *We did it?* Or *I duped you again, you fool?*

No, she thought. *A.P. would never lead me astray.*

As the prince and Ren both stood, the knot fell away with a faded, unintelligible whisper, and Jade Is Her Skirt said to the prince, "You are now the King Lord."

King what?

Jade's eyes turned to Ren. "And do you know what that means for you?"

Ren shrugged. Common sense told her that her new title might be the Queen Lord (bleh), but that would be too obvious, and nothing about Jade was obvious.

"Your duty is to complement the king's light," Jade said.

Ren fought the urge to roll her eyes. *Psh.* As if she'd *ever* do anything to make Mr. Sunshine shine brighter. "So, like, what does it actually mean," Ren said, "to be king? Does he make all the rules, or what?"

The other lords stared straight ahead, ignoring the question, but there was a flicker in Jade's eyes that told Ren being king was about more than a title or a crown. "You talk too much," Jade said.

Serena sniffed and tugged on her own tunic. The gestures were tiny, maybe even unnoticeable to the lords, but to Ren they meant something, and she had never wanted to get into someone's head more.

"Tonight, before the moon vanishes," the Prince Lord added, "the crown will call to you."

And I'll be long gone by then. And news flash—I am so not your queen of anything!

The Smoking Mirror stood by Jade's side, staring at Ren with a smile that managed to look both murderous and amused. "Did you really think you'd get away with it?" he asked.

The Maize and Fire Lords inched closer, like two jewel thieves who had just caught sight of an enormous emerald.

Ren's skin went cold. "It?"

"We know about the escape from Cuauhcalli," Jade said. "That you helped your wretched friends."

All of Ren's nerves felt like live wires ready to spark. "You were stealing their magic!"

Jade and the Smoking Mirror shared a fleeting glance. If Ren was ever unsure about their alliance, she was certain of it now.

The Prince Lord stepped away from Ren, rubbing his chin. "You think you freed them, but all you did was condemn them."

Jade smiled. "You see, we have a law here—anyone who escapes Cuauhcalli must be put to death immediately."

"That wasn't our deal!"

"And neither was breaking out the scoundrels," the prince/King Lord/whatever said.

The Smoking Mirror's stony expression cracked with a cruel smile—one that told a story Ren finally understood. "You did this!" she cried. "You knew I would help them." This was Jade's way of getting out of her promise to Ren.

"You are clever," the Smoking Mirror said, "but your intelligence comes too late."

"Someone was played!" the Maize Lord said with a snort.

Ren forced herself to stand taller. To not shrink under the lords' powerful gazes and brilliant double-crossing minds. Played? She wanted to laugh, to swim in the satisfaction that she had played them, too, and hopefully even the crown. Well, if Serena's illusion was as good as Ren hoped, that is.

"Let them go!" Ren insisted. "You don't need them. You got what you wanted."

"Ah, but they could create problems for us," the Smoking Mirror said. "Can't leave any loose ends now, can we?"

Ren could feel her jaguar magic rising, expanding, scorching her insides like flames. She breathed evenly through her nose. *Think, think. The godborns are smart*, she told herself. *They're safe, in hiding, and they won't fall for any tricks. They'll stick to the plan. And if anyone can find Edison, it's the hunter.*

"They aren't going to be your loose ends," Ren said.

"We'll see about that," Jade Is Her Skirt said.

"Then I will bring this entire place down." All it would take was one fierce roar.

"I don't think so," the Smoking Mirror argued. "Not when your friends are under this roof."

At the same moment, Ren heard footsteps. She turned to see two bald, scowling ghosts leading a shadow-chained Edison into the chamber. His face was that of a demon—his fangs hung over his lip, and his claws were hooked, violent-looking things. But Ren didn't care how monstrous he appeared on the outside. She knew her friend; she knew the sound of his beating heart and the goodness of it.

"Let him go!" Ren commanded, feeling herself sliding into a pool of desperation. "Or . . . or . . . I won't look for the crown."

"Oh, but I think you will," Jade said. "You see, you are mine to control."

"You'll never control me!"

"The moment you broke the vial that led you here . . ." Jade said eagerly, like she'd been waiting a long time to spew her words. "The moment you breathed in its contents, your mind belonged to me. All I have to do is think the thought and you will get down on your knees. Just as this *monster* will."

In an instant, Ren felt a powerful force buckling her legs, and as hard as she tried to fight it, she bent to the goddess's bidding and dropped to her knees.

Ren's eyes found Serena's, but the godborn gave away nothing, not even a flicker of surprise or emotion. Had she cast the illusion of the tied knot or betrayed Ren yet again?

Edison stood before Ren, but he wouldn't look at her.

"You're still Edison," she whispered.

At the same moment, a dagger appeared in midair, revolving slowly so Ren could see the details of the greenish-black weapon—an exact replica of the one from the vision she'd had in the Maze of Nightmares.

Her heart plunged. *No! No! NOOO!*

Edison blinked, and Ren saw the terrible understanding

wash over his face. He was remembering the murderous scene from the maze, too.

Ren balled her fists at her side. But the blade kept spinning, and her right hand unfolded painfully. The dagger found its way into her grasp, cleaving to her like it was an appendage, and the harder she tried to release it, the tighter it clung.

"This is wildly entertaining," Jade said with an eager look in her eyes.

The Smoking Mirror said nothing, only watched with fascination or curiosity while the Maize and Fire Lords grinned viciously. And the King Lord? He just looked bored.

The knife jerked Ren to her feet, propelling her forward, drawing her closer to Edison. She could feel the weapon's power, driven by a darkness like the one that had once possessed her. A terrifying panic gripped her.

The jaguar within her stirred, rolled to its feet, grumbled in the night. And as much as Ren wanted to release her inner cat, she could feel that the magic was suppressed, teetering on the edge of Jade's powers.

Serena, Ren said telepathically. *Please, help us.*

But the godborn didn't so much as flinch.

The shadow chains binding Edison forced him closer to the dagger, so close his chest was mere inches away from it.

The lords were chuckling now, sneering with a ruthless delight.

"No!" Ren cried. Tears snaked down her face as she thrust her hand back. "NOOO!" Her body quaked against the dagger's dark power.

A.P.'s voice drifted into her consciousness just then, his words so clear it was as if he was there with her. *I know a thing or two about the dark, Ren. It's all-consuming, and it tricks you into making you think you want it, that you'd rather dwell in its depths than . . . seek the light.*

A.P.?

Seek the light.

Ren clung to the message, to its hope. Suddenly, it was as if she could *feel* the magic of the Maya god's words snaking around her ribs, vibrating with an energy that was all-consuming. Flowing into her jaguar magic.

Rising. Rising. Rising.

Jade gasped. The criaturas' cages began to swing back and forth.

A golden light pulsed from Ren's fingertips. So barely there, she wasn't sure if she was imagining it. Imagining the force of her own will returning, of her hand dropping the blade.

A bee buzzed near Ren's ear. *Kenji?*

And the son of bees asked, *You ready?*

30

Everything happened at once.
A flash of blue light whizzed past. An arrow pierced Jade's chest, bringing the goddess to her knees with a hideous wail. Immediate chaos descended.

Hordes of bees flew out of nowhere, engulfing the Maize Lord. Shouts and grunts echoed across the chamber, now filled with the godborns. A cold wind gusted. Diamante threw out her hands, fingers dancing in the air as she painted what looked like steel animal traps. Ezra raced passed Ren, circling her arm above her head like she was roping cattle. The cages sprang open. The criaturas burst out, flying up and away.

Edison's chains vanished. He instantly returned to his human-looking form, but then . . . he collapsed to the floor.

Marco was at Ren's side. "You going to stand there gaping all day?" And then he whipped across the chamber with the speed of light, pummeling the Prince Lord with his fists so forcefully, the god fell back.

Ren threw off the top and skirt covering her ninja outfit and ran through the pandemonium toward Edison. The Smoking Mirror hurled a black net at Monty, ensnaring the hunter instantly before the lord vanished into a trail of black smoke.

"Ren, behind you!" Monty shouted.

Ren spun to find the Smoking Mirror reappearing, taller than before, darker and more terrifying. Oh, boy. He looked like an enraged madman.

A part of Ren knew she could never go up against him, not in his own realm. And as powerful as Monty's magic was, her arrow would only paralyze Jade for so long. At best, the godborns would only be able to contain the gods for mere minutes. *I need more time!*

A smug Prince Lord waltzed toward Ren with purpose and like he had all the time in the world. It was obvious he still thought the knot had been tied and she belonged to him. Diamante rolled across the floor, slinging a steel trap into his path. He missed stepping into it by just a few centimeters. Ren raised her boot to stomp and create a time gap, but the prince, in a blaze of supernatural speed, took hold of her leg and flung her into the air.

Ren flew past the cages, her body writhing, changing, shifting. Ears sprouted from her head, and claws grew from her fingertips. She became the jaguar.

Her long body spun—one revolution, two, three—each one more sluggish than the one before. Ren blinked, hyperaware of the fact that time seemed to be coming to a gradual halt. She had a rare vantage point of the scene below, which was playing out slowly, allowing her to see her comrades' inevitable defeat in excruciating detail. Though they were powerful and determined, the godborns were no match for the dark lords.

She flicked her gaze to Serena. The godborn had morphed back into herself. Her hands were thrust out in front of her body. What magic was she channeling?

Ren looked at her paws, still pulsing with golden light. As she began to descend, she shifted back to her human form and grabbed hold of the time thread around her boot. She snapped it free and clutched it in her palm. Heat and light radiated through her.

Ah, came a familiar voice.

Pacific?

I see you have finally activated the true essence of the time thread. Well done.

Activated the...? Is that why her hands had glowed? Ren wondered.

Wait, she said to Pacific. *Where are you? Help me!*

I did help you, when I gave you that thread. And now that you have awakened it, you must use it.

How?!

Is it necessary that I provide you every answer?

That's not an answer!

This is no different from your shadow magic, the goddess said evenly. *Let your instincts guide you.*

And then Pacific was gone. Typical!

Just as Ren landed on her feet and the last bit of dust twirled onto the ground, the entire chamber transformed into a jungle.

Time resumed.

"The illusion won't last!" Serena shouted. "Hurry! Let's get out of here."

That's when Ren realized the jungle was a screen of protection meant to confuse the lords, to give the godborns more getaway time. Ren raced over to Edison, who was pulling himself to his feet with effort.

Jade's laugh echoed through the trees. "Your magic will never save you."

And in a blink, the jungle began to fade, to bleed at the edges like paint dripping down canvas.

"Are you okay?" Ren asked her demon friend.

"Good as new," he said, swiping his hands together. Then, "Hey, you got the time rope free?"

There was no time to talk about the how or why of it, not when the jungle was vanishing. Marco, Kenji, Ezra, Monty, Diamante, and Serena stood next to her and Edison now. A wall of power.

"My arrows can take out those horrible lords," Monty asserted.

"We can't beat them," Ren said. "Not here."

"I can feel their powers breaking down the illusion," Serena said, frowning. "I...I can't hold it."

Edison said, "Their dark energy is building."

Marco, uncharacteristically calm, stared through the fading trees. "Then we'll fight them on our own turf." Ren could see his wheels turning—he'd already come up with a strategy. "But not tonight."

"Ren and Marco are right," Ezra said, her gaze falling to the time thread still in Ren's grasp. Still pulsating with power.

Let your instincts guide you.

Ezra began to twist her hands in the air, creating sparks of purple light.

"What are you doing?" Monty asked. "I thought we were getting out of here."

"We need a head start," Ezra said. The jungle vanished, and

the only thing now separating the godborns and the remaining lords were four glass walls that enclosed the lords. For now.

"Enjoy your prison," Ezra said with a growl.

"Whoa," Kenji said as he backed away.

Marco pressed a hand to the glass. "The next time I see you, I'm going to end you."

Jade Is Her Skirt stood tall, her expression one of terrifying composure. The Smoking Mirror's body heaved, dark swirls of magic rising from his back. Flames bled from the Fire Lord's eyes.

"You will never escape," the Prince Lord said.

"Go!" Ren told her friends.

"Aren't you coming?" Monty cried.

"No way, Ren!" Marco argued. "You're not staying behind."

"I'll just be a sec. Please," she said, staring into the son of war's eyes. "Trust me."

After a brief hesitation, Marco led the others out. But Edison remained. "What are you doing? This prison's already weakening. We have to go!"

Trust your instincts.

Ignoring the demon, Ren stepped up to the glass. Threads of light bled from her fingertips. The time rope pulsed with raw energy.

The glass began to crack.

"Uh, Ren . . . we really gotta go," Edison said again.

Ren took hold of his hand. *I know what I'm doing.*

Sort of doesn't seem like it.

Jade walked over to stand mere inches from Ren, the cracking glass between them. "Your little prison will never hold us."

The Smoking Mirror's darkness began to spread across the window. He smiled as the chamber shook mightily, as stone fragments fell, as the only exit was quickly choked by all the rubble. "Now we can enjoy this space together," he seethed.

The prison walls began to split open.

No different from your shadow magic.

Ren snapped the time thread into the crevice, letting her light feed its power.

The air, charged with electricity, sizzled and flashed.

Jade and the other lords lunged, grabbing for the time thread like it was some kind of lifeline.

An instant later, they froze. Still as stone statues. Their expressions were contorted, enraged.

Ren nearly collapsed with relief as the rope snapped back around her ankle. She asked Edison, "How long will it hold?"

The demon raised a single hand to the glass. "Wow."

"Edison..."

"Nine and a half minutes."

"That's really precise," Ren whispered as she backed away. She was still stunned by the magic—at how good it had felt, how natural.

"So is your magic." Edison grinned. "How'd—"

"I'll tell you *after* we get out of his rotten realm."

Together, they spun toward their next problem—the avalanche of rocks blocking the exit.

"We don't have time to dig ourselves out!" Ren shouted.

Edison clenched his jaw. Ren heard a groan and a grunt. He began to pace.

"What?" Ren said.

"I have a way out."

Ren's heart pounded like it was trying to kick its way out of her chest. "Now would be a good time to show me!"

Another grunt.

Then, in a blaze of silvery-blue light, Edison transformed into his monstrous form, wrapped his arms around Ren, and said, "Hold on."

And the two were whisked away by his magic.

31

Ren had stepped through magical gateways before, but she had never experienced the blaze that was Edison.

One second, she was standing in the disintegrating chamber with a bunch of dangerous gods, and the next she was zooming through a brilliant flash of what looked like exploding stars.

With a loud *POP!* they landed on the docks beneath the palace.

Woozily, Ren stumbled. Edison, back in human form, caught her by the arm.

"First time is always kind of dizzying," he said. "Hey, you stopped glowing."

"That was . . ." Ren didn't have the words to continue. *Amazing, like hurtling through space* didn't seem to be accurate enough.

"Lords, it took you long enough," Zulema said nearby. Ren noticed her, standing on the trajinera with a pole in hand, for the first time.

"Where are the others?" Ren asked, regaining her footing and breath.

"Already took them to the site," Zulema said. "Come. We must make up for lost time."

"So it's close," Ren said, stepping aboard the boat with Edison.

"Why would you say that?" the woman said.

Ren remembered how long it had taken Zulema to navigate the channels when they first arrived here.

"Buckle up," Zulema said, stretching her spindly arms over her head like she was some athlete getting ready to run a sprint. "This could get tricky."

Ren and Edison shared a confused glance but did as they were told. As soon as they sat on the bench, seat belts appeared and hooked around their chests in a crisscross fashion.

The palace trembled; fragments of stone fell into the water all around them.

"That's our cue!" Zulema cheered. And before Ren could say another word, the trajinera took off like a missile.

The little boat zoomed through the channels so fast, the entire world was a haze. Every inch of Ren's body felt like it was being squeezed by a vise, but that didn't compare to how her face seemed to stretch to her feet.

By the time the boat finally came to a halt at the edge of a small landmass, Ren had stopped breathing. Or maybe her heart had forgotten how to keep beating.

The seat belts released her and Edison, and as they stood, Zulema said, "Nice ride, yeah?"

Ren leaned closer to the demon. "You're faster."

He chuckled to himself. "Pretty wicked, Zulema."

"Indeed, but no rest for the wicked," Zulema said. "We must hurry."

They took off on foot, and as they made their way through the thick trees, Ren heard a hair-raising wail in the distance.

And then another, and another. Each howl closer than the last.

"I think our nine and half minutes are up," Edison said.

The trio ran, zigzagging through the woods until they came to a clearing where Monty and the godborns awaited.

"Now!" Monty ordered the little criaturas. The feathers came together in a mass and began to spin like a giant circle of red light. A circle that expanded vertically, stretching itself wider and wider. But all Ren could see on the other side was white light.

Great gusts of wind sped across the meadow. The trees bent and twisted with the force of the criaturas' magic. But the moon—it held fast to the sky.

Before the moon vanishes, the crown will call to you.

Ren waited for the crown to summon her. She listened through the chaos, but there was nothing, and she suddenly worried she had missed a step.

One by one the godborns stepped into the circle. Well, more like they were sucked into it.

There were some screams (Kenji and Diamante), some choice words (Marco), furious groans (Serena and Ezra), and a *hee-haw* (Zulema).

Jade's voice echoed through the dark. "There is nowhere you can go that I will not find you."

"One way ticket to Devils Tower!" Monty shouted over the deafening gales as Edison was pulled into the gateway. Then the hunter turned to Ren. "You're up next."

Ren shook her head, struggling against the headwinds. "I'll be right behind you!"

"I'm not leaving without you!" the hunter yelled.

"You can't stick around for this part."

A look of understanding swept across Monty's face. She nodded, and just when Ren thought the hunter would vanish into the gateway, Monty lifted her chin and said, "I am Valentina Montero of the Jaguar Warrior tribe, descendent of the great Aztec king Itzcoatl. Your roar can't hurt me."

Ren was stunned silent. Monty had never revealed her true name before, and Ah-Puch had said it was where much of the hunter's magic lived. To tell it to someone was to give them access to her true powers. But Monty had once told Ren she would share the secret if she were ever to become a full-fledged Jaguar Warrior. Which meant they shared a bond now, one of not only friendship but also of ultimate trust.

"So can we do this thing and get out of here?" Monty asked.

Ren turned. There would be time for all her questions later. Right now, she had a realm to bring down.

Ren's hair whipped around her face. Her body vibrated with the rising power of her jaguar magic. The hunter anchored her stance, nocked an arrow, and took aim into the darkness, readying herself in case her magic was needed.

Black shapes consumed the sky, like giant splotches of ink. Spreading and swirling and writhing. The lords!

Ren clenched her fists as her magic intensified and expanded. And when she could no longer contain the power of it, she threw her head back and roared. She roared with a ferociousness that shook the earth, demolished the trees, split the night.

Monty tugged on Ren and pointed to the portal.

Just as the sky fell, the two of them leaped into the gateway.

32

Ren landed in a bank of fresh powdery snow.
Face-first.

With a shiver and a groan, she stumbled to her feet as a scowling Monty sat up next to her and shook out her hair. "I hate snow!"

Ren helped the hunter to her feet and looked around the small meadow bordered by a thick pine forest. The sky was dawning: a warm swirl of pink and orange with streaks of pale blue. The moon was a mere trace, an outline of itself. "Where is everyone?"

Monty glanced about, hiking her quiver higher onto her shoulder. "They have to be here somewhere. The gateway was a one-way ticket to..." Her gaze rose as she pointed. "That."

Ren turned. There in the distance was a massive rock formation made of hexagonal columns. Devils Tower. The monument was so grand, so imposing, she understood where it got its diablo name.

And then, as if the stone mountain knew they were there, it began to emit a green glow. "What...?" Ren blinked. "Do you see that?"

Monty whispered, "Oops."

"Oops? What's oops?"

"Er, well, remember when I told you that lots of places in our world are actually mirrors of enchanted places?"

"Wait, are you saying that we landed at the wrong Devils Tower?"

"This must be the magic-world version," Monty said, scratching her head. "I bet the others landed in the real world."

Ren tried to pick up Edison's or Marco's scent. "Well, not only are they not here, but they've also never been here."

"But how? I was super clear with the criaturas. Like, why—"

"Because this must be where the crown is." Ren was certain of it. "It's the only explanation for why we'd be separated."

Monty groaned. "Did the crown really have to come to the Aztec land of the dead?"

"Maybe whoever busted it thought this would be the best hiding place." Ren's eyes darted about the snowy forest. "But this underworld—it's so different from Xib'alb'a. It's so..."

"Dead?" Monty snickered. "That's because it's closed for business. When the Aztec gods died out or were put to sleep, this place and all its energy collapsed." She gestured toward the still-glowing mountain. "Well, except for that, I guess."

"What happened to all the souls who were here?"

"No one knows exactly. There are theories. . . . My dad told me that they're catching some z's, too—that the dead are waiting for the lords to come home."

"That's creepy!"

The hunter's eyes scanned every which way. "I'm freezing. So do you hear the crown or what?"

Ren looked up at the sky. The moon, thin as tracing paper, was disappearing like rising steam.

Before the moon vanishes, the crown will call to you.

Shimmering flakes began to fall, forming a glittering path.

"Hey—the snow is gold!" Monty shouted.

And then Ren felt it. . . . Not a voice calling to her like she had imagined, but a magnetic pull she had no choice but to follow. Which made her wonder if Serena had actually tied the knot that would make her the Queen Lord, or if the godborn's illusion was so good it had tricked even the crown of jade and shadow. "If Serena actually tied that knot . . ." she began.

"She didn't."

"How do you know?"

"Because, after our escape from the fake wedding, she told us. Well, actually, she bragged at how good her illusions are."

Ren's chest nearly collapsed with relief. "Okay, then! This way," she said.

"Keep a lookout for spirits."

"You said they were asleep!"

"Well, they could wake up. I mean, they might sense our magic. Your magic as queen of the lords—woof!"

"Monty, stop being so wired for catastrophe."

"A good hunter warrior anticipates all possibilities."

"Perfect," Ren said. All she needed was to stir awake a bunch of ghosts.

The godborn and the hunter picked their way across the snowy landscape. "Hey, Monty?"

"Yeah?"

"Didn't you say this is the place where souls remember the saddest moments of their lives?"

"Yeah, but you don't need to worry about that because you're not dead."

The words reminded Ren that she'd be joining the ranks of the deceased if she didn't bring the crown to Ixtab in the next two days.

"Did someone say *dead*?" Zyanya flew up from the Obsidian Blade, still wedged into Ren's boot.

"You're awake!" Ren cried.

"And freezing!" The bird glanced around. "Did you not remember I was in the blade? Your boot offers no protection from that dreadful ice!"

"Oh, yeah—sorry," Ren said, keeping her voice low. "How are you feeling?"

"FEELING?! I can't feel anything, because I'm a Popsicle! Well, let's see.... I used up all my precious magic on your ungrateful friends and I've never slept for so long and there were these nightmares with giant bird skeletons—"

"Zyanya," Ren said, "you need to keep it down."

The shadow bird glanced around, then hopped onto Ren's shoulder. "This is the fourth level of Mictlan!" Zyanya let out a small shriek. "Do you know what you've done?"

"What do you mean?" Monty asked.

"You are alive," Zyanya explained. "This is the land of the dead. The living and the dead don't mix. Get it?"

"Not really," Ren said as they continued their sluggish hike up a hill toward the glowing Devils Tower.

"I'll explain it nice and slow for your puny human brain. Your life force will awaken the dead. They are going to want it, to *feed* on it."

"EW!" Monty screwed up her face. "Like zombies?"

Zyanya pointed a wing at the hunter. "Who invited her?"

"Hey, I'm a walking alarm, okay?" Monty gestured to her magical arrows. "If these babies glow blue, that means that I'm in danger. Do you see any glowing arrows?"

The bird sniffed as Ren took a deep breath. "Okay, so we go slow and quiet," Ren whispered. "We follow this path." Then, "Are you all better now, Zyanya?"

"You mean do I have the strength to put the lords to sleep?"

Ren nodded. Plumes of white fog floated from her mouth. Her feet were numb, her bones number, and her teeth had begun to chatter.

With a glower, the bird said, "Not yet."

Ren's heart felt like a thick hunk of dough clogging up her chest.

They walked in silence a few more paces—the only sounds were Monty's and Ren's breathing and the snow crunching beneath each step.

The golden snowflakes continued to twirl in the gray streaked sky. And for the first time, Ren allowed herself to think about what had happened back in the wedding chamber—how that strange light poured from her fingertips, how she had stopped time and frozen the lords.

You have finally activated the true essence of the time thread.

Pacific's words rattled Ren. As usual, her mom had spoken in a maddening riddle.

"This is too easy," Monty whispered as she turned in defensive circles every few feet.

"Which means it's a trap," the bird said. "I mean, truly, who's ever heard of golden snow?"

Ren felt a niggling in the core of her gut—a warning that something was off.

"We're almost there," Monty said as the ground became icier.

And still the golden flakes swirled down, sticking to the earth, creating a path that was growing steeper and steeper.

"Hey!" Monty growled. "I think the ground is moving."

"Well, you're the one who went and said this was too easy," Zyanya said.

"You're right," Ren agreed.

"I'm always right," the bird said. "Well, almost always."

"I meant Monty. The ground is shifting, getting steeper."

Monty slid back like she was on roller skates. "And slippery-er!"

"I'm not saying a word," Zyanya sang.

Ren dug her feet into the frozen earth, but every movement felt like a desperate, futile struggle.

"Try harder," Zyanya said, before mumbling, "This is why wings are better than feet."

Time and time again, Ren and Monty slipped and slid.

"I don't think this place wants us here," Monty whispered.

Ren blew out a frustrated breath. The crown was close; she could feel it. "Okay, listen, Monty. I have an idea. Can you stay here and keep watch?"

The hunter's eyes widened, asking the question *why?* or maybe *how?*

"And what about me?" Zyanya said.

"You stay with Monty."

"That is absolutely not going to happen. Did you not hear the part about my wings?"

"Fine," Ren said, not wanting to waste her breath on an unwinnable fight. "Then everyone give me some space."

Ren closed her eyes and channeled her jaguar magic; it rose faster than ever before. She curled into its warmth and power, and a blink later, she transformed.

Monty stood taller, clutching her quiver. "I won't let you down."

Ren snorted once and climbed a nearby tree. Then, using the branches, she launched herself into the next tree and so on like a strangely coordinated dance. Her muscles sang with her magic. Her heart soared with joy—as if this was who she was always meant to be.

Zyanya circled above. "Impressive."

A moment later, Ren sprang from the last tree, sticking her landing right in front of Devils Tower. The mountain's long fissures pulsed with light and heat. It was like looking at a city grid at night from space.

She inched closer, lifted her paw.

It was then that she realized the mountain wasn't made of rock, but of something else.

And it was moving.

33

Ren gasped.

The mountain was made of spirits—hundreds and hundreds of ghosts sleeping side by side and floating up and down the columns as if on a watery current. Their sunken faces were illuminated by the eerie green glow.

"Well, that's just gross," Zyanya said, landing on Ren's back.

Ren shifted to her human form, but her nerves still buzzed and her muscles tensed. And all the while she felt the crown urging her forward, like an invisible thread was tugging her closer.

"The crown is past them, isn't it?" Zyanya said.

"It's just a bunch of dead people," Ren said, trying to convince herself.

"Have you ever walked through the dead?" the bird asked.

A blue arrow whizzed past them, stabbing a tree. A rope was tied to it, and Monty gripped the other end and began hauling herself toward Ren, grunting and cursing all the way.

"Monty, you're supposed to keep watch."

The hunter rolled her eyes. "I'm a warrior, *not* a security guard." Her eyes alighted on the sleeping ghosts. "Oh. Getting serious Hercules vibes now."

"What is she talking about?" Zyanya asked Ren.

"You mean when he goes to the underworld to save Meg?" Ren asked Monty.

"Yeah, and all the dead suck the life out of him and—"

Zyanya flapped her wings frantically. "Very bad things happen if you pass through the dead."

"Like with Hercules?" Monty said.

"I've never heard of the guy," Zyanya said. "But if you mean freezing cold, loss of appetite, cramps, high blood pressure, permanent goose bumps—"

"You sound like one of those medicine commercials," Ren said. "It can't be that bad."

Monty frowned, gripped her quiver, stood taller, and said, "I'm ready."

"Okay," Ren said, steeling herself. "We go in together."

"I'll keep watch here," Zyanya said.

"See you on the other side!" Monty shouted to Ren as she grabbed hold of the bird and launched herself into Devils Tower.

Ren shifted back into her jaguar form. She crouched low, closed her eyes, then jumped through the ghosts, hoping they weren't light sleepers.

She hurtled through a dark space filled with echoing moans. The air was biting and getting thinner. Cold hands reached for her. Ren tried to shake them off, but she found she couldn't move.

She couldn't even scream. Another cold hand clutched her leg. And another. Would she be stuck among the dead forever?

The world tilted.

Ren was sinking in what felt like quicksand. Deeper and deeper, until she couldn't breathe. Still paralyzed, she used the only thing she had left—her mind. She reached for her magic, imagining its warmth radiating through her, envisioning its power bleeding from her skin. Her vision was all blurred edges. Ren refocused, willing her brain to overcome the reality in front of her.

I can defeat the dead became her mantra. Over and over she spoke the words internally. Until she felt the pulsing of her magic in her fingertips, until heat radiated down her spine and legs. Until she felt the ghosts release her.

In the next blink, she landed in a barren landscape made up of black sand and tangled white driftwood—piles and piles of it. A large golden orb hung in the gray sky. The place was spookily silent.

Just as she shifted into her human form, Ren heard, "Take my blood pressure," Zyanya said. "Is it high? Do I have goose bumps? Have I lost any feathers?"

Ren spun to see Monty and the bird coming toward her. Monty scowled at Zyanya. Then her face brightened. "No goose bumps," she said, "but I definitely think that's a zit on your face."

The bird shrieked.

"Guys," Ren warned. "Keep it down."

"No one's here," Monty said. "But I scoped out an exit."

"You mean *I* did," Zyanya argued. Then to Ren she said, "Can we please get the crown and vámanos out of here?"

Standing still as stone, Ren searched the landscape. Finally, she felt a tug in the center of her chest. The crown was here, calling to her. And then she saw it—a mere twenty feet away.

A shadow that didn't belong. The broken crown hanging from a twisted piece of wood.

Ren walked toward it gingerly, afraid that one wrong move, one wrong breath would make it disappear. Thankfully, Zyanya and Monty walked in silence, too. A few paces later, Ren reached out and lifted the crown off the branch.

"Looks like a hunk of junk," Monty whispered.

It was no longer a brilliant jade—it was more like a scorched and tarnished piece of tin wrapped in shadow.

Zyanya said, "Are you sure you should touch that thing?"

The sombra awakened.

"I guess so," the bird muttered.

A single ribbon of black rose from the crown, twisted in the air, and drifted ahead like a tendril of smoke. And then it curled into a bony hand, gesturing for her to follow.

Monty nocked an arrow.

"That won't work on a shadow," Zyanya reminded the hunter, but Monty retained her defensive stance anyway.

"If I ask you guys to wait here, will you?" Ren asked. "Please?"

"No way," Monty said.

"I could absolutely wait," Zyanya put in.

"You have to trust me," Ren pleaded with the hunter. "I have to do this part alone."

"Fine," Monty huffed. "But be fast or I'm coming after you."

Ren trailed the shadow. Her body tingled all over, and with each breath she felt as if she were outside of herself. As if she were walking across memories she didn't have yet.

"That's just loca," she whispered to herself as she followed.

"Not entirely," the shadow said.

Ren stopped cold. The shadow sounded just like Ren. How was that possible?

"You can talk?" she managed.

"I am the magic that doesn't sleep."

Ren's pulse skyrocketed. "How do you have my voice?"

"I am you. And you are me."

And then the sombra swirled into a circle and stopped at the edge of a wide gorge. "The rest of us is there," the shadow said, floating over the rocky chasm. "On the other side."

Us?

Ren lifted her eyes, but all she saw was a wide expanse. "There's nothing over there."

"Look again."

Ren focused harder, searching the flat horizon. And then she saw it. The other piece of the crown, swinging dangerously on the ledge on the opposite side. Her heart leaped in her chest.

Until reality settled in. The gorge was at least fifty yards across and infinitely deep. There was no way to climb across, and no way to leap safely even with a mighty roar.

"I . . . I can't make that jump," Ren said.

"Command it."

"What?"

The shadow curled around Ren like a blanket; she felt its darkness but also a strange comfort. She didn't know if she should be repelled or . . .

"Call it to you," the shadow said.

Ren lifted her gaze to the other crown piece again. She chewed her bottom lip, wondering how you call a magical object to you when you're stuck in the land of the dead with a shadow that sounds exactly like you.

Ren held up the first half, and before she knew it, she was

uttering words into the air. "The magic that doesn't sleep, the magic of old beings."

"Yes," the shadow whispered as it grew into a long tail, whipping across the space. Ren chanted the same words over and over. Like a mantra she had always known.

The broken crown trembled in her hands. Winds gusted. The earth trembled. Piles of driftwood beside her burst into flames one after the other.

But Ren wouldn't lose her concentration. She repeated, "The magic that doesn't sleep, the magic of old beings."

Louder and louder her voice grew, until the shadow had taken hold of the other half of the crown, until it had carried the piece across the chasm and set it in Ren's free hand.

"Now," the shadow whispered.

Trembling, Ren brought the two pieces together.

There was a brilliant flash of white, an explosion of stars, a colliding of worlds. Gray mist enfolded Ren. And then came a voice she had hoped she'd never hear again.

"Hello, Renata Santiago."

34

Ren froze.

She knew that voice. It belonged to the all-seeing calendar, K'iin, the timekeeper of the entire universe. The ancient being Ren and her friends had sought out to learn where the Maya gods had been hidden, so many months ago.

As though she could reach across Ren's memory, K'iin said, *"You will repay me with a favor someday, Renata Santiago.* Does that ring a bell?"

Ren flinched, wondering what an omniscient presence would ever need from *her.* "Right. But, uh...can it wait until after this quest, because—"

"The time is now."

The godborn knew there was no arguing with the powerful being that was created at the very inception at time.

Instantly, the mist thinned enough that Ren could see a figure materialize. She blinked and sucked in a sharp breath. "Abuelo?" His hair was a shocking white, and his honey eyes were just as warm as they had always been.

"Not exactly," K'iin said in Abuelo's voice. "How do I look? It has been eons since I took human form. I forget how dreadful and limiting it is."

Even though this version of her grandfather was an imitation, it didn't stop Ren from wanting to hug him.

K'iin screwed up her face like she was testing its muscles before she said, "I thought this would be easier for you if I wore a friendly visage."

Ren's stomach twisted with nerves. "What would be easier?"

"To collect on the promise you made me."

Ren's mouth went dry. For a wise, mighty, timekeeping being, K'iin really had the worst timing. "Are you going to kill me?"

K'iin laughed. It sounded just like Abuelo, with the little hitch at the end that always made her wonder if his laughter was just beginning. "I am not in the business of murder. Why would you ever think that?"

"Because the Maya love a good sacrifice, and I thought the only payment you took was blood and—"

"I am not Maya."

"Wait. But..." Ren took a breath. "My mom created you at the beginning of time, so doesn't that sort of make you Maya?"

"Your mother did not create me."

Ren was stunned silent. Not that she should have been surprised. In her experience, the Maya gods' stories were built on lies and half-truths, all so muddled together it was hard to tell legend from reality.

K'iin sighed. "I have much to divulge, many myths to dispel, truths to speak. But let us begin with this: I am light and day and time. I am without labels and names. I am everything and nothing."

Perfect. A riddle-spouting calendar.

"So, if you're not here for my blood, then..."

"Are you hungry?" K'iin asked.

"Uh, no, but thanks."

"I wasn't offering you food. I just wanted to know if you had a full stomach in case you throw up once I tell you the truth."

"What does the truth have to do with the favor I owe you?" Ren really hoped it wasn't another quest, or some impossible feat.

"The truth is this: I am here to take the crown."

Ren's heart lurched. No way! She'd come too far to just hand over the prize to someone she hadn't even promised it to. Well, not literally, anyway. The godborn inched back. "Well, here's the thing..." she said with a strained smile. "I promised it to Ixtab, and if I don't take it to her, I...I'm going to die."

"You're going to die anyway," K'iin said casually. "Everyone is."

Well, that wasn't comforting. "Look," Ren began, "I know I promised you a favor in return for you helping us find the gods and all that, but that was before I knew the stakes. I mean—"

"Would you have done things differently had you known the outcome?"

Ren wasn't sure. Would she have saved the Maya gods, her mom and A.P. included, if she'd known it would mean giving up her own life? Probably yes, but who really knew? And then a more pressing question bubbled up. "Why do you want the crown so bad? You're, like, all-powerful. You can see across time and space and—"

"Because the crown doesn't belong to you or Ixtab or those wretched Lords of Night."

Ren didn't want to sound disrespectful, but it just came out. "It doesn't belong to you, either."

"That is not entirely true."

"What's that supposed to mean?"

"That object in your hands holds many secrets. Its very history is intrinsically tied to the universe."

"History... Like that it's made from the magic of old gods—the Lords of Night."

K'iin snorted. "Please! As if they would ever have the consciousness, the power, the..."

Ren's pulse was rising, her mind was whirring, and her heart was pounding with disbelief. She gripped the crown tighter. "So if the lords didn't make this, who did?"

"The Maya gods and the Unknowns."

It took Ren a second to absorb this new truth, to connect the dots, to stitch her memories together.

And then she remembered what the mermaid had told her. *The crown of jade and shadow is a blend of two ancient magics, neither of this world. The jade carries the magic of old gods. And the shadow carries the magic of old beings.*

Beings... or Unknowns.

Ren's legs felt wobbly. Her entire center had been thrown off-kilter.

"You look rather pale," K'iin said. "Are you going to vomit?"

Ren shook her head, trying to regain an ounce of composure as she gripped the crown. She stared at its jade and the shadow. "The shadow magic..." she whispered with a tremble. "It... it doesn't come from Jade Is Her Skirt but from the Unknowns."

"That is correct."

Ren's heart pounded violently. "So that means my shadow magic"—*POUND, POUND*—"it...it comes from"—*POUND, POUND*—"aliens?"

And then she threw up all over the all-seeing calendar's shoes.

35

"They do NOT like to be called that!" K'iin growled, waving a hand over the vomit to make it disappear. "They are beings your human brain cannot comprehend, greater than gods, a fact that made the gods jealous. And now it is time to relinquish that which does not belong to you."

Ren heard K'iin's words, but her brain was in full-blown panic mode, and all she could manage was "Does that make me part ALIEN?! I mean, it makes total sense. How I'm obsessed with them and love space and started a blog to investigate UFO sightings and—"

K'iin dragged a hand over her face with a grunt. Then she grabbed hold of the godborn's shoulders and shook her once. "YOU ARE NOT AN ALIEN!" Abuelo's voice ricocheted across the world that was still so thick with mist Ren couldn't see more than a few feet in front of her.

Ren stepped back, clinging to the crown that was no longer a piece of tarnished tin—the piece glowed a brilliant green as bits of shadow swirled around and through it. "But Jade Is Her Skirt . . . She said that she created the shadow magic, that she hid it in humans, that . . ."

Had Ren's entire life been a lie?

K'iin rubbed her wrinkled forehead. "Why, oh why must humans be riddled with questions they are not wired to accept the answers to? This is just your brain clinging to a story that makes more sense to your consciousness. Now, please hand over the goods."

Ren wasn't going to give in so easily, not when she had the sage calendar right here in the flesh (so to speak) to answer her questions. "This is my life and my history, too, and I deserve to know!"

She imagined K'iin snatching up the crown and leaving Ren there to rot for all eternity. But the timekeeper just stared at her with Abuelo's warm honey eyes, and it gave Ren the courage to go on. "Why did the lords have the crown if the Unknowns and the Maya gods made it? And weren't the Unknowns allies with the lords?"

"Why do you ask me questions you already know the answers to?"

"But I *don't* know!"

"You know that the Unknowns helped the Maya gods create the Fifth Sun, what you call human existence today."

Ren pushed her bangs from her face. "Okay. Yeah. They were all friends until a demon had a baby with an Unknown."

"And a new race was born, one so powerful they could over-throw the Maya gods, so a war was waged. The Unknowns van-ished, and they returned a few hundred years ago and became friends with the Aztec Lords of Night."

Ren said, "That's when the Unknowns put the lords into a deep slumber to save them from dying out."

K'iin leveled Ren with a stony gaze. "That is where your story goes wrong. The Unknowns did not put the lords into a slumber to save them. They did it to punish them."

"For what?"

"For stealing the crown. The end."

Ren's jaguar magic stirred—every instinct told her *this* was the truth she'd been waiting for, the truth she knew existed but could never quite reach.

And yet there were still holes in the story. "I'll give you the crown," Ren said, thrusting her chin forward, "as soon as you tell me everything about the shadow magic."

K'iin inched closer, a small grin playing on Abuelo's lips. Ren thought the calendar was going to shred her to bits for her defiance, but K'iin simply said, "Are you sure? Sometimes the truth is too much to bear. It changes futures and demolishes pasts."

Ren stood taller. "I want to know."

"Very well." K'iin placed a warm hand on Ren's shoulder. "This will feel strange."

The world faded away, and Ren could no longer sense her body; she could no longer see or hear. She felt as if she were an hourglass being filled with sand, one speck at a time. Words didn't come to her. Neither did feelings or images.

Instead, what came was a deep understanding, an awareness that told her all she wanted to know. Warmth filled every crevice of her being, and a moment, maybe several, later, Ren blinked back into consciousness and whispered, "I saw it all."

"Tell me—otherwise, the memory will not stick. Or perhaps you do not want to remember."

"Jade Is Her Skirt stole the shadow magic," Ren began. "She placed it into a few humans to hide it until the day came when one of those humans could activate the crown." Ren's eyes flicked to K'iin's. "And on that day, the lords would have the power to reinvent themselves and create a new pantheon, one that could take its revenge on the Unknowns."

Ren heard the words coming from her mouth, but it was as if someone outside of her was speaking them—someone with no connection or attachment to this story. She went on, pouring out the knowledge.

"Ixtab thought she removed my shadow magic, but that kind of power can never be contained. That's why the crown still called to me. I still have a remnant inside." Ren inhaled, exhaled. "But it also means I'm not linked to the Lords of Night. All that darkness I felt was Jade's poisoning of the sombras."

"You saw something else," K'iin said. "Do you not wish to remember it?"

Ren rubbed the edges of the crown, realizing her story couldn't be told by anyone else; nor could it be kept locked away in the recesses of her mind.

"A prophecy . . . spoken by you," Ren managed. "A day would come when a Jaguar of Darkness would be born. A powerful being who would become an illuminator of truth, and . . . and she would bleed magic." Ren shook her head, hardly able to believe what she was saying. "She would be the only chance to save the world from chaos. . . ."

"And . . . ?" prompted K'iin.

"And if she succeeded, she would be known by one name."

"The Jaguar of Dawn."

Ren's cat instincts shook her core, vibrating with the awareness of a truth her human mind could never have conjured. "A *chance* to save the world?" she said quietly. "That doesn't sound so great."

K'iin said, "Prophecies seldom do."

Ren finally understood why the Smoking Mirror was afraid of her blood. Why he had said *There is only a chance*. He must have known about the prophecy, too, but he couldn't kill her before she had found and activated the crown.

While Ren knew *what* the lords wanted it for, she still didn't understand its exact power. When she asked K'iin, the ancient one hesitated, before dropping the words "It gives the wearer the ability to do anything they can imagine."

Like create a new pantheon.

"Who would want to destroy it, then?"

"Someone who doesn't want the lords to possess such power."

"Do you know who that is?" Ren asked.

"I do."

Ren waited for the answer, and as the seconds passed, her hope waned. "You aren't going to tell me."

"You will find out soon enough," K'iin said. "One more thing—when you return to your friends after this, things will feel strange."

"Strange how?"

"While you've been here with me, you've also been there with them. Better if I show you than waste my breath trying to explain it." In an instant, images flashed in midair. Images of Ren, Monty, and Zyanya leaving Mictlan through a rusted gate in the side of the mountain.

Ren peered closer. "Is that the future?"

"It is the current moment."

Ren didn't know how to break it to the cosmic calendar that

she was totally certain she was *not* with Monty and Zyanya. "Uh—but I'm here."

"A part of your consciousness is, yes."

It reminded Ren of the way Ezra could astral travel, how she could be in two places at once.

"For your friends, you got back thirty minutes ago," K'iin said. "And if you were practiced in this sort of magic, then you would remember that. You would see through the other Ren's eyes."

Ren didn't like thinking of some part of herself floating out there somewhere without her permission or memory. She much preferred being in one piece. "How much time has passed?"

"A few hours. Maybe fourteen."

"Fourteen? That's not a few hours!" And it also meant Ren had only one day left before she had to deliver the crown to Ixtab.

"You aren't actually going to argue about time with me, the great all-seeing calendar, are you?"

She had a point.

"Okay, so, like, how does this work?" Ren asked. "I mean, getting back to myself."

"Yes, that is the trickier question." The calendar sighed just the way Abuelo always did; it made Ren's heart heavy with missing him. "Everyone is different. And before you ask, the process is much too difficult to explain. Just know it can take time, and you might feel disoriented while you wait for it. Until then you will be a mere spectator no one else can see, so don't be alarmed. Well, no one except for a god." Then, with a shrug, she added, "Or an Unknown, which of course is impossible, because they do not bother interacting with humans."

The calendar extended Abuelo's wrinkled hand. "Now let us conclude our business. Give me the crown."

Ren chewed her bottom lip, wishing she could spend more time with the cosmic all-seeing calendar, asking questions about the secrets of the universe and its exceptional beings. But even if she had that kind of time, she knew K'iin would never reveal that kind of information.

Slowly, Ren extended the crown of jade and shadow. It was the right thing to do, despite the potentially devastating consequences for herself. At least it would thwart the lords' grand plans to reinvent themselves. Ren would have to find a way out of her deal with Ixtab. Maybe if she really could save the world from the lords' chaos, that might be enough to convince Ixtab not to steal her life.

But probably not.

The moment the crown was in K'iin's worn hands, the skies morphed into a palette of pink and purple and silver. Ren nearly gasped at the otherworldly beauty. Where had she seen this before?

She looked back at the crown, now sitting on a silken pillow. Gone were the swirling shadows, and in their place was a glorious shimmering piece of jade. Mesmerized, Ren asked, "Why . . . does this look so familiar?"

"The night your abuelo sent you in the boat toward your future, this moment played across your memory, as if it had already happened. Perhaps it had. Time is funny like that."

Had Ren really seen the future that night?

"Can I ask one more question?" she said.

"I'd rather you didn't."

"Since you can see the past and future and pretty much everything, can you tell me . . . will I succeed? I mean in putting the lords to sleep?"

K'iin shook Abuelo's head. "Knowledge like that is dangerous. Do you really want to know? Even if what you learn affects the outcome?"

Ren swallowed. "Yes."

"Very well. There are many possible scenarios, many variables, and in all but one you and your friends lose the battle. Death blooms like a great shadow over the forest, and you return to the underworld like you did before."

Ren's insides turned cold. "But there is one chance?" Tears stung her eyes. "What is it? How?"

"I cannot change consequences. Now, you must go. You will soon find a corridor. Follow it to the door."

"Please. Just one clue!"

K'iin said, "I will give you one word: *fuse*."

"Fuse? Like an electrical fuse, or . . ."

K'iin held up a hand, silencing the godborn.

Ren deflated and stared at the crown in Abuelo's gnarled hands, knowing she'd never see it again. How could one object cause so much trouble? "When I said the crown didn't belong to you, you said that wasn't true. Why?"

There was a moment of silence before K'iin vanished, before Ren was plunged into darkness, before the calendar's voice echoed all around.

"Because I am an Unknown, too."

36

!*&%$?

Ren found herself in a narrow corridor where a pink neon arrow flashed up ahead, along with messages: THIS WAY. NO DETOURS. DO NOT TOUCH WALLS. Then, YOU'RE NOT PAYING ATTENTION.

Great. A mind-reading sign, Ren thought as tremors snaked through her. You don't just go dropping the bomb that you're an ALIEN! Or exceptional being or whatever, and then—poof!—disappear.

The floor lurched and began to move like a conveyer belt, carrying Ren slowly toward a little green door. A moment later, shifting images appeared on the walls, just like when K'iin had shown Ren, Monty, and Zyanya leaving Mictlan.

But this time all Ren saw was the lords in shadow form—tall, misshapen, menacing figures. And then she heard the Smoking Mirror's voice: "Those little predictable fools."

"It is now only a matter of time," Jade Is Her Skirt purred.

The path continued to carry Ren toward the exit while her gaze never left the shadowy walls. How much did the lords know? What were they up to?

Ren reached the door, which had a knob in the shape of a gold hand. She took hold of it, and just as she turned it, its fingers squeezed hers. She flinched, pulled the door open, and jumped over the squatty threshold.

She found herself at what appeared to be abandoned circus grounds. Up ahead was a decrepit big top, the red-and-white scalloped edges of its awning flapping in the breeze. Ren stood on a cracked asphalt road that was lined with a row of empty game stalls. Beyond that were derelict trailers, a rusty Ferris wheel, and a ramshackle fun house.

The place was a hollowed-out version of what should have been all sound, smells, and color. But the only sound Ren heard was the mumbling of voices. She quickly followed them to find the godborns and Monty siting on some wooden benches eating chicken wings and yakking up a storm.

Ren shifted her gaze—Zyanya, Edison, and Zulema were nowhere to be seen. . . . And then she caught sight of *herself* sitting with the others.

For your friends, you got back thirty minutes ago. And if you were practiced in this sort of magic, then you would remember that. You would see through the other Ren's eyes.

The whole thing was like a bizarro dream. Why was everyone at an old circus, and how did they get here? Where *was* here, anyway? Somewhere near the real world's Devils Tower?

It took Ren a few moments to collect any sense of calm as she watched her other self talking to the group, telling them what had happened with the crown and Devils Tower and K'iin.

"HELLO!" Ren shouted to test it out. No one turned in her direction. *Great, so I really am invisible.*

Serena said, "Those lords deserve everything that's coming to them!"

Kenji snorted, tossing a bone over his shoulder. "Let's just hope the plan works."

Plan. What plan? Ren felt like her life was being lived without her in it. "No!" she shouted uselessly. "They said you're predictable!"

Ezra stood and swiped her hands together. "I can't wait to see their rotten faces when they learn the crown is adios."

"What do you think happened to the Unknown race of demons?" Diamante asked. "Are they, like, waiting in hiding, or do you think they're all dead, or...?"

Marco groaned. His eyes scanned the area with the weight of the fight he knew was coming. His gaze met the other Ren's, and it made spectator Ren's stomach drop. They weren't even close to being out of the woods. He was aware of it, and so was she. But did he know just exactly how terrible the odds were?

There are many possible scenarios, many variables, and in all but one you and your friends lose the battle. Death blooms like a great shadow, and you return to the underworld like you did before.

Kenji patted his stomach. "Yo, Ez—you should one hundred percent open a Magic Dash business. Those wings were killer."

"I didn't make the chicken," Ezra said. "I just got it delivered. And don't call me Ez. Ever."

Ren searched the air for Edison's scent. He was nearby, and so was Zyanya. Ren rushed beyond some empty animal pens and toward the center of the circus grounds, where the Ferris wheel stood, its lonely cages groaning in the breeze.

She came to the edge of a wooded area and saw Edison stooped over a few yards away.

"Hold still!" Edison said. But his back was to Ren so she couldn't see what he was doing or who he was talking to.

She drew nearer, curious.

A soft blue glow pulsed all around the demon. That's when Ren got a better angle and saw that he was cradling Zyanya in his hands.

The demon's light poured into the shadow bird the way it had once poured into Ren's wound. When she'd asked him if he was a healer, he'd said, *I can only feed magic back into someone.*

Ren couldn't believe she hadn't thought of this! If it worked, Zyanya would be restored enough to put the lords back into their forever slumber. But wouldn't it deplete Edison of his powers? How long had he said it usually lasted? *Only for a little while, depending how much energy I have to use.*

Zyanya grumbled, "Are we done?"

"Not yet."

"Now?"

Edison chuckled.

"And to think," the bird said, "that my sleep magic might return at the hands of a demon!"

A breath later, Edison shook out his hands and the glow vanished. "There. Better?"

Zyanya hopped down to the packed dirt and pranced around, fluttering her wings and shaking her head. "Not bad, demon."

"Do you think it worked?" Edison's demeanor seemed suddenly wilted.

Zyanya gave a tiny snort. "Well, you said your energy just feeds my already superior magic, right?"

Another chuckle. "Right. Except that you had almost none left."

How much of your own power did you have to use, Edison? Ren wondered.

"I feel supercharged!" Zyanya said gleefully. "It's extra-ordinary, truly. Before, I could only knock out one god at a time, but now?" She stretched her wings wider and wider, until their span was at least twenty feet. "I am certain I can do it in one fell swoop!" And then Zyanya vanished into the night sky, singing a happy tune Ren had never heard from her before.

Edison watched the bird as he shook out his hands. Then, slowly, he turned. His gaze met Ren's. "How long have you been standing there?"

Ren startled. "You can see me?"

"You feeling okay?"

"You're not supposed to be able to see me—I'm outside the strands of time."

And then the memory crashed into Ren like a tidal wave: *You will be a mere spectator no one else can see.... Well, no one except for a god. Or an Unknown...*

It took a moment of stunned silence, then, like dominoes falling, the memory triggered another and another.

His father is of undetermined origin.

The Unknowns had a kid with a demon and started a new race of very powerful creatures, so powerful that their offspring could overthrow the Maya deities.

"Ren?"

She couldn't move or speak.

Edison was a descendant of exceptional beings! Did he know? Did A.P.? Was that why Edison had been forced to hide out in the underworld? And why he was so different from any of the other demons she had ever met? He *was* extraordinary. . . .

"Edison, I just realized you—"

Edison cut her off. "Don't worry. My powers will come back. We were running out of time, and we couldn't wait anymore."

"Can't you recharge using some energy around here?" She looked around. "Maybe we could find a generator, or—"

"Ren, you know this is all an illusion, right? Serena made it look like a circus, but we're really at Devils Tower. It's all part of the plan."

Ren was already shaking her head. "I think the lords know whatever the plan is—they called it predictable," she said before spitting out everything she had heard after leaving K'iin. "And I could tell something was off when I got here. If that's true, don't you think the lords will know, too, and—"

"Hey," Edison said calmly. "It's all good."

A new blend of panic and fear gripped Ren. "We're standing in an illusion that's an abandoned circus and the lords are probably on their way and I already gave away the crown and you've got no powers and you're telling me to be calm?" Ren gulped in the cool night air.

Edison blinked. "You gave away the crown?"

With a nod, Ren told Edison about her visit with the all-seeing calendar. "K'iin told me she was an Unknown, but how could that be, if my mom created her?" She lifted her gaze to meet the demon's. She wished he didn't look so pale and weak.

"She said that only a god or an Unknown could see me while I'm outside the time strand."

The demon's expression tightened.

"So...you know," Ren whispered.

Just then, Marco and Serena appeared.

"Hey, Eddie," Serena said, oblivious to Ren's presence. "You're the tiebreaker. Does this look like the real thing?" She held up the crown.

"Tell her it needs more shadow," Marco argued.

"Ha!" Serena barked. "This might be the best illusion of my life. Well, other than this place."

"I still think you could have conjured something better than a hollowed-out circus," Marco said. "It's, like, totally creepy."

"Look," Serena said, "illusions take tons of energy, and the details I have to come up with are mind-numbing, so I like to create places I've been to or know a lot about. Anything that has loads of emotion tied to it."

With a smirk, Marco said, "Are you telling me you hang out at abandoned places?"

Serena scoffed. "No. This was last night's nightmare."

Ren felt like she was living in her own bad dream, because she still couldn't talk directly to Marco or Serena. "Why couldn't we just face the lords at Devils Tower?" she asked Edison.

He leaned closer and, taking her hand, spoke to her telepathically. *According to Serena, her illusion will bewilder the lords—you know, throw them off their game—at least for a few seconds, and that'll give Zyanya time to do her thing.*

Ren knew Serena's illusions were powerful, but she had no idea they could mess with someone's mind like that.

Without warning, the air grew impossibly thick and moist. Swirls of blue and green floated around Ren, and for a blink, it was as if she were looking through a giant soap bubble. The sensation was strange, like she was swimming underwater toward her other self. And in that moment, she saw the plan the other Ren had been privy to. Ezra, using a beacon of magic, had already alerted the lords about where to find them.

When the lords arrived, each of Ren's friends would assume a different role. Marco would turn himself into a carbon copy of Ren while he lured the lords to the big tent, using the illusioned crown as bait. Diamante would paint in the details Serena left out, and Ezra would create a magic perimeter to act as an alarm system to tell them when the lords were moments away. Monty, Kenji, and Ren would wait in shadows as backup if things went south. Which was more than likely.

Ren sucked in a breath. "I just saw the whole plan," she told Edison. "And it might seem good, but it *is* too predictable, just like the Smoking Mirror said! You have to tell Marco."

Edison turned to the son of war. "Look, Ren is here—well, a part of her, anyway—and she told me she heard the lords talking about our plan. They're onto us."

"I knew something was off when we were wolfing down those wings," Serena said.

Marco's eyes shifted back and forth. "Too late to change things now. And no way could the lords know what we're doing."

"Maybe we should have a plan B, just in case," Edison suggested.

"It's going to work," Serena argued.

Marco was starting to look less convinced. "This is nearly foolproof."

Nearly foolproof wasn't the same thing as *airtight.*

Ren felt like her insides were being twisted into a million tiny knots. Every one of her senses was on fire, screaming that this was too obvious, that they could do better. She reached for the time thread around her boot and wrapped it around her wrist like a bracelet. The rope pulsed with warmth and magic.

"We've got trouble," Monty announced, rushing toward them. Her arrows glowed a familiar blue shade of danger. "The lords are close."

"They're early!" Serena growled.

"I told you to be prepared for any- and everything," Marco said. "Serena, call the others."

Serena wedged two fingers into her mouth and released a high-pitched whistle, which brought Kenji, Diamante, and Ezra running down the path. "Yo," Kenji said. "Ren's, like, out of it."

"She's having an absence seizure," Ezra clarified. "So we hid her in a trailer. But we can't just leave her like that, all defenseless."

Monty frowned. "I'll guard her."

Ren's heart melted, thinking Valentina Montero was the truest friend she could ever hope for. "Tell her not to bother," Ren said to Edison. "The lords will be put to sleep before they can go looking for me." Or at least she hoped so.

Marco shook his head at Monty. "We need you here."

But Monty wasn't having it. She scowled and backed up and shook her head . . . all the way up until Edison told her about Ren being outside of the time strand and repeated her words.

"She's here?" Monty asked, wide-eyed.

The demon nodded while Diamante walked around as if she didn't have a care in the world, dancing her fingers through the air, filling in the empty spaces of the illusion, like the missing parts of the big top and the faded seats of the Ferris wheel.

Zyanya zoomed over out of nowhere. "I just want to go on the record that if this doesn't work, I am not going to do a plan B or C or D. This is a one-shot deal. Got it?"

"Everyone, take your places," Marco commanded. A minute later, everyone was inside the big top. The son of war stood in the makeshift center ring, while the others retreated to dusty corners and Edison tugged Ren into the shadows. She felt like she was going to explode from the feeling of helplessness, but all she could do was watch and wait, hoping she wouldn't be outside the time strand much longer.

The air went still and silent. Specks of dust floated across the beams of moonlight pressing through the tent roof's holes. Ren held her breath, feeling more nauseated by the second.

A moment later, the Lords of Night appeared at the edge of the stage where Marco stood waiting. They were too composed, too compliant.

"Something's wrong," Ren whispered to Edison. His body was so cold, she could feel his temperature coming off him in icy waves. But she couldn't worry about that now, not when Marco-as-Ren was already extending the crown to Jade and backing away, not when Zyanya was casting a careful shadow across only the lords.

Not when Ren realized too late that these Lords of Night weren't real.

37

The false Jade Is Her Skirt vanished in a trail of smoke along with the fake crown as five narrow mirrors rose from the floor of the center ring.

Each mirror held the image of a different real lord.

Marco shed his Ren identity and drove a fist into the looking glass that held Jade Is Her Skirt, but even with his strength, he didn't leave so much as a scratch.

Serena appeared, her expression tight and focused as she tried to maintain the illusion of the circus, but it was cracking under the weight of the lords' magic.

The Jade in the mirror laughed, holding the fake crown at her side. "Did you really think we would walk into your pathetic trap without armor?"

Zyanya had used her sleep magic on mere projections! Was it all gone? No. Ren held fast to the bird's own feeling that she'd been supercharged. Thanks to Edison.

But now the demon was depleted, and he looked that way as he stood at Ren's side.

The Smoking Mirror's mouth fanned out into a sickly smile. His eyes scanned the tent. Ren knew he was looking for her. She also knew the godborns' plan was now up in smoke, and that meant they had to pivot. But how? What was the one outcome that would ensure their success and wouldn't mean death, like K'iin had warned her about?

A slew of arrows whizzed across the space. Each flew into a column of glass before it dropped harmlessly to the ground, deader than dead. Ren sucked in a sharp breath. She had never known Monty's arrows to fail, and now all their magic had been absorbed by the mirrors. Kenji's bees were next. They zoomed right into the glass and disappeared.

"Seriously?" the Maize Lord laughed. "That's all you've got?"

Frowning, Edison flexed his fingers as if searching for his magic.

Ren was desperate to shift into her jaguar form, but no matter how hard she tried, she couldn't do it while she was outside the time stream.

"Did you really think your pathetic little magic could defeat the greatest gods of all time?" the Fire Lord said.

Serena's illusion had done nothing to disorient them!

Zyanya, hidden in a dark crevice high above, tucked her wings to her sides and dove forward furtively. Was she going to try again? But how, if the lords were in the mirrors?

At the exact same moment, ribbons of black shadow snapped out of the mirrors like tentacles, seizing Marco, Monty, and Serena with tremendous speed. Other tentacles grabbed Kenji and then Diamante.

Ren saw the horror of the lords' plan too late. Just as Edison lunged in vain and Zyanya cast another shadow, the lords' images vanished, and the godborns and hunter were sucked into the mirrors, now prisoners of the bird's sleep magic. Then the real five lords appeared in person and stood before the mirrors like a line of sentries.

Ren couldn't breathe or blink or speak. She was lost in the memory of Zyanya's words: *Once I put someone to sleep, it's*

lights-out forever unless you awaken them in less than five min-
utes. Six minutes and beyond is when it gets ugly.

But there would be no awakening the godborns, because
there was no way for the shadow bird to get into the mirrors,
not with the lords guarding them.

Desperate, Ren snapped the time thread, hoping to buy
them a few more minutes, but the string fell limply.

And then Ren went cold all over. In a flash, she felt herself
reaching across the darkness for her other self, connecting, and
blinking back to the moment. She became whole just in time
to see the Smoking Mirror cast a dark web of magic at Zyanya.
Fortunately, the bird escaped it, flying up and away through a
hole in the tent's roof.

"Forget the bird!" Jade Is Her Skirt shouted. "We've been
deceived. This isn't the real crown!"

The tent faded as the illusion collapsed, and all that was left
was a thick forest leading toward Devils Tower. Thankfully,
Ren and Edison were tucked behind a boulder while the lords
stood a few yards away.

The Maize Lord said, "We must find the queen. She'll have
the crown."

The Prince Lord nodded. "I'll do it." And then he took
off.

Ezra stalked up behind Ren and Edison just then. "I can't
hold the binding much longer," she whispered. "So we better
come up with a plan, like, ASAP."

Ren whirled toward Edison. "Do you have any magic left
at all?"

He shook his head miserably. "But I won't give up."

Resisting the panic that threatened to pull her under, Ren said, "We don't have much time to free the others. Five minutes, to be exact. Ezra, can you find Zyanya?"

"The chicken who ran away?"

"She's just spooked," Ren said.

"What are you going to do?" Edison asked her.

"I'm going to find the prince and lure him back here while Ezra binds these lords with her magic long enough for her to find Zyanya."

"I'm going with you," Edison insisted.

"To get him to trust me, I have to do this alone." She turned to Ezra. "Any chance you could magic up some kind of recording device?"

The daughter of spells and magic narrowed her eyes suspiciously. "Why?"

"Because I want proof of the prince's lies."

"Lies?" Edison said.

Ren huffed, "There isn't time to explain."

"Knowledge is power," Ezra said. "Talk fast."

"The Prince Lord thinks he became the King Lord when we got hitched, but he doesn't know that Serena only made it *look* tied," Ren spilled. "And his title gives him absolute power over the other lords."

Ezra shuddered. "And that means he's the only one of the lords who'd have something to lose if they all reinvented themselves as a new pantheon. He's *already* reinvented himself by becoming king... or he thinks he has."

"So he must have been the one who destroyed the crown," Edison put in.

"And when the others find out," Ren said, "they'll be mad and preoccupied with him, and that will be our one shot."

Edison frowned. "Except that doesn't solve the issue of the captives running out of time."

Ezra nodded. "Can't you use that time thread of yours, Ren?"

"Say that again," Edison commanded.

"About the time thread?" Ezra asked.

Ren could tell an idea was blooming in the demon's head. "What is it?"

"Ezra," Edison began, "if you can put this moment to sleep, and Ren can create a time gap at the same instant, then—"

"We'll have the perfect spell for time turbulence," Ezra whispered. With an approving grin, she said, "Not bad, demon."

A sudden thrill rushed through Ren. In her training at SHIHOM, she'd heard of time turbulence—a rare occurrence when the tiniest of ripples expands on a single thread of time and holds a moment prisoner, like someone pinching a water hose to stop it from flowing.

"Let's do it!" Ren said, gripping her time thread.

Ezra took Ren's free hand. "Snap the thread the second the air heats up." She gave Ren's fingers a squeeze. "Let's hope this works."

Just then, a spine-tingling clicking echoed around them. The Maize Lord! Followed by the Smoking Mirror's amused voice. "Do I smell godborns?"

Ren spun to find four lords floating toward them.

Edison ran in their direction. "Just your friendly neighborhood demon!" he shouted.

Ren was grateful for the diversion and the fact that it bought her and Ezra a few precious seconds. In a panic, she said to Ezra, "Hurry!"

The daughter of spells closed her eyes. A moment later, the air was so hot, Ren could barely breathe. Instantly, she snapped the jade thread, merging it with Ezra's stream of magic.

The air exploded with the sound of thunder, and then the world went still. But not in the way it usually did when Ren stopped time. This was different. Everything had lost all color, and the forest looked more like a drawing than reality. The lords were now pixelated versions of themselves suspended in the air. And so was Edison.

"Whoa!" Ren breathed, wishing the demon hadn't been caught up in the magic. "Do you think it hurts them?" she asked Ezra.

"No, but I'd never want to be in itty-bitty pieces like that."

Ren hoped Edison was feeling nothing. "How long will it last?"

"We just bought ourselves another fifteen minutes," Ezra said. Then, "Here." She removed a gold stud earring, spit on it, and handed it to Ren. "This will record and broadcast your conversation. Even while the lords are frozen, they'll hear it."

Ren admired the godborn's confidence, even if it was delivered in a trembling voice. With a nod, Ren pocketed the slimy earring and took off running in the direction the prince had gone.

Though she was in her human form, her body pulsed with jaguar magic, rolling through her in powerful waves. Without slowing, she caught the Prince Lord's scent. Her feet slammed against the cool earth as she raced through the trees, leaping over fallen branches, carving her own path.

When she was sure the prince was close, she let out a low rumble, alerting him to her presence as she stalked into a clearing and waited.

He surfaced from the woods.

With a forced grin, he slowed his pace, coming closer. "If it isn't the Jaguar of Darkness. Hiding out while her friends are ensnared."

"I'm not hiding."

He stood a mere few feet away now, still wearing that false smile. "This reminds me of the day I met you in the garden of the Black Flowers. Remember? When the clock was ticking, and I had to save your friend's life as well as your own."

Ren remembered. She had spoken the words *I am your queen* to save Monty's life, not knowing that it was a promise to *be* queen. Now she definitely got the hint he was dropping. "I'm not cutting a deal with you."

"Very well," he said in that signature bored tone of his. "I guess your friends will be stuck in a forever slumber." His gaze fell to Ren's clenched fists. "I see you don't have the crown."

"You never wanted me to find it."

The Prince Lord clasped his hands in front of him. "Do you know what it means to be the King Lord?"

"That you've got all the power."

"It means that I have the *greatest* of powers—greater than the other lords, enough to create a new kingdom, to force them to their knees," he said. "Of course, they hated the idea of giving me such a title, but it was necessary."

"Because it was the only way to find the crown," Ren said, hoping Ezra's recording device was working and the prince's words were playing into the other lords' ears. "So you set them up. You destroyed the crown, knowing that if I ever returned—"

"Oh, I knew you would return," he said. "I knew you'd overcome that wretched darkness Jade subjected you to. I knew that death couldn't hold you, not when your friends' lives were on the line, not when there was so much unfinished business. And not when you possessed so much untapped power."

As much as Ren hated his diabolic plan, she couldn't help but marvel at its brilliance.

"So," he said with a small bow, "thank you for not finding the crown."

It was Ren's turn to smile. "I never said I didn't find it."

The Prince Lord stiffened. His eyes searched her face. "Then where is it?"

"In the safest possible place."

"You're lying."

With a small shrug, Ren spoke with cool indifference. "What do you think the other lords are going to do when they find out you betrayed them? And they can't reinvent themselves? I bet they'll be super bummed and furious."

"Oh, Reina." The Prince Lord laughed. "They'll never find out, because you can never tell them."

Ren had a terrible feeling she was getting ready to be sucker punched.

The prince inched closer. "You tied the knot with me."

"So?"

"So, the queen can never do anything to harm her husband—it's a law of magic."

Ren took a deep breath to steel her nerves, bracing herself for his wrath when she told him the truth. "I'm not your queen. We never tied the knot. It was an illusion, and that means you're *not* the king."

His blank expression revealed no emotion, not even a glimmer of surprise when he said, "I don't believe you."

"Okay, but it's true. Want me to prove it?"

"How do you propose to do that?"

"If I were bound by your rule of no harm, would I be able to do this?"

Ren snapped the time thread around the prince's ankles and yanked, bringing him to his knees. His face contorted in agony as he froze.

She enjoyed a small moment of victory . . . until she was blinded by an explosion of white-hot heat. Until she felt a dark magic gripping her arms, pinning her in place. He had broken free of her time magic.

The prince moved with the speed of light. He now stood behind her, whispering in her ear, "You WILL make me king."

"Well, well, well," a distant voice said.

Ren forced her eyes open. Just in time to see Ah-Puch stroll into the clearing as he said, "This looks familiar."

38

"You!" the prince growled.

"Me." A.P. smiled as the prince tightened his reins of magic around Ren, making it impossible for her to squirm, or roar, or even wiggle a finger.

The god of death cast his gaze toward her. "Tell me, Ren, how does it feel to be trapped like an animal, to think that your salvation is mere inches away only to find that your savior is actually a traitor?"

Seriously? He was going to lecture her *now* on the merits of loyalty? And for the record, what she did to him was *not* the same thing! She had been trying to protect the quest when she'd left A.P. on that ship, when she'd asked Monty to momentarily disable him with a magical arrow. If he wasn't such a hothead, then maybe she could have told him the truth about her intentions to marry the prince.

"She *is* a traitor," the prince snarled.

"Humans always are," A.P. put in, like he and the dark lord were all buddy-buddy now.

Ren's heart thrashed against her ribs in frustration and fury. She reached her mind across the space between her and the god of death, forcing herself into his mind telepathically. *We need to hurry. Monty and the godborns were put under a slumber spell, and it'll last forever unless Z wakes them. So how about some help now, and you can hate me later.*

"I'm not so sure I should interfere," A.P. said aloud, drawing out his words slowly. "I mean truly, Ren, you had me shot."

Ren gritted her teeth. She didn't have time to massage the god's huge ego. *Do you want Monty to waste away forever?* she asked him.

"That's right, Ah-Puch," the prince said. "She betrayed you, left you without even a backward glance."

"I remember," A.P. said, shifting his dark eyes to the prince now. "And I remember you told me that she would choose you. That I was a . . . What was the word you used? Oh yes, a *pathetic* god who would be *a mere sentence in the annals of history.*"

"Oh, come, now," the prince said with a chuckle. "As one dark lord to another, surely we can come to amicable terms. Perhaps this godborn could serve as a sacrifice to you. Imagine what her blood is worth."

Ren struggled against the prince's power, wondering why it was taking the other lords so long to get here. Had they not heard his confession? Were they still bound up? Had Ezra located Zyanya? Ren hoped the godborns had been awoken by now, because more than six minutes had passed. . . .

A.P. folded his arms across his chest and took a deep breath, considering. "Yes, her blood is unique, and of course such a sacrifice would be quite an honor. But there's a problem."

"A problem?" The prince's eyebrows shot up as he walked closer to A.P.

"You see, I am quite fond of this little rebel."

Ren thought she was going to burst with joy and relief. But that would have to wait, because in the next blink, A.P. plunged the world into blacker-than-black darkness. The absence of all light was terrifying and debilitating. But so too was the sound of wailing demons. Their cries were so loud, so horrible, it was as if their shrieks alone could consume the world. That's when Ren understood that this was A.P.'s truest darkness, a magic that was uniquely his, one that was so crushing, Ren worried she might collapse under the unbearable weight of it.

She felt the god gently touch her arm, heard his voice whisper in her ear, "Sorry for the pain, but you'll only have to endure it a moment longer."

The prince's magic struggled to contain her. Ren closed her eyes against the agonizing dark. She went as still as death and drew up her jaguar magic, with its warmth and light and power.

"You think your dark can hold me?" the prince spat. "I am Piltzintecuhtli, the great god of the rising sun."

Instantly, the blackness was swallowed by a stream of golden light. It surrounded the prince in a circle of protection; it poured across the forest, reaching into the shadows, consuming every ounce of darkness it touched.

A.P., do something! Ren shouted telepathically.

Must you always doubt my superiority?

His light is winning!

The god snorted. *Or maybe it is taking all his power to sustain it.*

Yes! Great thinking. Drain him so he can't fight Zyanya's magic.

That is not the plan.

Then what is?

And by the way, A.P. said, ignoring her question, *this does not mean you're forgiven.*

Just then, three things happened at once: the god of death, darkness, and destruction vanished; the shadow bindings around Ren disappeared; and the prince's ribbon of light came to a halt.

A.P.? No way would the god of death abandon her now . . . unless this was his twisted way of paying her back for her so-called betrayal. *Is this like an invisibility trick?* she asked. *Hello?*

But A.P. didn't answer.

It was then that Ren saw why the light had come to a stop. There, at the edge of the woods, were the other four lords.

"Just in time, my friends," the Prince Lord said jovially, basking in the glow of light still encircling him.

Jade Is Her Skirt drew closer, followed by the others. "We know of your betrayal, Piltzinteuctli."

"That it was you," the Smoking Mirror said flatly. "You who destroyed the crown, you who sought to rule us all."

"It really was a brilliant plan," the Maize Lord said. "And normally I would admire such treachery. But not when I am on the receiving end."

The prince maintained his youthful smile against the accusations. "Who has been spewing such lies?"

"They heard it all." Ren held tight to the enchanted earring. "I made sure of it." She felt the heat and pain of sudden panic and wished the mega-charged Zyanya would show up NOW.

The lords stood a few yards from her, in a formation that would be so easy to cast a sleep shadow over.

If the prince was alarmed, he didn't show it. "Surely we can put this behind us," he said to the lords. "No harm, no foul."

Jade fanned out her long, shimmering skirt. A massive wave of water formed, reaching toward the night sky before it crashed over the prince. When it retreated, he was sprawled on the ground, choking and spitting like a drowning man. "Now you can slither in the slime like the worm you are."

At the same moment, Ren caught Zyanya's scent.

While the prince gagged on Jade's magic, the goddess turned to Ren. "WHERE is the crown?"

Ren was caught in the wicked glares of four Lords of Night, each one probably wanting nothing more than to throw her face-first into a vat of sizzling oil.

She took a deep breath. "It's somewhere safe."

"Yes," the Smoking Mirror growled. "We heard that in your little broadcast."

"Where *exactly* is that?" the Fire Lord spat.

Ren felt like she was standing in front of a firing squad that was shooting hate and contempt. But she knew one critical thing: as long as the lords thought she could still lead them to the crown, they wouldn't kill her. No, that task would fall to Ixtab, because Ren had failed to keep her promise.

"If you do not tell us," Jade put in with a sneer, "we will smother your little shadow friend."

The Smoking Mirror waved his hands through the air and produced a glass cage. One that held Zyanya.

No! It was a trick. There was no way they could have caught the shadow bird. Or at least that's what Ren believed until Jade said, "We trapped the little beast when she circled back to wake your friends, which of course was a monumental mistake and made her easy prey."

Ren's heart crumbled into a million tiny pieces. Did that mean that Monty and the godborns were asleep forever now?

"Such a foolish child you are," the Fire Lord said to Ren as the prince continued to writhe on the ground in front of him. "Thinking you could outwit us."

The Smoking Mirror smiled, staring into the cage where the shadow bird beat her wings futilely against the glass. Each flutter broke Ren's resolve and heart a little more. "The creature will be freed once you tell us where the crown is," he said.

Ren didn't believe that for a minute. Her jaguar magic rose to the surface, coiling around her ribs, snaking through her blood. A barely there light pulsed from her fingertips.

"You aren't strong enough to stand up to us, jaguar," Jade warned. "So either tell us what we want to know, or we kill the bird *and* you."

Okay, so maybe the lords *wouldn't* hold off after all. She tried so hard to come up with a way out that sharp pains stabbed her brain. *Fuse.* That had been K'iin's clue, but what did it mean?

Zyanya threw herself against the glass as Ren felt the pressure of her own magic rising, spreading. Maybe K'iin had been right. The odds of Ren winning this battle were stacked against her. . . .

Even so, she would die trying.

She shifted into her jaguar form, threw her head back, and released a roar so loud, so powerful, that the glass cage shattered. Zyanya raced out, and the lords fell to their knees, covering their ears.

Now! Ren shouted telepathically to the bird. *Cast the spell!*

But the bird only flew in woozy, confused circles.

Instantly, a blinding burst of blue light engulfed the area. Edison!

Just as Zyanya hovered closer, the lords got back to their feet. With shouts of rage, they brought on violent winds, bursts of fire, and tremors in the earth that battled against the demon's magic.

How had he recharged himself? Ren wondered.

The lords' gusts threw the shadow bird off course and out of sight.

"The rope!" Edison shouted as he flung streams of energy at the lords.

They kept coming at him.

Ren understood. She leaped into the air, extending her paw and snapping the time thread to connect it to Edison's power the way she had with Ezra's earlier.

The air sizzled and popped as the two magics united in an explosion of blue and gold light. It was enough to force back the lords, but for how long?

This is what K'iin had meant by *fuse.* Fuse the magic!

But it wasn't enough. They needed more energy.

Ren spun to see Monty, Marco, Serena, Kenji, and Diamante running toward the clearing. Then a slimy black vine grew from the Smoking Mirror's mouth and wrapped around Ren. She fell to the ground, flipped onto her back, and slashed the vine with a claw.

Terrible hisses filled the air. "Your magic can't hold us long, demon!" Jade Is Her Skirt hollered.

Ren shifted into human form, jumped up, and raced toward her friends, reaching into their minds: *Fuse your magic!* She halted in front of Monty, grabbing hold of the hunter's hand to demonstrate. *We're stronger together.*

The others followed suit. Clasping hands, the godborns and hunter stood in a row before the lords, joining all their combined powers to keep them at bay. The result was suddenly dizzying, so much so that Ren felt like she might be sick. Still, she held fast to Edison's and Monty's hands. Scorching heat coursed through her veins.

"It's not working!" Diamante shouted.

More flames erupted in the field.

"Don't let go!" Ren commanded through the excruciating pain.

Monty nearly buckled, but Ren held her upright.

Their combined power began to weaken. The lords pushed back against the magic with their own. Ren knew they couldn't hold the line much longer.

"Try harder!" Marco yelled.

We need Zyanya! Ezra cried telepathically. *Now!*

She was right. Ren looked up. Zyanya was battling the lords' headwinds and not gaining a single inch. And she was flying too high for her magic to reach the lords.

Ribbons of black smoke snaked closer, penetrating their wall of magic.

"Enjoy the poison!" the Smoking Mirror snarled.

Ren, acting on pure instinct, broke free of her friends, shifted into her jaguar form, and raced toward the lords. Flames continued to erupt around them in violent blasts of heat. Smoke continued to spread. She held her breath, darting between the infernos.

"Ren!" Monty cried.

Just as Ren got within a few feet of the lords, she leaped supernaturally high into the smoky air and caught Zyanya gently in her jaws.

Time for a loop, she told the bird as she landed with a thud. Then she spun in a circle with such velocity, the world was one enormous blur of chaos.

Zyanya's shadows burst forth, enfolding the lords in her magic. They thrashed mightily, screaming in anguish. But they didn't fall into a slumber.

"It's not working!" someone shouted.

Edison threw his hands out in front of him, drawing on all the magic of the godborns and Monty, channeling it into a lightning rod of power.

And then he thrust it at the lords.

39

The world went still.

The flames died instantly, and the smoke vanished, clearing the air enough for Ren to watch in amazement as the lords, reduced to a single long shadow, were sucked into...Ren blinked. A small red leather suitcase?

Ren searched the sky for the shadow bird, but Zyanya was nowhere to be seen. Had she flown back into the Obsidian Blade in Ren's boot? Ren was about to check when the other godborns and Monty rushed over to her, cheering their victory.

"We took down those gods!" Kenji shouted with glee.

"Let's do it again!" Serena said, smiling with pure elation.

Ezra high-fived Marco. He was wearing his signature frown, but between the lines, Ren could see his relief and joy. "Zyanya woke us up," he said. "She saved us."

Monty turned a few cartwheels. "That was amazing! Like, we really did it."

"Together," Edison said.

Everyone went quiet then and glanced around at the others, letting that single word settle over their celebration.

That's when Ren remembered her promise to Zyanya, to destroy the Obsidian Blade and give the bird her freedom. A seed of an idea began to take root.

"What do we do with the luggage?" Diamante asked.

"Toss it in the ocean?" Serena suggested.

"Good call," Marco said. "But first, I'm starving. Who wants pizza?"

"Ezra could order it like she did the wings?" Kenji offered.

Ezra groaned and rolled her eyes. Then she grinned and said, "Extra large?"

Ren wanted to join the fiesta, but she still had a crown to deliver to Ixtab by tomorrow. She had to face the goddess, tell her the truth, and accept her fate as a ghost lost to the darkness of the underworld. Maybe it would be okay. Maybe A.P. and Edison would still visit her. If there were any visiting hours in Xib'alb'a, that is.

And speaking of Edison, how had he gotten his powers back? It was still a mystery.

Just as Ren was about to make her way to the underworld to get the truth-telling over with, Ixtab saved her the trouble. The goddess appeared, dressed in a black fur cape and long gloves, and sauntered over without even acknowledging Ren. Ixtab's companion, one of her demon soldiers, retrieved the suitcase and vanished with it before the goddess could remove a single silk glove.

"What's she doing here?" Marco whispered.

"This can't be good," Serena said.

Ezra muttered, "Wow. She's so much prettier in person."

The goddess finally turned her attention to Ren. "I understand that you gave away my crown."

Ren's insides buzzed with terror. So K'iin had been right. Death *would* bloom over the forest, because Ren was for sure headed to Xib'alb'a.

"Uh . . ." Ren began, twisting her fingers anxiously. "I made a promise to K'iin before the one I made to you."

"We can get you another crown," Monty suggested, which earned her a few groans from the group.

The goddess flashed angry eyes at the hunter. "I do not accept secondhand prizes. Which is why I have taken something better."

"Indeed," A.P. said, appearing next to the goddess. "You are getting five vicious lords as pets, and their magic is so much better than a crown."

Ren's heart nearly burst with love for the god of death. This, she knew, was his way of showing forgiveness. He hadn't abandoned her—he had gone to fetch Ixtab and save Ren from the underworld. But she couldn't celebrate right now, not when Ixtab was still glaring like that.

Ixtab said, "True enough," as she drew her silk glove across her palm.

"How do we know those lords won't escape again?" Marco asked.

Ixtab grinned. "No one escapes *my* underworld."

Except Edison, Ren thought. She looked around for him, but he was nowhere in sight—no doubt hiding from the goddess.

"And even if they did somehow manage to get out," Ixtab went on, "they would not have an ounce of magic left. Not by the time I'm done with them." Her gaze fell on Ren. "And you . . ."

Ren held her breath. Here it was. The goddess was probably going to turn her into a pile of ash or sentence her to toilet cleaning duties in the underworld or some other deplorable chore. Ren was making a list of all the hideous possibilities when Ixtab said, "You did much with so little."

Ren's eyed went wide. Was the goddess actually complimenting her?

Maybe this speck of admiration would make Ixtab want to give back Ren's shadows—without the lords' darkness attached, if that were possible. It emboldened Ren enough to say, "So, about my shadow magic..."

Ixtab straightened. "Your shadows will remain with me. Forever."

Ren's heart dropped, but a part of her knew this was for the best. She couldn't risk giving herself over to the dark ever again. And besides, she was eager to explore more of her jaguar powers. She would definitely have to hit up her shape-shifting friend Brooks for some tips.

Ixtab said, "I don't want to see you in my realm before it's your time, understood?"

Ren nodded enthusiastically.

"ANY of you!" the goddess warned. She turned and disappeared into the dark forest without even a backward glance.

A.P. watched Ixtab go, then turned to the godborns. "Away with you all. I have unfinished business with the jaguar."

The others retreated while glancing over their shoulders. Ren averted her gaze, in some ways wishing she could avoid the god of death, too.

"If you're going to chew me out, can you wait until I've slept and eaten and—"

"This cannot wait," A.P. said evenly. "You deceived me. Betrayed me."

"I tried to explain—"

"And I still care for you." The god cringed, touching his chest. "How is that possible? I should want to demolish you."

Ren's heart filled with affection for a god who had become like a father to her. "It's called love and forgiveness," she whispered, afraid the statement would throw him into a tirade.

A.P. looked away, nodding. "It's why I had to help you, why I convinced Ixtab to let you out of that horrendous deal you made, and why I gave Edison back his power."

"YOU did that?"

"His magic would have returned eventually, but it would have been too late, and you needed him."

Ren threw her arms around the god and squeezed him tight. He allowed her indulgence for a single breath and then backed away. "That is enough of deplorable human emotion for one day. Now, I am off to a sublime vacation."

"When will I see you again?"

"You have my number."

"You never answer."

The god blinked. "I'll be around, here and there. But could I make a single request?"

"Anything."

"Stay out of trouble. No more quests or catastrophes."

"In other words, be normal."

The god's face broke into a knowing smile. "That, jaguar, is an impossibility."

Ren and the other godborns huddled around a fire, no one ready to go back to their lives quite yet. And how could they? They had just battled the powerful Lords of Night and won. All because they had worked together, joined forces, and fought for something greater than their own gains.

Everyone sat in silence in the glow of the flames.

Until Ezra cleared her throat, stood up, and said, "I want to say I'm sorry."

Everyone turned their gazes up to her, but she only stared at the ground.

Diamante rose to her feet next. "Same."

Kenji followed.

The rogues all glared at Serena. "What?" she exclaimed. "Didn't we already do this back in prison?"

Marco tossed a twig onto the fire. "That was before it meant something."

"Before we were friends," Edison offered.

Monty chewed on a hangnail. "When's the pizza coming?"

"It's okay," Ren said. "No need to apologize. It's over now." Unlike Ah-Puch, she was terrible at holding a grudge. She understood that letting go sometimes meant replacing anger and hate with love and trust and forgiveness.

Serena exhaled dramatically. "I'm not going to say sorry again because that would just be pathetic, but—"

"Serena!" Diamante growled.

Serena shushed Diamante and turned to Ren. "I would totally go on another quest with you."

Ren smiled. It was the perfect apology for the girl who had once wanted to be queen.

Marco barked out a laugh. "I'd be more than fine if Ren never called on me for another quest."

"I think you're safe on that front," Ren said. "But I have one more favor to ask all of you."

Everyone groaned.

She tugged the Obsidian Blade from her boot. The bird flew out of it, stretching her wings as if waking from a long nap. "What did I miss?" Zyanya said. "Your undying adoration? Gratitude? Did you see how I saved the day? How I woke the godborns? How I put those nasty gods into a forever slumber?"

Ren chuckled. "And now I owe you what I promised."

Zyanya perched on a branch above. "Truly?"

To the group, Ren said, "I promised I'd destroy this blade, to give Zyanya her freedom."

"That's an ancient magical object," Ezra said in a rush of breath.

"A forbidden one," Serena put in.

Ren nodded. "And I think we could do it—together."

"Not sure I want to expose myself to that kind of pain," Kenji admitted, reminding everyone how awfully their last united stand had hurt.

Monty stood up. And, faster than the flare of a flame, she nocked an arrow and pointed it at the blade, now lying in the dirt. "We'll do it for Zyanya."

Ren understood, and the others must have, too, because wordlessly they formed a line behind the hunter, each touching the shoulder of the person in front of them. Ren gripped Monty. Edison gripped Ren.

Zyanya threw a wing over her eyes. "I cannot watch."

Instantly, Ren felt the power flowing between them,

infusing Monty's arrow with extra magic. And, just as the weapon ignited with white light, the hunter let it fly.

The blade burst into flames before turning to a pile of white ash. Ren spun to Zyanya. Did it work? Was the shadow bird now free?

Zyanya paced along the branch, and for a split second, Ren thought something had gone wrong. But then the bird morphed into the most beautiful blue jay Ren had ever seen. Zyanya burst up into the sky, streaking azure across the night with a single chant: "I'm FREE!"

As the godborns waved good-bye, Monty called out, "Steer clear of ancient arrowheads!"

That night, Ren slept in her own bed back home, comforted by the fact that Abuelo was snoring away on the other side of her bedroom wall. He'd been so happy to see her, he hugged her for way too long, and when he finally let go, he had tears in his eyes.

"I was so worried," he'd said.

"I was fine," Ren lied. "Just a little quest. All is good now."

He smiled brightly. "You look hungry. Come. We'll eat, and you can tell me all about your *little* quest."

Ren hadn't shared everything, of course. Eventually, she would tell him about losing her shadow magic and gaining her jaguar magic, but for now it was enough to be home.

Monty and the others had gone home, too, until the meeting they were supposed to have at SHIHOM the following week to recap and record the quest. As for Edison, he had taken off before Ren could get some alone time with the demon/ Unknown, to ask all the questions about his heritage that had been piling up. She missed him already. She wasn't even sure if he'd be at the meeting. And what if he wasn't? She'd have to ask A.P. how to get in touch with him. Maybe the demon was living with the god of death. Surely he hadn't gone back to the underworld. Ixtab would kill him!

A light rain tapped along the roof, waking Ren from a strange dream in which her mother's voice echoed. *Jaguar of Dawn...*

At the foot of the bed, in a beam of moonlight, stood her mother. "You have questions."

Ren didn't bother launching into how her mom had once again left her to fend for herself. Instead, she sat up, rubbing the sleep from her eyes. "You told me that you created time and the calendar and—"

"All true," Pacific said. "What I left out was that I did it with the help of the Unknowns during our period of alliance."

"You mean K'iin," Ren guessed.

Pacific nodded. Her blue gaze intensified. "K'iin is their eyes and ears. A guardian, if you will."

"Will the Unknowns ever come back?" Ren asked.

"They have many worlds to explore and are quite done with this one and all its trivialities."

"And will the crown be safe now?"

"Nothing is ever entirely safe, Renata. You should know that by now. But the crown is in its rightful place, so take heart and don't look sullen."

"I'm not sullen."

"Is this about your shadow magic? Do you miss it?"

Ren considered that for a moment. Then, rolling her blanket between her fingers, she said, "I did, but now . . . I . . . I don't think so?" The admission filled her with a surprising feeling of guilt, but she had learned something during this quest. She had realized that her shadow magic had always felt borrowed and never as natural as her jaguar magic. And she couldn't have defeated the lords without her feline powers. Powers that still felt so unexplored.

"What now?" Ren asked. "Are you going to teach me more about my magic?"

"Time is like a river," Pacific said. "It creates constant change, whether you like it or not. Nothing will ever stay the same, not even your magic."

Uh, that wasn't exactly an answer. "So, no?"

"Your magic will unfold as you develop and grow. It will shift and stretch and retreat," Pacific said as she morphed into her jaguar form. Her blue eyes glowed through the darkness. *But do not count on me to train you. It would be far too dangerous.*

Ren knew her mom was right. She couldn't risk the Maya gods discovering Pacific's true identity.

Ren thought about how much she had changed in the last year. It wasn't all because of the magic and the quests, or even her own death. It was because of the friends she had made along the way—their betrayals and gifts, their sacrifices and selfishness. They'd been motivated by power, love, and loyalty, but also by greed, anger, and revenge. Like her, they were flawed. But when they were united, they were a powerful force.

And she would hang out with them soon. But that made her wonder...

"Will I see you again?" Ren asked. She didn't expect Pacific to be like a real mom, but maybe she could visit every now and then?

Pacific's mouth curled into a small smile. "Look for me in your dreams. There we can run wild. We can test the limits of our great jaguar magic without fear of exposure."

Ren's breath hitched in her throat. The idea of sharing this ancient feline magic with her mom was...enough.

Just as Ren blinked, the goddess vanished, leaving her alone in the moonlight. Ren put herself back to sleep by repeating her mother's words over and over: "Nothing will ever stay the same, not even your magic."

40

The following week, Ren found herself in the magical jungle of SHIHOM.

The mysterious forest was just as beautiful as it had been a few months ago, and it felt more alive than ever. She rushed across one of the suspension bridges that connected all the god-borns' treehouses, down the rope ladder, and into the dense woods. Ribbons of mist curled around the massive tree trunks. Vines grew in great heaps across the rock-strewn path. The sounds of bird calls, rushing waterfalls, and squawking monkeys brought a smile to Ren's lips as she made her way to the ancient library.

The massive stone structure looked abandoned, but Ren knew that the answer to every question rested within its chipped blue walls.

Ren stepped into the massive tri-level room with floor-to-ceiling bookshelves encased in glass and a domed ceiling made of stained-glass windows. The air smelled like old cigars and worn leather.

Yeah, the place was impressive, but not as much as Saás, the all-knowing holographic orb that glowed blue as it spun in midair.

"It's you again," the globe said by way of greeting.

Ren knew it was protocol to give her account to the globe,

but she felt edgy, like a million bubbles were rising and popping in her chest. "Where should I start? Let's see. . . ."

"Oh gods—is this going to take all day?"

Ren took a deep breath and began. The cranky orb waited until Ren was done with the tale before she said, "Is that the entirety of it?"

Ren nodded. *I am absolutely not going to tell you about my mom's or Edison's secrets.*

"I truly believe you are not telling me everything," Saás said, glowing a faint silvery blue. "I will have to call this a missing information case, which will definitely raise red flags."

"There isn't any missing info," Ren argued. "I told you—"

"What you wanted me to know, yes, but I have my ways of finding out the rest."

Ren heard the threat, but she was so tired of fighting and arguing and cajoling. There had to be an easier way. "Saás?"

"Mm?"

"You once told me that you're the greatest understander of all time."

"Es cierto."

"And don't you agree that some things are secrets for a really good reason and should stay, you know, secret?"

"Perhaps I agree with this assessment. But perhaps not."

Ren tried a different tactic, one that was more personal to the globe. "Maybe it's time you got a break, a vacay. I mean, aren't you tired of holding so much information and so many secrets all the time?"

"It *is* rather exhausting."

Ren held her breath. "So can we call this case closed?"

Saás was silent. Just as Ren was about to repeat her question, the globe sighed and said, "Very well."

"Great!"

"And do tell the Water Lily Jaguar I said hello."

"I will!" Ren immediately froze, realizing her mistake. "I mean..."

Saás snickered and then blinked offline.

So the globe knew the truth about Pacific and, more than likely, Edison, too. But clearly, she was going to keep the secrets. Maybe she already had been all this time.

Outside the ancient library, clouds gathered in the distance. Ren could hear voices and laughter drawing nearer. Marco and Serena emerged from the jungle.

"Yo, Ren," Marco said, eyeing the library behind her. "How'd it go? Is Saás still a big grouch?"

Ren chuckled. "What're you guys up to?"

Serena folded her arms across her chest. "We're collecting wood for a bonfire later tonight. Wanna come?"

Ren found herself nodding. But as much as she wanted to hang out with the godborns from the quest, she missed Monty and Edison. She had tried to reach A.P. to ask about them, but his cell phone kept going to voice mail. And he hated texting, so she didn't even try that. A part of her was hurt that Edison had left without a good-bye. Would she ever see him again?

"Sure," Ren said, shaking herself out of her reverie. "I'll be there."

"Don't forget the hot dogs and marshmallows," Serena said.

Once Ren was alone, she shifted into her jaguar form and broke into a run through the thicket of trees, marveling at the

way her paws pounded the earth with such ferocity and purpose. She climbed up to the highest cliff, where she sat as the
sun crept lower. Seeing the world through her jaguar eyes was
astounding, as if it had been painted in streaks of undiscovered
colors. Everything was richer, more vibrant.

She shifted back into her human form, measuring the dif-
ference of how her human eyes registered the same view. The
world was definitely more muted.

Her phone vibrated. She reached into her pocket to retrieve
it and saw a text from an unknown number displaying the message *HIII!*

Who is this?

It's me! VM.

Monty?

*My parents let me get a cell phone! Cool, right? So now we
can talk whenever.*

Ren's fingers danced across the screen. *Very cool. Are you
doing okay?*

Yes! But I gotta go clean my arrows now. And then an up-
close-and-personal photo of the hunter's nose appeared.

Ren laughed. She lifted her phone to take her own selfie for
Monty, and as she did, she saw something behind her.

She spun to find Edison walking toward her. "What are you
doing here?" she asked. "Where have you been?"

"Here and there. Sorry I didn't say good-bye. I had to think
through some stuff." He sat next to her. "So, uh—I need to tell
you some things."

Remembering Saás's generosity in keeping secrets and not

pressing for more, Ren said, "You don't have to if you don't want to." But she really wanted him to.

"I didn't know I was part Unknown until I found some old notes in my mom's things a few years ago and I sort of put two and two together. It's why she kept me hidden in the underworld." He raised a single shoulder and blew out a half-hearted chuckle.

Ren wasn't sure what to say. "It must've been really hard to keep that secret."

"Yeah, it made me feel like something was wrong with me." He turned his gaze to hers. "But then A.P. showed me my powers could be a good thing. He taught me more about how to control them and—"

"You helped save the world."

He smiled and squinted one eye closed against the setting sun. "You're the only person I've ever told about this."

Ren beamed with pride that he felt safe enough with her to share something so intimate and so monumental. She had lots of questions, but they had plenty of time. "I won't tell anyone."

"Not even your blog followers?"

"Especially not them," she said. "In fact, I've decided to shut down the blog. Let someone else report on alien sightings. Some things should just stay a mystery. Right?"

Edison took her hand. "For sure."

"Besides, I'm going to be too busy learning how to be a jaguar."

They sat like that in silence as the sun faded away. She made a mental note to thank A.P. for introducing her to Edison. Even though the god would always be her BFF, she knew she had room in her heart for another.

When it grew dark, Edison got to his feet. "I'm starving," he said, helping her up. "Race you to the bonfire?"

Ren laughed lightly. "Edison, you're an exceptional being. You can vanish at will."

"And you're a jaguar with ancient magic in her blood." Edison's mouth twisted into a playful grin. "I'll race you fair and square. No vanishing tricks."

Ren sighed theatrically. Then, in an instant, she shifted into a jaguar and took off through the trees.

"Cheater!" Edison called out, laughing.

Ren's heart smiled as her paws pounded the earth. Not because she was so going to beat Edison, but because she was racing through an enchanted jungle, her best friend was a descendant of extraterrestrials, and she was the Jaguar of Dawn.

She had never felt more like herself.

El Fin.
Really.

GLOSSARY

Dear Reader,

This glossary serves to provide some context to Ren's story. It is merely a bird's-eye view of a vast and complex mythology that has been passed down for generations and in no way represents the enormousness of this lore and culture. I was captivated by these myths growing up, by the way humans sought to understand their place in the universe and their relationship to something greater than what they could see, touch, and hear. I grew up listening to various narratives of the same tales, featuring the same Aztec and Maya gods, and with each iteration my fascination grew. My grandmother used to speak of spirits, brujos, gods, and the ancient civilizations that further ignited my curiosity for and love of myth and magic. I hope you, too, are inspired and fascinated by these tales, that they lead you to open your heart to the possibilities of what-if.

abuelo (*uh-BWAY-low*) grandfather.

Ah-Puch (*ah-POOCH*) Maya god of death, darkness, and destruction. Sometimes he's called the Stinking One or Flatulent One (oy!). He is often depicted as a skeleton wearing a collar of dangling eyeballs from those he's killed. No wonder he doesn't have many friends.

Akan (*ah-KAHN*) the Maya god of wine.

Aztec (*AZ-tek*) the term often used now for Mexica, one of the peoples indigenous to Mexico before the Spanish conquest of the sixteenth century. The word means *coming from Aztlán*, their legendary place of origin. The Mexica did not refer to themselves as Aztecs.

Cehualoyan (*seh-wah-LOH-yahn*) fourth level of Mictlan, where a spirit is said to relive the saddest moments of their life.

Centeotl (*sen-THE-oat*) one of the nine Aztec Lords of Night; also called the Flower Prince or Maize God.

criaturas (*kry-ah-TOO-ras*) little creatures.

Cuauhcalli (*kwau-KAHL-lee*) part of the Aztec prison system, also known as Death Row.

Eréndira (*eh-REN-dee-rah*) according to legend, a princess captured by the Spanish conquerors. They imprisoned her in the forest, where she cried night and day, begging the gods to save her. The gods sent her a flood of tears that transformed into a beautiful lake. She dove into it and became a mermaid.

espejo (*ehs-PEH-hoh*) Spanish for *mirror.*

Itzcoatl (*ITZ-coat*) fourth King of Tenochtitlan and founder of the Aztec Empire.

Ixtab (*eesh-TAHB*) Maya goddess (and often caretaker) of people who were sacrificed or died a violent death.

k'iin (*KEEN*) Mayan for *sun* or *day.*

Mexica (*meh-SHEE-ka*) a Nahuatl-speaking group of people indigenous to Mexico before the Spanish conquest of the sixteenth century. Now commonly referred to as Aztecs.

Mictlan (*MEEKT-lahn*) underworld of the Aztec mythology.

Piltzintecuhtli (*peel-tseen-TEK-wit-lee*) one of the nine Aztec Lords of Night; also called the Prince Lord; god of the rising sun.

Puksik'al (*pook-SEEK-ahl*) Mayan word for *heart*.

reina (*RRAY-nah*) Spanish word for *queen*.

saás (*sah-AHS*) Mayan word for *light*.

Scorpion River a river in Xib'alb'a filled with scorpions. No thanks.

sombra (*SOHM-brah*) Spanish word for *shadow*.

Sparkstriker also known as Saqik'oxol (*sock-ee-kh-oh-SHOLE*), a being who lives in the woods, wears a red mask, and dresses entirely in red. The Sparkstriker pounded the lightning into the first daykeepers (diviners).

Tenochtitlan (*teh-nosh-TEE-tlahn*) capitol of the Aztec Empire and what is now the historic center of Mexico City. According to legend, the Mexica founded this place after leaving their homeland of Aztlán.

Tezcatlipoca (*tes-kah-tlee-POH-kah*) one of the nine Aztec Lords of Night; also called the Smoking Mirror; god of the night sky.

trajinera (*TRAH-hee-neh-rah*) a type of small, colorful boat maneuvered with a pole.

viva la reina (*BEE-bah lah RRAY-nuh*) Spanish for *Long live the queen*.

Xib'alb'a (*shee-bahl-BAH*) the Maya underworld, a land of darkness and fear where the soul has to travel before reaching paradise. If the soul fails, it must stay in the underworld and hang out with demons. Yikes!

Xiuhtecuhtli (*shee-wit-EK-wit-lee*) one of the nine Aztec Lords of Night; also called the Fire Lord; god of fire, day, and heat.

Xochimilco (*sow-chee-MEEL-kow*) Nahuatl for *field of flowers*. The last remnants of a water canal system built by the Aztecs. Today, a borough in the southeastern part of Mexico City made up of artificial islands.

Yohualli (*yoh-WAL-lee*) the Nahuatl word for *night*.

Zirahuén (*see-rah-WEN*) a lake in the central highlands of Mexico, also known as the Mirror of the Gods.

Other Rick Riordan Presents Books You May Enjoy

Aru Shah and the End of Time by Roshani Chokshi

The Spirit Glass by Roshani Chokshi

The Storm Runner by J. C. Cervantes

Dragon Pearl by Yoon Ha Lee

Sal and Gabi Break the Universe by Carlos Hernandez

Tristan Strong Punches a Hole in the Sky by Kwame Mbalia

Race to the Sun by Rebecca Roanhorse

The Last Fallen Star by Graci Kim

Paola Santiago and the River of Tears by Tehlor Kay Mejia

City of the Plague God by Sarwat Chadda

Pahua and the Soul Stealer by Lori M. Lee

Outlaw Saints: Ballad & Dagger by Daniel José Older

Serwa Boateng's Guide to Vampire Hunting by Roseanne A. Brown

Winston Chu vs. the Whimsies by Stacey Lee